The DREAM

JILL ROWAN

snowbooks

Proudly Published by Snowbooks in 2013

Snowbooks Ltd.
email: info@snowbooks.com
www.snowbooks.com

British Library Cataloguing in Publication Data
A catalogue record for this book is available from the British Library.

ISBN 978-1-907777-82-0

For my mum, Peggy, with love

For my 'Uncle' John in New Zealand, whose friendship with my dad inspired some of this story.

PROLOGUE

The invisible man, that's me. At least that's what I thought, until I met you. Talk about a shock. But I suppose I'd better start at the beginning.

There I was, all innocent, heading *out* to get on with my search. That was the routine most days, as long as I could make it. I did what I always do: closed my eyes, concentrated, and pushed at the boundary. Not that long ago it used to be as easy as flicking a switch, but now it's more like wrestling with one of those feet-thick doors into bank vaults. I pushed until it started to give, and then I visualised some familiar features of Dunedin City Library: a certain pattern on a stained glass partition; a carpet with the shape of New Zealand on it; the words above the entrance. This was always more than enough. After a couple of seconds' pause there was the familiar rush *across,* and then I waited until the world felt steady around me before opening my eyes.

I wasn't at Dunedin City Library. No, I was perched on the edge of the pavement of a wide, busy street while cars shot past just inches away. Now, okay, it's not as if I've never misfired, made a mistake; the process isn't foolproof. I'm working with memories of places I've been, and memories can be faulty, but up until then any error had sent me to my parents' old house; it was like a failsafe. So you can guess I was a touch surprised to have no idea where I'd landed. I scanned around in a bit of a panic, trying to get my bearings. There was a bridge just down the road and a cluster of shops. I recognised the bridge; I *had* been there before, but it must have been a while. I scanned for road signs, anything that would give me a clue. It wasn't as if I could ask a passing stranger, although as passing strangers go, I certainly would have liked to talk to the gorgeous woman who was walking fast in the direction of the bridge. She was wearing a large backpack and a frown, as if her thoughts weren't too happy. I stared at her as she got closer, mainly because I can, and besides, she was *hot*. To my amazement, she stared right back. She didn't look through me or glance away, like people always do. Incredibly, she stopped and gave me a sort of concerned look.

'Are you okay?' you asked in an English accent, your face screwed up as if you really cared. I turned to check behind me, but we were alone. You were definitely looking at me. You could see me! I was too stunned to answer, but you carried on watching me, waiting for a reply with a sweet smile on your face. All I could think was: *who the hell are you*?

Chapter One

I'd got myself into another fine mess. I'm good at those, or so my mum would have me believe. Only *I* could be so foolish as to go out on my bike and forget to take my mobile phone, then get a puncture and have to walk nine miles home in the pitch dark; only *I* would be so stupid as to tell my boss to stuff his job just as he was about to recommend me for promotion; and only *I* would find myself on the verge of homelessness when my landlord decided to evict me from my flat so that he could sell the house.

My mum certainly wasn't going to react well to this latest debacle. As far as she was concerned, giving up my job just to spend a year travelling in New Zealand and Australia was yet another act of idiocy, especially at my age. I could already hear the satisfied tone of her voice as she told me that she'd known it was all doomed from the start.

I readjusted my backpack and lengthened my stride; I had no idea what I was going to do now, but running back to the UK with my tail between my legs wasn't on the list of possibilities. My long hair swung in its utilitarian ponytail as I headed down the noisy street and rewound the last hour in repetitive detail. It had ended with me walking out and leaving Niall behind for good. It had begun with our tenth row of the day.

I glanced down at the white band on my left hand where my engagement ring used to sit. Now it was lost, rolled into some cranny in the motel room, a tarnished remnant of our twelve months together. It was a shame we'd had to come eleven thousand miles before I finally saw the writing that had been blazing away on the wall like a set of Catherine wheels, but such a relief to have finally got up the nerve to call everything off. I'd even thrown the ring at him, just like all those women in TV dramas and soap operas, and it had felt good.

We'd arrived in the town of Alexandra just two hours earlier, after a fraught four-hour drive punctuated by bickering and smouldering resentment, and now I was looking for some cheap backpackers' accommodation appropriate to my newly impoverished status. I headed rapidly towards the town centre, through a stifling evening that was cooling very slowly. The only other person around on foot was a tall, blond man who stood on the edge of the pavement, regarding his surroundings in total bemusement. As I approached he turned to stare at me as though I might hold the key to a major mystery. Something vulnerable in his posture made me stop hesitantly.

'Are you okay?'

He started, and his expression altered to one of incredulity. 'Ah, I…' He began, and then he looked away, surveying the scene: the traffic passing, the struts of the nearby bridge, the river reflecting a sky now fading to rose, until at last the confusion on his face cleared and he grinned. 'Yeah, I'm fine. Just had a bit of a moment there.'

I nodded slowly, far from convinced.

'Tourist, are you?' he said, putting his head on one side. He was tall, tanned and good looking in that Nordic sort of way that I'd never gone for, preferring my men dark and brooding, like Niall.

'How could you tell?' I asked in a sarcastic tone.

'Pale skin, English accent, and just maybe the backpack,'

he replied, ignoring my irony. 'Besides, tourists are thick on the ground around these parts. More tourists than locals this time of year. You here for long?'

'I'm not sure yet. My plans are… um… a bit fluid, you could say.'

'Oh yeah? Mine too, *right now*,' he said, lifting his eyebrows significantly as if he expected me to understand the meaning of his emphasis. When I didn't respond, he added, 'So you're just here for a short time then? Just visiting?'

He seemed a bit nosy, but I'd been brought up to be polite. 'I've just arrived,' I replied, keeping it brief. I started moving towards the bridge just up ahead. Surely I'd seen an accommodation sign around there earlier, when we'd driven through?

'My name's Mark. Mark Juniper,' he said, falling in beside me.

I turned to look at him again, wondering what he was after, but his grin was disarming. 'Ollie Kimpton,' I reciprocated, with an inward shrug.

'Is that short for Olivia?'

'Yeah, but no one calls me that. I prefer Ollie.'

'So you're over from England?'

'Yep,' I said, in a discouraging tone. If he was trying to chat me up, he'd picked the worst possible day.

I stopped on the bridge to admire the river. Mark stopped too, standing silently at my side. His expression had become distant and pensive. I stared at the glassy surface of the water and replayed the moment when Niall, looking achingly, smoulderingly handsome, had glared at me as I stood at the motel room door.

'Are you sure this is really what you want?' he'd said. 'Because if you leave now, don't think I'll take you back.'

I'd glared at him. What kind of an idiot did he think I was? It's true I hadn't had time to think through the consequences, or even to pack all my belongings, but I had no intention of returning.

'I suppose you'll be heading back home?' he'd said, glowering. 'I mean, you won't want to stay in New Zealand on your own, will you? You won't even have any transport.'

'I'll cope,' I'd said, through gritted teeth. I just wanted to leave. It was typical of him that he wanted to manage even our break-up.

He'd held up his hands in a gesture of sullen surrender. 'Okay, fine. It's your bed, you go ahead and lie in it.'

When I'd opened the door the stuffy evening air had hit me at once. It smelt of freedom.

'You're staying in a motel?' Mark's voice interrupted suddenly.

'Er, no, I don't think so.' I chewed my lip. 'I'm looking for something cheaper.'

'Backpackers' hostel?'

I nodded. 'Know any?

'Yep, a good one. Stayed in it myself a few years ago. Want me to show you?'

I accepted his offer with relief, and as we walked the couple of streets to the hostel, he told me about his previous visits to Alexandra and his experience of cycling on the rail trail. I felt oddly at ease with him, as though he weren't a stranger at all.

'Do you know if there's any work I could find around here?' I asked.

He turned to look at me more closely. 'You said you were a tourist.'

I sighed. 'Yeah, but I'm a tourist fallen on hard times. I can either go home or seek my fortune here, and I have no intention of going home.'

He chuckled slightly. 'Seek your fortune, eh? I don't know about work. You might get something casual, but be careful. If you really want to seek your fortune here, you'd best not get kicked out of the country.'

'I suppose there'd be more chance of casual work in a bigger city,' I said, almost to myself. A slight sense of panic was setting in. My whole focus had been on getting away from Niall, but it was his redundancy money that had been paying for this trip. Without it, I was close to penniless.

We arrived outside a slightly run-down looking building, and Mark said, ‘Here we are. Don’t judge it by its cover.’ He gave me another lazy grin, which led me to wonder how many women had fallen for his effortless charm. ‘It was real nice to meet you, Ollie. Maybe I’ll come across you again.’

‘Maybe,’ I said, smiling back but wondering at his odd choice of words.

‘I’ll know where to find you if I hear about any work,’ he added and then turned, a little reluctantly, it seemed to me, and strode away, lifting his hand in a parting salute. I had a sudden certainty that I *would* see him again, and quite soon.

Over the years I’d become accustomed to this intuition of mine, although it was something I never talked to anyone about, not even my best friend, Suze. My mum knew, though; I couldn’t hide it when I was a kid. It frightened and worried her. It made me somehow not quite normal. Well actually it made me even *less* normal by my mum’s standards. She’d always seen it as her life’s work to mould me into her vision of a proper daughter.

I called it intuition because it wasn’t so scary that way. It was just that I often knew things I shouldn’t, or couldn’t, by normal means. All the same, the idea that I might have some sort of miraculous talent was too far-fetched for a sceptic like me, so I buried the whole concept under a blanket of disbelief. I’d even go so far as to ignore the odd hints and suggestions that came to me unbidden, and I avoided dwelling on it much, or thinking of myself as in any way gifted.

I hitched up my backpack and tried to dispel this latest unlooked-for hint as I entered the hostel.

‘You’re in luck,’ said the man who greeted me at the reception area. ‘We’ve got a small single room left, if that’ll do?’

I smiled in relief and followed him to a tiny box room. After pointing out the location of the common area and cooking facilities a little further down the corridor, he left me to myself. I dumped my backpack on the floor with a sigh. I really didn't want to be on my own tonight; I was guaranteed to sit and dwell. After a quick wash and change, I went in search of other backpackers to talk to, and as the hostel was full, finding some wasn't too difficult. I joined a group watching an old episode of Doc Martin, and it was only when the credits came up that I realized this was the first time in months I'd been able to enjoy anything on TV without the accompaniment of Niall's critical comments. He'd usually spend the whole of any programme of my choice complaining that there was something on another channel he'd rather be watching.

I returned to my tiny room more convinced than ever that splitting up had been the right decision; I should have done it long ago. Nevertheless, I sat on the edge of the bed and rested my chin on my hands, darker thoughts crowding back now that I was alone again. When Niall and I had planned our trip, the intention had been to spend six months in New Zealand and six in Australia. Obviously Australia was now out, but there had to be a way to survive six months in New Zealand. I had no friends or relatives in the country, and only my minuscule savings to live on. I didn't want to break the law and work on a tourist visa, but what else could I do?

***

I sat up in bed, shaking, the dream memory still playing through my mind. It had been fifteen years, but the dream was just the same.

I was on a beach. It was hot and sunny, and the sky was a perfect blue. Tiny waves lapped gently at the greyish sand, there were half-submerged tree stumps around the little bay, and across the wind-ruffled water was a distant shore fringed with odd-looking trees. I was sure I'd never been to a beach that looked even remotely similar. It bore no resemblance to the beaches of my childhood memories, which included Clacton's windswept groynes and the fascinating rock pools of Broadstairs. Nor was it like any of the beaches I'd visited on package trips to France or Italy in more recent years. No, this beach looked rather exotic. It certainly wasn't in the British Isles or anywhere in Europe.

As ever, despite the vivid scene, the dream was really about what I was *feeling*; it was a backdrop to a powerful sense of devastation. Back in my teens I always used to wake up crying. My mum had been concerned enough to take me to see the doctor, but he'd assured her it was natural distress at witnessing my dad's decline. I'd believed that too, when the dream stopped after his death. I thought it had died with him, and now, out of nowhere, it was back.

I shuddered and pulled the duvet around me, even though the room was far from cold. Perhaps it was just a fluke, a one-off, but nevertheless all the awful memories of my dad's illness were flooding back. It was still early in the morning, only just after six, but I could think of one sure-fire way to take my mind off those bad memories. I picked up my mobile with a wry grimace. It was evening back at home; my mum would be hoping I'd phone. What was I going to tell her?

'Ollie, about time,' she said in her Jean Brodie Edinburgh accent, almost before I'd heard a ring tone. 'I wondered where you'd got to. Are you in Alexandra now?'

She always wanted to know where I was, as if she feared some terrible fate awaited me that she could avert somehow by tracking my movements.

'Yes, we got here yesterday.'

'And how is it? How was the journey?'

I told her all about it: innocuous descriptions of the scenery and the baking heat.

'And Niall? He's okay? You were a bit edgy the other day.'

I willed myself to answer blithely in the affirmative, but I couldn't bring myself to do it. Lying just didn't come easily to me.

'We've broken up for good,' I said finally.

There was a stunned silence, and I listened to the crackle and hiss down the phone, waiting for the storm.

'You've split up?' she said at last, sounding strained. 'So where is he?'

'He's at the motel. It's the best thing. It wasn't working out.'

'What do you mean, *he's at the motel*?' Her voice was suddenly pitched an octave higher. 'Where are *you*?'

'At a backpackers' hostel. I'm fine. You don't need to worry.'

'I don't need to worry?' she squeaked. 'You're in a foreign country on your own. What about money? Your savings won't go very far. Now don't be an idiot; get back here ASAP. You can change your return flight and be home in a few days, and you can stay with Ron and me until you get back on your feet again.'

I gathered my breath. 'I'm not coming home. Not yet.'

There was another silence. I could imagine my mum's lips tightening as she prepared herself for battle. '*Ollie*, you've no money; you're on your own. What on earth are you proposing to do?'

'I'm looking into my options,' I said carefully.

'Oh, for goodness' sake, get back home and look for another job. Don't be so stubborn.'

'There's hardly a big demand for general dogsbodies,' I said, the usual resentment rising. 'We *are* in a recession.'

'You've got years of experience –'

'Of being a dogsbody.'

She tutted. 'I mean of office work. Don't put yourself down. You were doing quite well in your last department; I don't know why you hated it so much. It was a secure job, too. If you're lucky they might even take you back on.'

I winced. 'I couldn't bear to go back to that. Better to try my luck here.'

I could hear her exasperated sigh. Arguing with my mum was pointless; we were never going to agree on anything much.

'You're living in a dream world,' she said. 'I've told you a million times that life's about hard work and sticking it out. If you'd done that you'd probably have your own house and car by now, instead of living in a rented flat and rattling around on that old bike. And how are you going to get about in New Zealand, I'd like to know? You've barely driven in years.'

'I'll just have to find other means of transport,' I said, swallowing down my nerves.

'You're a funny girl, you really are. I can't make you out sometimes.'

I know you can't, Mum. And it's not just sometimes, either.

When we'd finally hung up, I felt exhausted. Trust my mum to point out all the flaws in my new found resolution. I headed for the showers to try to wash away all my fears, and by the time I stepped out of the hostel into another bright blue morning I'd almost managed it.

Chapter Two

A bike. That was what I needed. As Mark and several of my fellow travellers had reminded me, in Alexandra I was at the apex of the rail trail, an old railway line now turned into a cycle track. When Niall and I had planned our trip, I'd pored over the maps and pictures, fired up to do the whole thing and cycle from Clyde to Middlemarch.

'You want to *cycle*? Don't you get enough of it every day?' Niall had said. 'We'll have a rental car, for God's sake.'

Well, I was free now, although despite his threat last night, Niall obviously had other ideas. There were a mounting number of texts and missed calls from him on my mobile. The texts claimed he was concerned about me and asked to meet up to discuss the situation, but I had no intention of cooperating. I didn't even want to be in the same town as him any longer.

Before the morning was over, I'd hired a bike, stocked up on essentials, booked my accommodation ahead, and begun skimming along the rail trail towards Chatto Creek. I knew one thing for certain: notwithstanding his phone calls, Niall wouldn't be in close pursuit.

Like Niall, my mum had never understood why I loved cycling. According to her well-thumbed copy of the Book of Outstanding Womanhood, women should glide around glamorously in cars, not bump about on bikes, getting sweaty and grubby, having their hair disarranged by the wind and those highly unattractive helmets that look like giant cockroaches. 'You're a good looking girl,' she was always saying. 'You just don't do yourself justice.'

I frowned to myself as I pedalled down the trail. That was the main problem with Niall as well. I was never going to be the woman he expected me to be. Our final row was the culmination of my pent-up frustration.

'What kind of woman are you anyway?' he'd said, setting my hackles up at once.

What kind of woman? Not a *normal* woman obviously. A *normal* woman wouldn't be cycling to work at the age of thirty-three. She'd have a nippy little town car, or even a sports car. She'd like make-up and high heels and hairdos and handbags. She'd be keen on fashion and her idea of a great day out would be shopping for clothes and grooming products. She'd have a high-powered job, too. Rushing from meeting to meeting, hair immaculate, high heels tapping. Not like me, condemned to a call centre as an alternative to redundancy.

'You're starting to embarrass me when we're out,' Niall had continued. 'Why do you have to be so bloody different? The other girls are all dolled up, and there's you with no make-up, no heels, hair just anyhow. I'm surprised you even bother to put on a nice dress. Might as well wear a black bin bag, the way you go on.'

'Is there something you want to tell me?' I asked in as flat and unemotional a tone as I could manage.

'What d'you mean?'

'You seem to have decided I'm not of a satisfactory standard to meet your needs. As you knew what I was like when we first got together, I fail to comprehend this sudden change in your attitude.'

He rolled his eyes. 'Swallowed the dictionary again, have we? You always do that when you're pissed off. Look, all I'm saying is why can't you be more girly? You know. Just be more feminine.'

'More feminine,' I said slowly.

'Yeah, you know, it's not much to ask. I mean, look at Yvonne and Mandy. You're better looking than either of them, and you've got a great figure, but you just don't make the best of it.'

'So you're saying I'd make a good bimbo.'

He nodded haplessly. 'Yeah, you know, just do yourself up more.'

'Right.'

'Oh, c'mon, you're not going to get all huffy now are you?'

My hands were clenched tightly at my sides. 'What is it you want out of our relationship?'

'How d'you mean?'

'Do you just want someone to show off to make yourself look good? Is that it? Because I thought it was more than that. I thought maybe there was a bit of love involved.'

'Well,' he looked confused. 'Of course there is, but there's nothing wrong with wanting you to look good.'

'It never used to bother you. You used to say I didn't need make-up.'

'Well yeah, but you're a bit older now, and anyway, it's not normal is it? I mean, how many other women in their thirties just let it all go like you do?'

That was just the *beginning* of the row, but now I could think more clearly, it was obvious that I was also culpable. Why had I gone for Niall in the first place? There was no avoiding the truth: he was incredibly good-looking. Physically, he was my ideal man, and I suppose I'd tried to ignore all his other, less attractive attributes. He'd suffocated me, or tried to, but I had only myself to blame.

I stopped halfway to Chatto Creek and leaned the bike against a tree while I sipped water and ate a sandwich. It was still sunny, but the heat of the day was ebbing. I sighed with satisfaction. This was the life, even if I had no idea what was going to happen next – or maybe *because* I didn't know what might happen next.

I was just finishing my sandwich when there was a movement from the trail up ahead. A tall, blond figure appeared around the corner and wasn't long reaching the small grove of trees I was standing under.

'Fancy seeing you here,' I said sarcastically as he came to a halt and regarded me with the same bemused expression as yesterday.

'Yeah – do you come here often?' he answered with a grin.

'No – this is a one day only event.'

'Oh yeah? You off to Dunedin or Queenstown?'

'I'm cycling the trail for now – then maybe I'll get the train from Middlemarch to Dunedin.'

He lounged against a tree. 'You're in a bit of trouble aren't you? I could tell that yesterday.'

'*I'm* in trouble – what about you? You looked like you hardly knew where you were. Where are you from, if not Alexandra?' I asked.

'I was born in Blenheim.'

'Oh. I haven't been up there yet. We just came down the coast from Christchurch.'

'We?' he said, looking around as though my companion were about to pop out from behind one of the trees.

'I came with my boyfriend, but we've split up,' I told him in as blithe a tone as I could manage.

'Ah. I get it – that's why you're so hard-up. I guess biking is cheap, but it's hard work.'

'Doesn't matter – I don't like driving. The world would be a far better place without cars, in my opinion.'

He looked at me oddly but then started to smile. 'How do you get around then, in England?'

'It *is* possible to live without a car, you know,' I said sharply. 'I ride my bike.'

He laughed. 'What, everywhere?'

I gave him a withering look, which didn't appear to faze him at all.

'You still looking for work?'

'Yep.'

'You okay with bar work, waitressing, cleaning, even?'

I nodded silently.

'Well look, give me your mobile number, and I'll get back to you if I come up with anything,' he said.

I grinned. 'Okay, thanks.' I took a sip of water. 'So, how come you're out here? Isn't it a bit of a long way on foot?'

'Yeah, but I like the outdoors. I work for the DOC… normally. I don't like to be caged up for long.'

'The DOC?' I asked, puzzled.

He laughed and ran a hand through his hair in a way that reminded me unfavourably of Boris Johnson. 'The Department of Conservation. I'm a ranger.'

I was impressed. It sounded like the kind of job I'd rather be doing, so I asked him what was involved.

'We maintain trails and back country huts, things like that. I get to be outside all day; I wouldn't want to do anything else.'

'Can't be so much fun in winter.'

'It never gets too cold on the West Coast, but it does rain a lot.'

'So that's where you work, the West Coast?'

'Uh huh. Normally. I'm just… taking a break right now.'

He looked unusually vulnerable as he said this, so I decided not to press, and asked him if he'd been to Dunedin.

'It's a great city. I went to Uni there.'

'You've travelled around a bit. Born in Blenheim, Uni in Dunedin, working on the West Coast. And you don't look a day over twenty-five.'

He shrugged. 'The South Island's a small place. Most of us travel around a lot. And thanks for the two extra years. I'm twenty-seven. What about you – what did you do back in England?'

I grimaced. 'Worked in a call centre. I hated it.'

This sparked off an intense discussion about the relative merits of various jobs and the joys of being a ranger. I forgot all about the time until a trio of cyclists passed at some speed and gave us a *g'day* and a wave.

I wrote my mobile number on a slip of paper and handed it to Mark before I set off for Chatto Creek. He kept it in his palm and gave me another grin. 'Glad to have met you again, Ollie,' he said, emphasizing my name. He shook his head. 'Olivia suits you much better, you know.'

***

My mobile phone rang early the next morning as I prepared to set off for Omakau, the next stop on the trail. I flipped open the phone to see that it was a New Zealand number.

'G'day,' Mark's voice drawled. 'How's it going?'

'Okay,' I fibbed. I'd been up since before six, watching the sun rise painfully slowly over Central Otago's gold-green landscape. The dream had struck again, every detail picked out in Technicolor, accompanied by the same raw, formless pain. To my embarrassment, I'd woken several fellow travellers with my cries of distress. Why was I suddenly being plagued by this echo of my dad's last days?

'Well, I might have some good news for you. I checked around, and I happen to know that if you offer to help out at the Coffecup Café, they'll probably snap your arm off,' he said. 'They've got two staff off sick at short notice, and they're desperate. That's the only kind of thing you're going to get, I reckon, but it might just keep you going. You'll need to scoot along – it's just a small place off the trail, a few kilometres from Chatto.'

'Okay. Thanks for the tip; I really appreciate it. Should I mention your name?'

'No need. Just say you heard it from a friend.'

Mark hadn't mentioned that the trail from Chatto Creek included a few steep climbs that made it a bit difficult for even a hardened cyclist like me to 'scoot along', but I eventually arrived, sweating, at the café just at lunchtime. It was indeed small, with five tables inside and three more outside, but it was busy. Hungry cyclists and trampers were lining up to order, and I waited for a lull before asking the harassed girl who was serving if they needed any help. She looked me over and then called an older woman of about fifty who took me into a small office at the back.

'So you're looking for work? You're a tourist?'

I nodded, embarrassment making me blush. 'I'm struggling right now, and I just need something to tide me over. A friend told me you were having trouble.'

She raised her eyebrows. 'A friend?' She shrugged. 'Well it's certainly true we could use the help. You've been a waitress before?'

I nodded. 'Back in England, when I was younger.'

She appraised me with sharp blue eyes and then gave a decisive nod. 'Okay. We'll give you a go. Sixty-five dollars cash in hand for the day, and if you're any good you can come back tomorrow.'

I converted sixty-five dollars into pounds in my head and came up with about £30. Not a lot, but better than nothing. I smiled at the woman in relief, and at last she smiled back. 'I'm Val, by the way,' she said. 'Come on, we'll get you a uniform.'

It might look easy, but waitressing is tiring work, and I hadn't done any since I was eighteen. Even so, I welcomed the buzz and activity, and after a year engaged to a control freak, I was starting to appreciate the concept of living from day to day, with no idea where your life is going.

During a break in the late afternoon, Val asked me where I was staying and where I was heading, post rail trail.

I explained that I'd booked myself into a backpackers' hostel a couple of kilometres down the trail. 'It's the cheapest one,' I said with a small smile. 'As to afterwards – Dunedin, I think,' I added a little diffidently.

She gave me a thoughtful, considering look. 'If you're interested, I know someone in Dunedin who might be able to put you up for a few days or more, in exchange for a bit of help. Not paid work, mind, but at least you'd have a roof over your head. I could have a chat with her, see what she says.'

This was a huge relief. Out here I felt I could eke out my tiny funds, but I had no idea what to expect in a city like Dunedin. I nodded eagerly. 'That'd be great.'

The café closed at six, and I was pleased when Val handed over the precious sixty-five dollars without hesitation. 'See you tomorrow, then. Quarter to six. We get some early breakfast trade.'

My feet ached as I cycled the couple of kilometres to the hostel. The temperature was still high, and I couldn't wait to have a bath. For once, I took little notice of the landscape as I slogged to my destination. Halfway there, my mobile rang: my mum had got up early to phone me. Unfortunately, the information that I was now cycling the rail trail hardly provided the reassurance she was seeking.

As I arrived at the hostel, I was also forced to send further dampening texts to Niall, who was still in Alexandra and apparently had the idea that even two days on I would soon see the error of my ways and return to the comfort of his open arms. Apparently he'd been to all the hostels in the town looking for me, but luckily he didn't seem to have considered the possibility of my heading onto the trail. I made my last text as firm as I could. 'It's over. Keep the ring. Keep the things I left behind or throw them away, but I won't be back. Don't contact me again.' I bit my lip once I'd typed it. It sounded harsh, and we had had some good times, but they all seemed such a long time ago, back when we'd first met. I had to make a clean break now, or he could dog my steps indefinitely. I pressed *send.*

At the hostel, I paid a little extra for another small room to myself. I didn't want a repetition of that morning. Once

I'd finally had the bath I'd been craving, I lay on the bed, fending off exhausted sleep. I wasn't looking forward to having the dream again. Instead, I decided to ring Mark to tell him how things had gone at the café. The number he'd used earlier that morning was still on my mobile, but when I called it, the phone at the other end rang and rang without going to voicemail like most mobiles. I held on, thinking he must be driving or something and would eventually pick up, but to my surprise, a woman's voice answered. She sounded a little breathless.

'Um, I'm trying to get hold of Mark Juniper,' I said.

'There's no Mark Juniper here, love,' she said. 'Never heard of him. But then this is a call box. Sure you've got the right number?'

'Call box?' I shrilled.

'Yeah, outside Dunedin City Library.'

'This is definitely the right number. You're in *Dunedin*?'

'That's right. I just picked up because it wasn't going to stop ringing.'

I apologised and cut off with a slight feeling of disquiet. Mark was in Dunedin now? How had he managed that so fast? Not to mention a twenty-seven year old who didn't have a mobile phone! Okay, so he loved the outdoors and everything, but even ninety year olds have mobiles in the 21st century.

Chapter Three

It was just dawn the next morning when I hopped on my bike and set off on the short ride back up the trail to the café. The birds were beginning their morning chorus. I'd read up on the New Zealand birds before I left the UK, but my bird identification book was one of the things I'd left behind with Niall at the motel, so I now only had memory to rely on.

My fascination with wildlife, and especially the likes of snakes, insects and spiders was another big bone of contention with my mum. As far as she was concerned it was a woman's duty to be fragile and pretty, dependent on the big strong man to take care of any unsavoury tasks, particularly spider-removal. My habit of lifting logs to check out the interesting creatures beneath had always left her shuddering, and my eagerness to handle even the biggest of spiders was beyond her comprehension.

It was a busy morning at the Coffeecup Café and I was relieved when the time came to sit down for a brief lunch. It was the first chance I'd had to talk to Val about her friend, and she hadn't let me down.

'I phoned Shelly, and she said she'd be pleased to have you on the terms I mentioned: food and board for helping out with whatever's needed,' she said, as she ploughed through her pie and chips. 'She's been looking after her mum, who's had a hip replacement op, but now she has to get back to work, so she'd be eternally grateful if you could help out for a week or two – that's her words; she's always liked a bit of drama. I'll give you her phone number, and you can make arrangements. Zoë will be back here tomorrow, so I won't need you. Shell said could you get there as soon as possible – I think she's a bit desperate, poor love.'

I smiled. 'Her mum's really difficult?'

Val raised her eyebrows. 'Well, like I said, Shell's a bit of a one for exaggeration, but in this case I think that's only the half of it. Had any dealings with old folks?'

I shook my head. All my grandparents had died comparatively young, and my mum was only in her fifties. 'I'm happy to give it a go,' I said, with only a twinge of unease. 'If I take the train from Middlemarch, I reckon I can be in Dunedin in about three days.'

When I left the café that evening with over a hundred dollars in my hand (extra for the earlier start), I might have felt tired, but I was also oddly elated. Apart from the recurring dream, I was having the time of my life. The memory of the dreary call centre, with its constant pressures, was fading from my mind, and as for Niall and his ilk, I'd made that mistake too many times. Never again.

***

Two days later, the train rattled out of Middlemarch station in stifling heat. I'd cycled my backside off to ensure I caught the train on one of the two days a week it actually called at the station in what seemed to be the middle of nowhere. I leaned back in my seat and relaxed, enjoying the luxury of watching scenery pass without any effort on my part, for a change. I'd had a great time on the rail trail and had a camera full of photos to show for it. What I didn't have, though, was a purse full of cash. Staying at hostels should have been cheap, but the dream had forced me to elect for single rooms, which were far more expensive than the bunkrooms. And, of course, there was eating to take care of, too. I couldn't cycle 40 kilometers a day and stint on food. My earnings from the café were long gone. I shifted my sore buttocks on the seat and hoped all was going to be well with my new situation in Dunedin.

It had been a comparatively quiet couple of days cycling, with no further contact from Niall but also, disappointingly, none from Mark. I couldn't even explain to myself why I'd hoped to hear from Mark, but his silence and his odd communication from Dunedin preoccupied my thoughts. The one person who hadn't been silent had, of course, been my mum, who, in long telephone harangues, expressed her horror at my actions daily.

As the train moved closer to the city, the sun baked the broom that flowered all over the craggy hills of the Taieri gorge, resembling endless drifts of breadcrumbs. I listened drowsily as the train manager spoke over the intercom, telling us tales of the railway and the people who had built it and lived on it.

Val's friend had promised to meet the train and drive me to her house. We'd exchanged photos on our mobiles, so I knew who to look out for. Once the train pulled in at the station, I searched through the crowds for the plump, middle-aged woman with black corkscrew curls framing a pretty face. I spotted her quickly, and her eyes lit up at the sight of me.

She came rushing over. 'You must be Ollie? Please say you are!' she said in a theatrical tone.

I smiled. 'I'm Ollie.'

'Thank God for that! I was afraid you'd changed your mind. I'm Shelly.'

'No chance of me changing my mind,' I said, to reassure her as well as myself.

She led the way out to the car park and to a large estate car. She chatted all the way about her mother and how she hoped I wouldn't find her too intimidating. If I hadn't been nervous before, I was beginning to feel so now.

She filled me in on her mum's accident and current status as she drove us through the confusing streets of Dunedin. 'She's a lot better – she can get about slowly with a stick, but she's still housebound and fretting. I'm hoping you'll help by taking her out in the car. You can drive, can't you?'

I hoped my gulp wasn't audible. 'Yes, I can drive,' I said, and decided not to elaborate further and explain that while I had passed my test five years earlier, I'd barely sat in a driving seat since.

'At least we drive on the same side of the road here in New Zealand,' she said cheerily, 'so you shouldn't have any trouble at all.'

I was perspiring with anxiety by the time Shelly turned into a short drive outside a large, old-fashioned house that could just as well have graced a British street. Dunedin seemed much more like home than any of the other places I'd visited, even Christchurch.

She led the way through a large living room full of antiques and into a bright, airy kitchen. A woman of about seventy-five with grey hair cut severely short was sitting at the table, reading a paper, but she looked up as we entered and gave me a searing look out of piercing grey eyes.

'Mum, this is Ollie, who's come to help us out for a bit. Ollie, this is my mum, Diana.'

'Pleased to meet you,' I said, not sure I felt able to call this daunting-looking woman by her first name just yet.

Diana nodded curtly. 'My daughter seems to think I'm such a great encumbrance that she needs help to look after me. And what kind of a name is *Ollie*, might I enquire?'

'Oh Mum, really,' Shelly said before I had a chance to respond. 'Sit down, Ollie, and I'll get you a cup of tea. You must be tired after all that travelling.'

I sat down on the other side of the table and then met Diana's gaze. 'My name's really Olivia,' I said, 'but I prefer Ollie.'

Diana raised her eyebrows and then shook her head. 'I can't understand this need to abbreviate everything. I gave my own daughter a perfectly reasonable name, yet she persists in shortening it. Whatever was wrong with Michelle, that's what I'd like to know.'

'Not that old chestnut again, Mum,' Shelly groaned from her spot by the kettle.

'Shelly and Ollie. Sounds like a pair of poodles. Perhaps you'd like to reduce me to Diney?' She gave me a challenging look as she said this, but I'd already started to grin, and as our eyes met, she let slip a tiny smile of her own. She quickly dropped her gaze to her newspaper and resumed her disgruntled expression as Shelly came over with the tea and cake.

'Don't mind Mum,' Shelly said as she handed me a cup. 'She's pretty fed up since she broke her hip. She was so active before.'

'I *am* still in the room, surprisingly enough,' Diana said, her eyes fixed on her paper.

'So how can I help out?' I asked, taking a welcome gulp of tea. While Shelly had already given me a few pointers in the car, it seemed only polite to speak about it in front of Diana, who was obviously far from being in her dotage.

'I have to get back to work full time,' Shelly said. 'I've taken as much time off as I dare, and they're starting to make a fuss. Mum's getting back on her feet, but she needs someone around for a bit longer. Just helping her get out and about, making meals, clearing up, that sort of thing.'

'And how is it that you're at such a loose end?' Diana butted in, gimlet eyes fixed on me again.

I explained about being temporarily financially embarrassed and looking for a way to stay in New Zealand for a while longer.

'Val said you'd split with your fiancé?' Shelly said.

I nodded and glanced down at the white band still apparent on my ring finger. 'But it's all okay. It was the right decision.'

'No friends or relatives here?' Diana asked.

I shook my head. 'There's just my mum and stepdad at home. No brothers or sisters either.'

She looked me up and down again and then nodded. 'Well I suppose you'll do. Just your room and board and a bit of pocket money, mind.'

Shelly sighed with relief and pushed the Victoria sponge across to me. 'Have some cake, and then I'll show you your room.'

When we eventually headed upstairs, I was pleasantly surprised. A double bed covered in a flowered duvet took up only a small corner of the room, which sported a desk and chair, along with wardrobes and a chest of drawers and even a dressing table, all apparently antique.

'This is a big old house, so we have big old rooms,' Shelly said. She gestured towards the huge window. 'You've got a good view of Mount Cargill from there, and you even have your own bathroom.'

She left me to settle in and unpack, but one backpack doesn't hold much, so I lay back on the bed and contemplated the white-painted ceiling cornices with a sense of relief. Diana didn't seem as bad as Shelly had been hinting, and it looked like I was okay for at least a couple more weeks. I wasn't going to think any further ahead than that. I was just going to hope something else would turn up. I realized with a wry smile that I was starting to think like Dickens' Mr Micawber.

***

'Olivia, wake up.' Diana was banging on the door. 'Remember I need a lift to Pat's today, then you can amuse yourself as you like until four, when I'll need picking up. Hurry up – Pat's expecting me at ten.'

I groaned inwardly and mumbled in the affirmative, listening to the sound of Diana's stick receding as she limped away towards the stairs. She'd woken me from the dream, which I'd continued to have almost every night, and I was shaking, slick with perspiration and feeling more than a little put upon. Being Diana's helpmeet was no easy ride – not least the driving, which had me in a sweat every time I got behind the wheel.

I took a quick shower and started to cheer up as the dream memory receded and I contemplated my free hours. Yesterday, at the end of one week as chauffeur, cook, cleaner and general dogsbody, Shelly had handed me fifty dollars in pocket money, which seemed quite generous on top of room and board.

I'd seen a lot of Dunedin as I ferried Diana to the houses of friends and family and pushed her in her wheelchair around various shops in the city centre, but this morning she was visiting a friend who lived up the coast in Warrington, so I'd taken the opportunity to hire a kayak in nearby Karitane.

When I arrived in the kitchen, Diana gave me a keen look over the top of her coffee cup.

'Might be a good idea to do something about it, you know,' she said. I gazed at her blankly. 'These nightmares you keep having,' she continued. 'I didn't like to mention it before, but with my room being across from yours, it sounds like you're having them every night. Maybe you should see a doctor about it.'

'I'm not that loud, am I?' I asked in surprise. 'I'm not sure what a doctor can do, and besides, I can't afford one – it's not free here, is it?'

'You cry in your sleep. At first I thought you were homesick, maybe, or missing your boyfriend. Did you have nightmares back in England?'

I sighed slightly. Diana wasn't really the ideal confidant, but I could hardly refuse to explain. 'Not since I was a teenager, but it's just one dream. Always the same one. I don't know why it's come back.'

'Hmmm.' She took a thoughtful sip of coffee. 'Could be buried trauma. You shouldn't ignore it. GPs aren't free here, but you'll have some sort of reciprocal government insurance, I'm sure.'

I shrugged. 'I don't remember any trauma.' My childhood had been an averagely happy one until I was fifteen, when everything was blighted by my dad's illness.

'That's why it's called *buried*,' Diana said in her most sarcastic tone. 'You should at least think about seeing a doctor. It's affecting your sleep, making you cranky.'

I raised my eyebrows at this. Making *me* cranky? Spoken by the queen of crankiness herself. Thing was, Diana used to be a neuroscientist. She'd written papers and everything, and up until she broke her hip, she had still been enjoying an active life, albeit a retired one, so it was hardly surprising that she resented her need for help. As for me, having the dream every night was pretty draining, but surely going to a doctor was a step too far?

Diana spent the journey to Warrington regaling me with anecdotes about her former work as a professor at the University of Otago. My interest was tempered only by my usual nerves at driving through the alarming streets of Dunedin. Fortunately, once we were out of the city, it was just long hills I had to contend with, and I was able to relax my taut and sweaty grip on the steering wheel. We were just negotiating one of these giant switchbacks when I jolted in surprise at the sight of a familiar figure walking at the side of the road. *What was he doing out here?*

'Something wrong?' Diana asked.

'No, nothing,' I replied, as the figure receded behind us. He hadn't spotted me, but then he'd hardly expect to see me in a car.

Once I'd dropped Diana off I sat chewing my lip for a minute before deciding I couldn't leave it. Mark had stayed in my thoughts all week, even though I'd been kept so busy. I was still curious about the call box incident, and I felt drawn to him in an odd way that wasn't romantic or even sexual.

I drove back towards the main road where I'd seen him, and I was in luck, as he'd just turned into the Warrington road. I pulled up at the roadside and rolled down the window of Diana's white Nissan.

'Hey, Mark,' I called, and he turned sharply, but then his expression changed to one of relief, even pleasure.

'Well,' he grinned, raising his eyebrows and looking significantly at the car. 'This is a surprise.'

'Just what I was thinking,' I said. 'Do you want a lift anywhere? I'm free for the next few hours.'

He headed over and stared at me, running a hand through his hair. 'So how come you're driving a car?'

'I've got a job here. Just board and pocket money, but it's keeping me going for the time being.'

'That's great. I wondered how you were getting on. I would have phoned, but I… um… had a few problems.'

'Are you okay?' I asked.

'Yeah, I'm fine now.'

Somehow I didn't think he was fine. He was just as tanned and good looking as before, but he seemed vulnerable somehow.

'Is there anywhere I can take you?' I asked again.

'Well, to be honest, I'm um… I'm kind of…'

'Lost again?'

'Not quite, but I'm not headed anywhere in particular.'

'How come? Someone throw you out of a car or something?'

He grinned. 'Or something.'

Once again it was obvious that he was holding back. 'I'm heading for Karitane for some kayaking,' I said. 'Want to come?'

His face lit up, but then his features fell just as quickly. 'That'd be great but –'

'But? C'mon, I could do with the company, and the exercise.'

He hesitated, looking a little uncomfortable. After a moment he said, 'OK, let's give it a go.'

I shook my head in bemusement as he got into the passenger seat. Surely kayaking was harmless enough?

'What kind of work are you doing?' he asked as I accelerated away.

He listened with interest as I filled him in about Diana and Shelly and why I was driving despite my ethical objections, not to mention my sheer terror. I'd rather have picked up twenty tarantulas than drive, although my confidence was improving, despite Diana's constant instruction, otherwise known as back-seat driving.

'So I've got this job until Christmas,' I finished. 'They're having a lot of family over then, and I need to move out by the twenty-third.'

'You'll probably get lucky with another job, it being Christmas,' he said reassuringly.

I looked at him sideways. 'So what are you really doing up here? I mean, you know a lot more about me than I know about you.'

He smiled. 'Seeing as we're obviously fated to keep on meeting, we could trade stories if you like. I'll start. Like I told you, I was born in Blenheim. My mum couldn't keep me, so I was adopted. All I have of my real mum is my name. My adoptive parents were great, and I was an only child. I went to Uni in Dunedin and studied Environmental Management, but not long after I finished my studies, my mum and dad were killed in a car crash. After that I kind of threw myself into work and moved across to the West Coast to work for the DOC. That's it really, in a nutshell.'

'What about girlfriends? Isn't there someone?' I wondered if I was being too nosy, but as before, I felt quite at ease with him.

He turned to look at me with an oddly sad expression. 'No. I've had a few relationships over the years, but nothing that lasted. What about you?'

I was motoring through Warrington again by this time and hoped Diana wouldn't look out of the window and spot me with a strange man.

'Okay. I was born in Stratford-upon-Avon, where Shakespeare's meant to be from, and I was an only child too. I had a normal childhood until my dad got ill when I was fifteen. He had motor neurone disease, and it was horrible watching him deteriorate. I couldn't work too well at school or college with that going on, so it was a surprise when I got reasonable A levels. All the same, by the time I left college, I was too messed up to even think about going to Uni, and my dad died just after. I got a job in an office and hated it, and then I just sort of drifted along for years, changing jobs every now and again but never finding one I enjoyed. As for boyfriends, you know about Niall. That's about the closest I've ever got to a long-term relationship.'

'Never met Mr Right, eh?' Mark said after a long pause that had me turning to look at him.

I shrugged. 'I don't seem to be quite what men expect or want. And vice versa, I suppose. I always feel like they want to own me.' I stopped suddenly, concerned that I was talking too much. I looked aside at him again. 'So why *are* you here?'

'Like I said, I wasn't exactly planning to be here today, but I'm kind of looking for someone. Well okay, I *am* looking for someone: my real parents, or at least my mum. I don't know my dad's name, and I only know my mum's surname was Juniper.'

'Couldn't the adoption agency get in touch with your mum, ask her if she'd be willing to meet you?'

He sighed. 'I wish, but she didn't hang around. She did a runner just after I was born, and their records say they're not even sure Juniper was her real name.'

'Okay,' I said slowly, as I concentrated on one of the many bends in the coast road. 'So how do you search in circumstances like that?'

'Pretty hopeless ones, you mean? You go through all the records you can find, looking for the surname Juniper, and then you go and check out the people.'

'Check them out?'

'Yeah. I just kind of turn up and…' he sighed, 'look them over.'

'They don't think that's a bit odd?'

He laughed dryly. 'I'm pretty crafty about it.' He was silent for a moment and then added, 'I guess you're thinking I'm on a wild goose chase, but it's *important.*'

I wanted to ask why he was so desperate but sensed a deep reserve there.

'So was this what you were doing in Alexandra?'

He chewed his lip. 'Sort of.'

When I pulled up in Karitane at the kayaking centre, Mark was out of the car immediately. 'I'll get down to the boats,' he said, 'and leave the arrangements to you.'

I was puzzled and wondered if it was a problem with money. He seemed unduly tense until we were actually out on the water, but once we were well away from the shore, he relaxed visibly and began to enjoy himself.

It was a great afternoon. The kayak glided easily through clear waters with both of us paddling hard; the sun shone bright on our backs, and we talked about New Zealand, cycling, tramping, boating, kayaking – just about anything that wasn't personal. We paddled up the Waikouiti River and chilled out on a deserted sandy beach for a while. It began to seem as though I'd known him forever, but it was obvious that he still didn't want to reveal too much about himself, even to me.

When we finally got back to Karitane he insisted on heading off on foot but gave no hint as to where. Instead, he favoured me with his usual lazy grin. 'It was great to see you again,' he said. 'Good luck with the dragon lady, and if I hear about any more jobs, I'll let you know.'

As I drove away in the opposite direction, I couldn't help feeling that his receding figure looked incredibly lonely. Then I shook my head at my own fancy. He was a hot guy in his twenties. Surely he had everything going for him?

Chapter Four

'Having a very interesting time here,' I emailed Suze from a Dunedin internet café. 'Definitely no regrets about Niall – haven't heard from him for two weeks now. I hear it's a bit chilly back at home!' I paused, my fingers poised over the keyboard and my mind drifting off to Mark's harebrained scheme to somehow lurk around the homes of potential relatives. It seemed an odd, even desperate, way to go about it. On a whim I opened up a new browser tab and looked at a few genealogy websites, wondering whether Mark had his own laptop and had already done all this himself. I found nothing helpful that didn't require a subscription. Besides, Mark's mother must have been born in the 1950s or 60s, far more recent than anything available on the websites. My only surprise was that the name Juniper wasn't as uncommon as I'd first thought.

I left the café wondering if Mark had lost my phone number and why I cared so much, but at just that moment my mobile phone vibrated. I flipped it open quickly and felt a surge of disappointment as I noted that it was only my mum. I gritted my teeth as I answered. I'd avoided ringing her for over a week.

'So you're still alive then?' she said in a hurt tone. 'That's nice to know. Are you still in Dunedin?'

'Yes, still at the same place. I didn't ring because there was nothing new to report.'

'I'd still appreciate hearing from you, just once in a while,' she said huffily.

I headed through the streets towards Diana's house while she filled me in on all the news from Edinburgh. Once I was safely ensconced back in my room I said finally, and a little hesitantly, 'Um, do you remember when I used to have that nightmare all the time?'

'Of course I remember. Back when your dad was ill. You used to wake up crying, and the doctor said it was down to the stress. Why do you ask? You're not getting it again are you?'

'Well…'

'Oh Ollie, for goodness' sake, just come home. It's obviously doing you no good having to struggle there on your own.'

'I'm fine. Really. I'm enjoying it here. I just can't understand why the dream has come back – it's exactly the same, as well. There wasn't ever anything really traumatic in my childhood, was there?'

She was silent for a moment. 'Traumatic? You mean, like abuse? How could you even think it? You had a perfectly normal childhood, and your dad would never have hurt a fly. You know that.'

'But there wasn't anything else that could have happened? You know, any time when I wasn't with you and dad? Anything you can think of?'

'No,' she said firmly. 'You're going to have to face up to the fact that you're too stressed, never mind looking for skeletons in the cupboard. There just aren't any.'

After five more minutes of expostulation on her part, we eventually disconnected. I sat at the desk in my room and stared out at Mount Cargill; I was already dreading going to sleep. Maybe I would have to see a doctor after all.

'I'd say your mum's right,' Dr Piper said, detaching the blood pressure cuff.

'About which part? It being stress or me needing to go back home?'

He chuckled. 'About the stress. As to going home, I'm not sure that's necessarily the answer.'

'Thing is, it came on *after* I'd split up with Niall, which should have meant less stress, and it's not getting better. It's worse, if anything.'

He frowned as he made rapid notes. 'I could prescribe a few sleeping tablets, for when you're really struggling, but you should avoid taking them as much as you can.' He sat back in his chair and made eye contact. 'Being short of money in a foreign country *is* pretty stressful. Plus, don't tell Diana I said this, but I know from experience that she's a formidable woman. What are you going to do at Christmas? It's only just over a week away. You need to make some sort of plan – copping out might be making the nightmares worse.'

I knew he was right, but he hadn't really told me anything I didn't already know. In fact, he had made me feel even more stressed. I fingered the prescription in my pocket as I headed away from the surgery. Was it worth spending money on redeeming it? Maybe I'd just wait and see how things went.

The sky was grey and there was a bit of a drizzle. The weather in Dunedin reminded me of a British summer and seemed just as variable. I actually felt chilly in the wind and headed into a café for a hot chocolate. It was another of Diana's days out, so I had plenty of time to spare.

My mobile rang as I took my first sip. It was another unfamiliar New Zealand number.

'Hi Ollie, it's Mark.'

'Hi. Are you still in Karitane?' It had been five days since I'd last seen him.

'No, I'm in Invercargill, and I might have some news to your advantage.'

'You get about a lot.' Maybe he was chasing a new family lead there. 'What sort of news? A job?'

'I'll tell you about it when I get back to Dunedin. Will you have any free time tomorrow?'

I thought for a minute. 'Yes, in the morning. Diana's having her hair done.'

'Okay. Can you meet me at the Botanic Garden?'

As he gave me directions, I began to wonder whether he ever liked to be indoors at all. He'd probably want to meet on the top of a mountain or the middle of a field even if it were pouring with rain.

When I picked Diana up later, she asked me about my visit to the doctor.

'He just said it was stress,' I replied airily, hoping to close the subject.

'Hmmm,' she said grimly. 'Old Piper doesn't know what he's talking about. There's more to it than that. Let me guess, he prescribed some pills?'

'Yes, but I'm not sure that I'm going to take any.'

'Good for you, but I still think you ought to see a psychologist. I'm convinced it's post traumatic stress disorder, and I do have a bit of an idea of what *I'm* talking about.'

'But even my mum says there weren't any big traumas in my childhood, and this place I dream of, it's nowhere I've ever been.'

'The place might not be real, but the emotion is. You said it started when your dad was ill – maybe you've never really dealt with those feelings.'

I was beginning to feel uncomfortable. Okay, so Diana used to be a neuroscientist, and she knew a lot about the brain, but she wasn't a psychologist herself. Besides, where did she think I was going to get the money for lengthy consultations with one?

'I think I'm just going to play it by ear for now. Maybe it'll ease off soon,' I said, trying to put a note of finality into my voice.

'Hmph. On your own head be it. Now, I need you to stop off at the supermarket. I want to do my own shopping for a change. Michelle doesn't get the right brands.'

Mark was already at the Botanic Garden when I arrived the next morning. It was hot and sunny, a complete contrast to the previous day's damp chill, and we wandered around a duck pond, admiring the flowers.

'Did you find any Junipers in Invercargill?' I asked. 'I assume that's why you went.'

He shook his head. 'No luck.'

'What did you do? Go and speak to them or what?'

He frowned and stared across the pond. 'Sort of,' he said in a distracted tone.

'Weren't they a bit surprised at you just turning up out of the blue?'

He turned back to me. 'Nah, good as gold. Anyway, like I said, no luck.' His tone was final.

'So what are you going to do now?' I asked as we sat on a bench. The blazing sun was beginning to burn the top of my head.

He shrugged. 'I think I'll head to Christchurch for another ferret around. There's a lot more Junipers there.'

'What about the North Island? Couldn't she have come from there?'

He bit his lip. 'Thing is, the notes are pretty sparse. All they say is my mum came into hospital, gave the name Mrs Juniper, was healthy and presentable, showed no sign of being a druggie or anything like that, had me and called me Mark, and did a runner the next day. She never gave an address. She didn't even… you know, leave a blanket or anything, like they do in stories.'

I gazed at him with sympathy. 'This really eats you up, doesn't it? Can you afford to keep on looking? I mean, don't you need to go back to work?'

He smiled. 'No, I'm fine for now. I know it's like looking for a needle in a haystack, but like I said, it's important.'

'It's not because you need a transplant or anything, is it? You look pretty healthy.'

He gave me one of his usual grins and raised his eyebrows. 'Thanks. No, it's not that. I suppose it's been growing inside me ever since my parents died. Not having anyone or knowing where I really come from. I always wondered how she could… you know, just walk away like that. Why she did it.'

'She must have been desperate, I suppose,' I said, trying to think myself into a very alien situation. 'Maybe she couldn't cope. Did they say how old she was?'

'Late teens, maybe twenty. No wedding ring, they did mention that.'

'So Juniper could have been her maiden name?'

He nodded and then looked aside at me. 'I know what you're thinking: it's hopeless. But I have the time, and I'm just going to try everything and if I fail, well then maybe I'll be able to let it rest.'

'You don't want to be haunted by it all your life – blighted by it, even. It's a waste, Mark. And even if you find her, or some other relatives, how do you know they'll be willing to meet you, or want to know you? You could be opening up a real can of worms.'

He washed his face in his hands. 'I know, I know. You're right. But…'

'Okay. I won't keep on. I shouldn't anyway, really. It's not my business.'

'It's all right; I don't mind. Actually I'm really glad we met. But speaking of your business, I heard about a job for you when I was in Invercargill.'

He reeled off a phone number to me. I was amazed he could memorise it so well. 'If you phone that number and tell them about your customer service experience, you could be in with a chance of a temporary job in Manapouri,' he said.

'Manapouri? I've never heard of it – where is it?'

'In Fiordland. It's a little township on the edge of a gorgeous lake. I had a couple of weeks down there a few years back: great tramping country, too. You'd be helping out at one of the tourist boat companies. There'll probably be a fair bit of menial stuff, and they can't pay much, if anything, but if you play your cards right, you could get it for room and board. It's Christmas, and there aren't so many people looking for temp work down there.'

I was already getting excited; it sounded ideal, and I'd always fancied messing about in boats.

Mark smiled as he added, 'Who knows, after I've been to Christchurch, I might come and look you up.'

'I'd like that,' I said. He could be pretty intense under the cheery grin, but I felt more at home with him than with any man I'd met.

We wandered around the gardens for an hour longer, discussing our mutual interest in plants, nature and the outdoors. I wasn't sure what kind of relationship we were developing. I still didn't fancy him, and while he was distinctly not gay, he showed no overt sign of fancying me. Maybe we were having that elusive thing, a platonic boy/girl relationship. If we were, I couldn't quite see it ending like it does in *When Harry Met Sally*.

He refused my offer of a lift and left on foot, saying he wanted to look up a friend in Dunedin but would contact me again before too long. I still found it amazing that he didn't have a mobile.

In my room later, I phoned the number he'd given me for the job in Manapouri. A dry, male New Zealand voice answered and expressed surprise when I said I'd heard about a job.

'It's not a job exactly. It's true I do need some help, but – how did you hear about it?'

'From a friend,' I said, wondering if I should mention his name but deciding against it.

'Yeah? Well, he might have overheard me talking down the pub or something, I s'pose.'

'He said it was helping out with the boats,' I added, wondering if Mark had gone to Manapouri. He hadn't mentioned it.

'Yeah, true, normally it's me and the wife, but she's not too well, and the doc says she's going to be out of action for a few weeks. I do need someone to help out, but I can't pay, you see. So if you're looking for work I'm not going to be much use.'

'I could work for just a place to stay, and maybe food,' I said.

'Yeah?' the man said with a hint of interest in his voice. 'Any experience of boats?'

'Not yet, but I'd love to learn, and I'm fit and strong.'

'What about office work? Answering the phone, taking bookings, things like that?'

'Yes, I've done a lot of that sort of work. I was in a call centre for two years, and I worked in accounts for five years before that.'

There was a silence, as though he was thinking fast. 'Where are you right now?'

'Dunedin, but I'll be finishing on the twenty-third.'

'Well, look, I'm not sure yet, but give me your number, and I'll get back to you in a couple of days.'

I gave him the details and felt a bit dispirited as I ended the call. It didn't sound too hopeful. I was going to have to spend the next couple of days trawling around Dunedin to see if I could pick up any bar or café work, just in case.

***

My mobile burst into life, dragging me out of the dream. I sat up in bed, confused and sweating, and grabbed the phone, flipping it open in irritation.

'Why do I have to make all the calls?' my mum asked, sounding hurt. 'Are you still in Dunedin? It's almost Christmas. What are you going to do then?'

'I've got the chance of another job down in Fiordland,' I said. 'I'm just waiting to hear.'

'What sort of job?'

'Helping out with a boating business. He'll be getting back to me shortly.'

'I wish you'd just come home. I really don't like to think of you on your own in another country, especially not at this time of year.'

As I listened to my mum's complaints, I couldn't help succumbing to a feeling of panic. I'd already been waiting three days to hear back about the Manapouri job, and I only had three to go with Shelly and Diana. What was more, all my efforts to find other work had failed. I could end up having to stay in a motel, using what was left of my New Zealand dollars for just one night. Not that I was going to tell my mum any of that.

After she'd rung off, I got up and took a look out of the window and the dawn of another warm summer's day. I wouldn't admit it to anyone, but I was feeling a bit lonely. I hadn't heard from Mark; Shelly and Diana were getting ready for a family Christmas with all the trimmings; and I seemed to be heading for a solitary Christmas Day in a motel room. The day before, in a moment of weakness, I'd checked out the possibility of altering my flight and returning home, but there were no spaces on any flights for the next couple of weeks, which had spared me from making a decision I might regret, at least.

The dream had continued to plague me every night. I'd been trying to unpick it, to determine what it was that was bothering me, with no success. It started and ended with me sitting on the beach, feeling utter loss and despair. Apart from the clarity of the images, there were no other clues to what was going on.

I showered and dressed quickly and headed downstairs for breakfast. Diana was already up, as usual, and Shelly had gone to work.

'I'm expecting a visitor today, and I need you to be here,' Diana said, glancing at me obliquely.

'Oh. Okay.' She didn't usually want me around when her friends visited. I'd been thinking I might have some free time.

'Have you had any luck looking for a job?'

I shook my head and took a sip of coffee. Diana pushed over her copy of The Press, the newspaper she favoured.

'There are a few jobs in there you could do,' she said. 'Of course most of them will be permanent, but if you could get one you'd be able to apply for a work visa.'

I nodded and thanked her, perusing the headlines. 'NZ recession worsens,' one told me cheerily.

When the bell rang half an hour later, I opened the door to a short, slightly plump man a few years older than I was.

'Hello,' he said. 'You must be Olivia.'

'Um… y-yes,' I stammered in surprise.

'I'm Greg Manners, a friend of Diana's. She's expecting me.'

I took him into the living room, wondering why Diana had told this man my name. It wasn't that she treated me like a servant, exactly, but I was, after all, just a temporary lodger in her house.

She greeted him affectionately and then turned to look at me. 'Greg used to be one of my students at the university,' she explained. 'I asked him to come because he's a psychiatrist now.'

I exhaled sharply. So now she thought I needed a psychiatrist?

'I could see you weren't going to do anything about it, but I know it's no better. You could at least talk to him about it.'

'But,' I began, feeling completely exasperated, 'I really *don't* have any buried trauma.'

'That's what they all say,' Greg said with a smile as he seated himself on the sofa.

'I'm going out for a drive,' Diana said. 'So I'll leave you to it. It's time I had a go on my own.'

She was hardly limping anymore, so I couldn't really protest, but I listened to the front door close with a sense of being completely outmanoeuvred.

'I don't have any buried trauma,' I said again to Greg, sitting down reluctantly on the edge of an armchair. 'I don't agree with Diana that it's post traumatic stress disorder.'

He shrugged. 'She does seem to be very concerned about you. Are you that bothered about talking to me?'

'Would it mean something if I was?'

He smiled and shrugged again. 'Who knows? A recurrent dream *is* usually indicative of some kind of traumatic event.'

'Diana thinks I haven't dealt with my dad's death properly, but that was fifteen years ago.'

'It was traumatic, though?'

'Yes, to the extent that I was really close to him, and he went downhill so fast. I was only fifteen when he was first diagnosed with motor neurone disease, and I'm sure it had a big impact on me. The dream started then, when he was ill. But that's the point; it started when he was still alive.'

He nodded slowly. 'And then?'

'It went off after he died but started again just after I broke up with my boyfriend. And no, that wasn't a traumatic event; it was a huge relief.'

'But now you're having the dream every night?'

'Just about.'

'Can you tell me about it?'

I sighed. 'There's not much to tell.'

He regarded me stolidly but didn't comment. I shrugged in defeat and described the scene on the beach and how it made me feel, watching as he frowned.

‘You’re assuming the scene is significant?’ he asked.

‘It’s too vivid to be imagined. I’d know the place as soon as I saw it.’

‘Well, it does sound to me as though you need to talk about your dad, at least. Of course, we don’t have much time if you’re about to leave Dunedin.’

‘I don’t have any money either,’ I said.

‘Don’t worry. I’m doing this as a favour to Diana. It was more than my life was worth to refuse.’ He laughed. ‘We’ve got a couple of hours now anyway. What was your relationship with him like?’

I took a deep breath. What *was* it like? It was difficult to remember how our lives were before my dad’s illness. Was I Daddy’s little girl? Not exactly. My dad never treated me like a little girl. He always talked to me as though I were an adult. We were more likely to be discussing population growth or free will or climate change than whether I wanted a princess dress or not. He had no interest in that side of things. Looking back, I couldn’t imagine how he and my mum ever got together. She was the ultimate girly woman, and sadly for her, I took after my dad.

‘So your relationship with your dad was quite unusual,’ Greg commented.

‘I suppose so. He was more like a friend. He was the only person I could talk to about those kinds of subjects.’

Greg nodded sagely, and I wondered what he was thinking.

‘And your mum? She’s still alive?’

‘Oh yes, alive and very well. We don’t have the best of relationships. We’re not much alike.’

‘Was that the case when you were growing up as well?’

‘Yes, I suppose it was, but she and my dad seemed to get on well enough.’

‘That sounds a bit qualified.’

‘Well, they didn’t show much affection towards each other, but I always thought they were happy. I suppose I could have missed any undercurrents there might have been. But I don’t see how this is relevant, anyway.’

'It might not be. I'm just trying to understand what your dad meant to you.'

'I suppose it was like I lost my best friend,' I said slowly. 'I never thought of it that way before.'

'Tell me more about him,' Greg prompted, and I found myself explaining how my dad was a thwarted intellectual who read widely and knew about almost everything yet worked as a repair electrician all his life.

'I don't know how happy he was doing it,' I said. 'He never used to talk to me about himself much. Not his personal life, anyway.'

'How did he meet your mum?'

I laughed. 'He went round to fix her washing machine. She must have beguiled him somehow. They were married within a few months.'

'You'd say your childhood was a happy one?'

'Yes, definitely. Apart from a few spats with my mum here and there, I don't remember anything bad happening.'

'Until your dad got ill.'

I nodded solemnly. 'Then everything changed. I was still at school, but my marks went from As to Cs. I only just scraped through college with decent qualifications.'

'And when he died, how did you react?'

'I know what you're trying to get at, but I really do think I dealt with it at the time.'

'Humour me anyway,' Greg said with a small smile.

'It was a relief by the time it happened; he'd been in such a decline. It was actually harder watching him deteriorate than it was when he finally died. By that time I just felt numb. I didn't cry a lot. It seemed to be too late for that.'

He nodded thoughtfully. 'I have to say, given what you've told me, that this problem does sound like a reaction to your dad's illness, rather than anything else.'

'So what do I do, apart from spend years in analysis?' I said flippantly. 'I dread going to sleep every night now.'

'We could try hypnosis,' he suggested. 'It might bring more of the dream to light.'

The idea made me uneasy, but given how rotten I'd been feeling after so many disturbed nights, I agreed, and settled down nervously on Diana's sofa. It took Greg quite a long time to get me to relax, and when he asked me to tell him about the dream, I became very uncomfortable. Next thing I knew I was pushing myself up into a sitting position, shouting 'No!'

I dragged my hair away from my face and wiped my sweaty forehead. Greg was regarding me with some concern.

'You're a tough nut to crack,' he said in mock-amusement. 'What happened there?'

'I was going to ask you that,' I replied, getting up and going over to the window to avoid his gaze.

'I assume you didn't want to talk about it. You only went into a light trance, in any case. You're not an easy subject. What did you feel?'

'Just... scared. I didn't want the feelings again,' I said, turning back to face him.

He nodded sympathetically. 'There's obviously something there, but perhaps it's best to leave it for now. I'd say you really do need to see someone properly about this though. You shouldn't ignore it.'

'So it's your opinion that it *is* some buried trauma?'

He fingered his chin thoughtfully. 'Are you absolutely sure you don't remember ever seeing this place – this beach – before?'

I shook my head firmly. 'It doesn't even look like a British beach. It looks foreign.'

'Did you ever go abroad on holiday when you were a child?'

I shook my head again. 'Mum and Dad were right home birds. While everyone else was jetting off to Benidorm or the Greek Islands, we were heading to Clacton or the Norfolk Broads.'

'So what makes you so sure it's foreign?'

I bit my lip, playing through the all-too-familiar images in my mind. 'I suppose it's the trees. They look exotic.' I paused as a sudden connection sprang into my mind. 'Oh. *Oh my God.*' I lifted my eyes to meet his, trembling. 'I just realized. Those trees look like New Zealand trees. You know, the real native ones? They're that same sort of greyish green. And those big plants that look like triffids with great big pods that grow everywhere here –'

'Flax?'

'Is that what they're called? Well, there are some of those growing by the beach, and tree stumps sticking out of the water. But I've never been to New Zealand before, and I know *that* for certain. What on earth can it mean?'

He smiled. 'You've got me there, unless it's an image you've seen on TV and you've associated the emotions with it, but that's a long shot I grant you.'

I was clenching and unclenching my fists. 'It definitely seems like I'm there. I can touch the sand under my hands. I can even feel the breeze blowing. It's warm – really warm.'

'Who are you grieving for?' Greg asked softly, almost insidiously.

'For her,' I found myself saying without realizing it. I snapped my head back up to look at him and then clamped my hands over my cheeks. 'Oh. How did you do that?'

'I didn't. The memory's there, but you don't want to recall it.'

'But it *never happened*. I don't know what I meant; I don't know *who* I meant.'

'It's in there, Olivia, and it's in your best interests to get it out, before it makes you ill.'

'Do you really think that's likely?'

'You told me yourself you're afraid to go to sleep.'

'Yes, but –' The front door opened, startling us both. 'Well, thanks for coming,' I added quickly, as Diana's limping step headed our way. 'At least talking about it to you has clarified something, even though it still doesn't make sense. I'll see how things are after Christmas.'

'Don't leave it too long,' he warned, his expression serious.

Chapter Five

I opened the car door and stepped out onto the roadside grass, taking deep breaths of clean air and shielding my eyes from the sun as I looked down towards the sea and the twin crescents of the Karitane beaches. It was one of my favourite spots around Dunedin.

This was my last day but one with Diana, and I still had no immediate future. I needed to book a motel, but I was putting it off, still waiting, Micawber-like, for that something to turn up. The one bright spot was that I hadn't had the dream the previous night. Something about Greg's visit must have helped, even though I was annoyed at Diana's high-handedness. I still had no idea what I meant about grieving *for her*, but it was a relief to be free of the dream for long enough to try to understand it.

My mobile rang, and I pulled it out of my pocket with a sigh, expecting it to be Diana, but I didn't recognise the number.

'Is that Olivia Kimpton?' a slightly familiar New Zealand voice said. My heart started thumping as I answered in the affirmative.

'This is Bob Haynes, of Manapouri Aquatic Adventures. You called me a few days back. Thing is, I thought I had the situation sorted out; my nephew was going to fill in for a bit, but he's had to pull out. You still looking for work?'

'Yes,' I said eagerly. 'I finish here tomorrow.'

'Well, I've got a small flat you could live in for a while, and I can give you a bit of money for food and essentials – it won't be much. If that's all okay with you, then the job's yours.'

I leaned back against the car with relief, and at once the sun seemed to shine even more brightly on Karitane far below. 'That's more than okay with me!' I said almost as dramatically as Shelly. 'I'm really looking forward to it.'

I filled Mark in on all the details when he rang me that evening. 'It's just him and his wife doing everything. They run these boat trips around the lake and stop off at a couple of scenic spots.'

'Sounds good. What about somewhere to live?'

'There's a flat over the top of his office I can use. There's even a bit of a lake view, apparently.'

'That's great.'

'Are you staying in Christchurch?'

'Just for a bit. I've still got a few leads to follow up.'

I was tempted to tell him about the dream and Greg's visit, but he started talking about the wildlife and landscape around Manapouri and warned me to look out for sandflies.

'What's a sandfly?' I asked.

He laughed. 'You won't be asking that for long. They're only small, but their bites are really irritating, and you don't feel them until it's too late. Get some bug repellent while you're still in Dunedin – you'll be needing it.'

I settled in bed later, feeling more light-hearted than I had for days, and I wondered suddenly whether the beach in my dream could be at Manapouri. After all, why would there be tree stumps on a sea beach? Maybe it was a lake beach, with all those trees on the other side. My stomach tightened with excitement. On the other hand, what would happen if I *did* find the beach? Would I end up experiencing the loss? It could have been a precognitive dream, couldn't it? Greg hadn't mentioned that, but I'd read all my dad's psychology books, and dreams of the future weren't unheard of. I sat up in bed suddenly. What if it was my mum? She seemed fine, happy with Ron in Edinburgh, never ill, but what if something was going to happen? I'd been so neglectful, hardly ringing her, avoiding her. I checked the time. It was midnight, so it would be late morning at home. I scrabbled for the mobile phone in the dark and called her, my heart thudding.

'Bit of a turn up, you ringing me,' she said, without preamble. 'What's come over you?'

My heart rate slowed. She sounded just the same.

'I just wondered how you were. How's Ron?'

I listened as she told me all about the current play she and Ron were taking part in for their local amateur dramatic society. She had to be okay; she sounded quite happy, if as exasperated with me as ever.

'Have you booked your flight home yet?' she asked eventually.

'No, I've got the job in Manapouri now. I'll be there the day after tomorrow.'

'How long do you think you can keep this up?' she said. 'Your money's going to disappear, and you'll be penniless. Then what?'

'I'll cross that bridge when I come to it,' I answered, quoting one of her own favourite catchphrases from my childhood. 'So you're okay, anyway? Fit and well?'

'Of course I am. Why the sudden concern?'

'I just had a bad dream, that's all.'

'Well you needn't worry about me. You should pay more attention to yourself. Are you still getting that other dream?'

'On and off,' I said, and hoped she wouldn't pursue it, only to be disappointed. I lay there in the dark and stared out of the window at the moon lighting the quiet side streets of Dunedin, listening to my mum's lecture with a small smile on my lips. As long as she was ranting like this, I knew she was fine.

***

'Alan… how could he… how could they…?' I groaned and woke up abruptly, staring around the room with a momentary lack of recognition. I sat up, rubbing my face. The dream had captured me again, but this time with added content.

I tried to dispel the uneasiness this new fragment had brought on as I got out of bed and padded across the room to the large window of the attic apartment. As promised, there was indeed a lake view if you ignored the houses and road in the foreground. The weather had taken another of its sharp about-turns and the sky was grey and oppressive. The lake looked quite rough in the blustery wind; there were even a few white-capped waves.

I was very much taken with my new loft, which consisted of just one room with a small bathroom at the side. Despite its size, it contained a double bed, sofa, table and a compact but well-equipped kitchen area. There was also a TV, although the picture wasn't too good, and you couldn't get all the channels, which I assumed was down to the signal, not the TV.

'My son lived here for a couple of years before he went to London to do his OE,' Bob had explained when he'd shown me around.

'Um… OE?'

'Overseas experience. Most New Zealanders go abroad for a bit before they come back and settle down.'

Hmmm. Mark had never mentioned doing any OE.

I popped a slice of bread into the toaster and continued to stare out of the window. Lake Manapouri was vast, amazing and beautiful, and it was nothing like the lake in my dream. It was bound by tree-clad mountains, but there were only distant, hazy mountains visible from my dream beach; I'd spotted a few lupins flowering at the lakeside, but no flax; there were no half-submerged tree stumps, and the long stretches of beach I'd already explored were shingle rather than sand. I didn't know whether I was glad or sorry.

I chewed my lip as I thought about the name that had suddenly appeared in the dream. *Alan?* I didn't know any Alan. I cast my mind back, searching for some recollection of the name, maybe in my childhood, but there was nothing. My appetite faded a little as I considered the possibility that Diana and Greg had been right, and I really did have some awful trauma in my past that even my mum didn't know about.

I'd been in Manapouri for a week, and things couldn't have been rosier, except for the dream. For five nights in a row I'd had no let up from the overwhelming emotions. And now, it seemed, there were two people involved: *her* and *Alan.* My toast started to burn as I squeezed the dream memory, trying to bring up more details. As ever, now that I was awake they drifted away.

I rescued the charred toast and buttered it absently. I doubted that there were any psychiatrists or psychologists in the area, but I couldn't carry on like this much longer.

Mark wasn't faring much better. His phone calls were becoming increasingly despondent as his search foundered in Christchurch. During one of these calls, I'd finally brought up the topic of his oddly outdated lack of a mobile, but he'd just laughed.

'Look who's talking, Miss I-want-to-ban-cars.'

'Well that's different. I mean, cars are horrible, noisy, polluting things whereas mobiles…'

'They come in handy though, cars. And motorbikes. I used to love my bike, travelled everywhere on it.'

'So where is it now? Every time I've seen you you've been on foot.'

'Yeah well, times change,' he said, and I sensed a hint of bitterness. 'Besides, tramping's better exercise.'

Why was he always so mysterious? Perhaps he'd had to declare himself bankrupt? But that didn't explain why he was on such a frantic search for family.

When I'd told him about the dream, and the beach, and what had happened with Greg, he'd seemed genuinely interested.

'Tree stumps in the water and a sandy beach? I've seen places like that on the West Coast. You sure it's a lake? There are spots like that around Haast, but they're on estuaries rather than lakes.'

After that, the idea of going to Haast kept popping into my thoughts. There was something about the name that kept tickling my memory; something that felt significant, and while it seemed ludicrous to travel all over New Zealand looking for a beach, I felt compelled to rid myself of the dream, and finally put it to rest. The job in Manapouri was going to last for a while, but once it was over, Haast had to be the place to go.

'You going down the pub later?' Bob asked as I helped him clean the cabin of his boat after my first trip out as his assistant. Up until then my duties had been all too familiar from my office days – answering the phone, dealing with bookings, e-mail, filing, paying bills. Bob's wife Marion had given me advice over the phone but was too ill to come in. She was due for an operation after Christmas but would still be unable to work for a while after that.

'Yes, sure,' I said, spraying citronella sandfly repellent all over the fittings and upholstery with considerable enthusiasm. Mark had been right; I was now very familiar with the little black devils and had enough itchy bites to remind me to plaster repellent onto any of my own exposed skin.

'Marion says she's coming down tonight – she's feeling a bit better than usual,' Bob said. 'If you're there, it'll give her a chance to tell you anything she's forgotten before she goes in for her op.'

'Okay, I'll be there.'

The pub was at the one big motel in town. From the start, Bob had encouraged me to join him and some of the other locals there in the evenings. I think he felt sorry for me, being on my own, and I was grateful to escape from my preoccupation with the dream. I was slowly starting to feel a part of the community rather than just a tourist.

Besides, it suited me to eat there sometimes, as cooking was another of the prime duties in my mum's lexicon of womanly tasks at which I didn't excel. I'd found cookery a complete bore at school and beyond. Naturally my mum was a great cook: I was never going to live up to her elevated standards. Still, living on toast, baked beans and scrambled eggs got a bit boring after a while, so the occasional blue cod and chips at the motel made a pleasant change, even though it ate into my small store of cash.

'That's good enough for now,' Bob said, looking around the cabin. 'You did well for your first time – you're good with the customers. It helps if there's two of us when we get a big group.'

'I enjoyed it.' Actually I'd more than enjoyed it. Being on a boat, watching the clouds drift below the mountain tops, seeing the water change constantly as we tracked across the lake was just the sort of thing I'd always dreamed of doing. Even those pesky sandflies couldn't ruin it.

Later, I left the small building that was both Bob's business office and my current abode and headed along the lakeshore in the direction of the motel. The lake was placid, with just a few skeins of lighter shading rippling across it as the sun grew lower in the sky. Its waters were a perfect blue, the forested mountains crowding around it tinted red from the evening sun and the furthest crags topped with snow. I watched someone practice water skiing, falling in and getting up again and again, and reflected on how unlike my dream lake it was. Even the colour was wrong, I realized suddenly – the water in the dream lake was a sort of tan, but Manapouri was completely clear.

I joined Bob and Marion in the pub and was enjoying a convivial time when Tom strolled over. We'd met a couple of days earlier, and he'd been quite persistent in his attentions. I scratched my hand absently – those wretched sandflies had somehow managed to break through my layers of repellent – and took a sip of my Coke.

'So what are you up to tomorrow?' Tom said, settling down on the seat opposite me. 'Me and Jake are planning to drive out to the Kepler Track and hike from Rainbow Reach to Shallow Bay and back. You could come with us.'

Damn. Seriously tempting, considering I didn't have any independent means of getting to the Kepler Track, but if I agreed, I'd just be prolonging the agony and giving him false hope. At least he was only going to be there for another day or two – he and Jake were British tourists themselves, just passing through.

'Ah, no, I can't. I've… um… arranged to meet someone in… um…Te Anau.' I lied, sounding beyond lame even to my own ears.

I was spared his response because Ed came over. 'Hey, Ollie, I'm taking the boat out fishing tomorrow, across to the West Arm. Wondered if you fancied coming – I could teach you to fish if you like.'

I didn't have a chance to reply, as Tom wasted no time telling Ed about my appointment. Ed was a friend of Bob's. He was a few years older than me but good fun to be around. I'd have loved to go out fishing, but instead it looked like I was going to be spending the day on my own in Te Anau, pretending to meet someone. The only good thing about it was that I'd be able to check out the lake. Mark had said it wasn't a likely prospect for the dream lake, but it was surely worth a good look.

'So you'll be cycling up there?' Bob asked. 'Or were you going on the bus? Is it your friend Mark you're meeting? I thought he was still in Christchurch.'

I wished I could sink into the floor. My face started to redden, and my palms were sweating. 'Er, well, he is, but no it's not him. It's just… um…'

‘I hope you’re gonna call in on me on the way,’ a voice butted in in a pronounced American drawl.

I turned in surprise to see a tall, shambling man of about sixty-five giving me a significant look.

‘Since when do you want visitors, Pastor?’ Bob said, giving the man a friendly push on the shoulder.

‘Yeah, I thought you got that electrified fence to keep people out as well as deer,’ Ed added.

‘Well, normally I wouldn’t, but cycling to Te Anau, that’s thirsty work.’

‘Pastor lives at around the halfway point on the road,’ Bob explained.

‘Well thanks very much for the invitation,’ I said, totally flustered. ‘Maybe I will.’

He smiled and drew me a map showing the location of his house before heading out of the bar to a chorus of goodbyes.

‘Is he a real pastor?’ I asked Bob and Ed. Tom had sloped off with Jake, and to my relief it looked like they’d found a couple of female backpackers to chat up.

‘Used to be, back in Alabama, but he lives like a hermit now. It’s rare to see him in town, and even more rare to get an invite to his house,’ Bob answered.

‘He lost his faith after his wife died, and he came out here to get away from everything,’ Ed said.

‘Yep, been here ten years, and that’s about as much as we know about him, but he’s a good bloke all the same. Always willing to help anyone out.’

I wondered if he was helping me out, trying to distract everyone from my economy with the truth? Maybe he was regretting it already, but then again, he had drawn the map.

I left the pub soon after that, giving tiredness as my excuse, and took a detour down to the shingle beach nearby. I stared out at the dusky lake, wishing it could reveal the answers to all my problems.

Alan who? I tried prodding my brain again. I skimmed a couple of stones aimlessly, watching tiny wavelets splash against the shore. A thought occurred to me in a flash of insight. Surely this dream couldn't be mine? Or rather, the event couldn't be a memory of mine. The more I experienced it, the more it seemed like a representation of a real moment in *someone's* life. Perhaps someone had sat on that beach in total despair, hurt by Alan, grieving for 'her', but I was convinced that that person wasn't me.

Chapter Six

Lake Te Anau glistened greyly in watery sunlight. I'd had to cycle through a misty drizzle on the way, but at last the sun had begun to break through. The town of Te Anau was deluged by tourists, even more so than Manapouri. I'd already traipsed around the town, perused the goods in all the tourist shops, been to the supermarket to buy as much as I could carry on a bike, eaten a snack in one of the many cafés and even been to the cinema to watch a short film all about the beauties of Fiordland that Bob had recommended to me. Now I was back on the bike and cycling as far as I could beside the lake. It looked like Mark was right; it was nothing like the dream lake. The parts I could get to were too tame, fronting the road, and those that I couldn't reach appeared, from a distance at least, to resemble Manapouri. The dream lake was smaller, and there were no boats, and no forested mountains sloping down. Although that should have narrowed it down, it just made me realize what a difficult task I'd set myself. Maybe not quite as hard as Mark's though. He'd phoned last night sounding more despondent than ever.

'Any luck in Christchurch?' I'd asked.

He sighed. 'Nope, and I've tried every route I can think of.' He paused and then added in a discouraged tone, 'It's always seemed like the most likely place. She could have been on the run from there, driven up to Blenheim and gone into labour.'

'So what are you going to do now?'

'I've already searched the rest of the South Island, so there's nowhere else to go, except maybe north. I suppose she could have run from Wellington, even Auckland if she was really desperate.'

'Mark,' I began, and then hesitated before plunging on. 'You said yourself you might even be looking for the wrong surname. Are you sure it's doing you any good to keep looking? Couldn't you at least take a break, a few days off?'

'It's kind of… urgent.'

'Why is it urgent? You're so driven it's scary.'

'It's hard to explain,' he said faintly, 'but look, I'll try and get down there to see you before I go.'

I was worried about him. I wondered when urgent was going to tip over into desperate, if it hadn't already.

As the sky cleared, I turned away from the lake and headed back down the road to Manapouri. It was when I stopped in the middle of nowhere for a rest and a drink that I remembered the invitation from Pastor. Strange how no one had told me his real name. I took out the piece of paper I'd thrust into my pocket that morning as an afterthought.

The road was bordered on both sides by huge farm fields, but according to the map, Pastor's house was down some long track that led to his own small piece of land. I shrugged to myself. *Why not?* I was intrigued, and I was tired, hot and sweaty now that the sun was out. I could do with a break.

I found the track without too much difficulty and cycled down to an unlocked gate, which led into what looked like a smallholding with a modern New Zealand house at its centre. New Zealand houses often look like prefabs, and I'd learned that that's because many of them are. A dog came out barking past the chicken coop and what I assumed was a pig pen, closely followed by Pastor himself.

'Olivia, glad you came,' he said, giving me an exaggerated bow.

'I wasn't sure if you really wanted me to, or if you were just trying to rescue me from an awkward situation,' I said, propping my bike against the wall of the pig pen.

He smiled. 'Both, I guess. Come on in.'

I followed him into the house, which resembled a cabin of the kind people let out as holiday homes, with ranch-style glass sliding doors, big picture windows and living room/kitchen, bedroom and bathroom. It was just slightly bigger than my garret above Manapouri Aquatic Adventures.

'You must be thirsty after all that bicycle riding,' he said. 'Something cool to drink? Lemonade?'

'Sounds great,' I said, and seated myself at the kitchen table. The window gave a view across swathes of farmland to forested, snow-capped mountains.

'So why was it an awkward situation?' he asked, handing me a tall, cool glass.

I bit my lip momentarily. It wasn't something I talked about. I mean, getting a lot of male attention, wasn't that just what most women wanted? How could I complain about it? On the other hand, he was once a pastor, so wasn't he supposed to be kind and understanding and all that?

'I get a lot of men inviting me out, but I'm not looking for a relationship right now,' I said carefully.

He sat down opposite me. 'Uh huh. Had a bad experience?'

'I've realized I need a break from it.' I took a gulp of lemonade. 'This is a nice spot,' I said, gesturing towards the window and hoping he'd take the hint.

'Sure is,' he said. 'We came to Manapouri on vacation, my wife and I. I guess I sound like an American through and through, but I was born in Invercargill, and my New Zealand citizenship was never revoked. We came over to see the country where I was born, and it was a great time, wonderful memories.' He sighed and looked up to meet my gaze. 'She was diagnosed with cancer not long after we got back, died a year later. You remind me of her – guess that's why I came to the rescue.'

'I do?' I said, startled.

He smiled sadly. 'Yeah, she was the real belle of the ball. Everybody at college wanted a piece of her. I was the gawky, geeky guy no woman ever looked at twice: too tall, too skinny, too intense. Rosalie had so many jocks hanging around her that I never dared to ask her out.' He smiled again, his gaze far away, reminiscing. 'In the end she had to ask me, but it worked; we just fit together, you know? We never looked back.'

'Bob said –' I paused. Should I bring it up? 'He said you'd lost your faith after…'

He nodded slowly, his expression serious. 'It was hard. Are you a believer?'

I shook my head. 'Not really, not these days. I don't think about it much. My dad was, though. He was pretty devout, I suppose.'

'Was?'

'He died when I was eighteen, of motor neurone disease.'

'That was hard too, huh?'

I nodded and took another gulp of lemonade. 'It's still causing me problems now, according to some.'

He raised his eyebrows. 'Who's the "some"?'

To my surprise, I ended up telling him all about the dream, including Diana and Greg's opinion that it was down to buried trauma, and my own view that it was someone else's experience I was reliving.

'The only person who seems to think that it might be real is Mark,' I said. 'He's a friend I met in Alexandra.'

Pastor took a sip of his own iced tea, nodding thoughtfully. 'Why do you think you came to New Zealand?' he asked.

'Um, how d'you mean? I came with my boyfriend. We were both looking for a change in our lives, an adventure I suppose, so we took a year out.'

'Your boyfriend chose New Zealand?'

I pressed my lips together. 'No,' I said slowly. 'He mentioned Australia, and then I threw in New Zealand. He just went along with it.'

'You threw in New Zealand because…'

'Because it's always interested me. It looked so beautiful and peaceful… and empty.'

'That's all?

I looked directly at him. 'You think there should be more?'

'Well, if this dream *is* real, and it's a New Zealand lake, seems to me you've been drawn here, kind of like a moth to a candle flame.'

'Maybe I have been,' I said slowly, with a sense of light dawning. It was true: New Zealand seemed to have been in my mind for as long as I could remember, but why? I put my fingers to my temples, trying once again to force my reluctant brain to reveal some answers. When had I got interested? Was there anything when my dad was alive?

A trickle of a memory rose to the surface. When I was young, really young, maybe eight, there was some holiday programme on TV, and we were all sitting there watching it when the presenter said something like, 'And now, Jeremy Scott visits the wild West Coast of New Zealand…' My dad had almost shot out of his chair and switched it off.

'What on earth's got into you, Paul?' my mum had asked, staring at him in irritation.

'We watch far too much television in this house. Why don't we all go out for a walk or something?'

The memory had come so sharply detailed that I was almost shaking. I looked back at Pastor. 'I think you could be right,' I said, and took a deep breath. *My dad... Alan... 'her'... the West Coast.* Was it *my dad's* memory I was dreaming?

'I wonder if my dad ever came here,' I said tentatively, thinking aloud.

'He never mentioned it?'

'No, he said he'd never been abroad and had no desire to go, either. He made a bit of a thing of it, telling us – my mum and me – how much money we were saving by going to Broadstairs instead of Benidorm, but…' I sighed. I needed to think about this alone and decide whether to talk to my mum or not. I looked back up at him. 'So you think my dream might be a real one?'

He nodded. 'If it was really trauma, why did it come back again now after so many years?'

'Just what I've been thinking. Have you ever been to the West Coast?'

'I've driven up there a couple of times since I've been living here. Sure is wild and beautiful.'

When we'd finished our drinks, he showed me around the smallholding and occasionally talked gently about his wife. I felt at ease with him, so when he said, just as I was getting on my bike to leave, 'You know, if you need a hiking companion who doesn't want a piece of you, I could do with some more exercise,' I took him up on it. We arranged to walk on the nearby Kepler Track the following weekend.

I pedalled fast on the final few miles to Manapouri, my mind running in its own circles. If it was my dad's memory, it made at least some sense, but then why did he make out he'd never been abroad? Given the 'her' element, which suggested another woman, it didn't seem like a good idea to consult my mum on the matter. It could have been a coincidence that my dad had turned off the TV at the mention of the West Coast, but my intuition was giving me a very different message.

***

The rowing boat moved slowly through the choppy waters of the Lower Waiau River as I headed across, planning to take a walk around a long, circular track everyone had been telling me about. It felt great to be active. Although I'd never been a fitness freak and didn't go to the gym, I loved to walk and cycle and swim, which were some of the reasons I'd been so keen to come to New Zealand. Stupidly, in Niall, I'd got myself engaged to a guy who didn't share any of those interests. I was beginning to wonder if I'd had anything in common with a single one of my boyfriends. Niall was the last of a long line of men who'd wanted me to be just like my mum.

I moored the boat and headed up the track. It was quiet, with few other trampers about, and I revelled in the peace and beauty of the New Year's Day evening as I looked down at the lake from a high viewpoint. Even though the sun was still shining, there was a stiff breeze blowing, and white crests were visible on the waves far below.

It had felt a little lonely to spend both Christmas and New Year away from friends and family, although when I recalled just how little fun family Christmases with Mum and Ron had been in the past few years, with or without a boyfriend along, it didn't seem so bad. It wasn't that I didn't get on with Ron, but he and my mum were so much of an item that no matter how hard they tried to make me welcome, I still felt like an intruder. I was glad my mum was happy with him, but I couldn't imagine ever having that kind of togetherness with someone myself. Although she never said so, I was pretty sure she hadn't had that with my dad.

Something moved just at the edge of my vision. Startled, I turned quickly.

'G'day,' Mark said, walking towards me with a sheepish grin.

I just stared, and put my hands on my hips. 'What are you doing here? I thought you were headed to the North Island. And how did you know I'd be out here?'

He looked a little taken aback at my reaction, but shrugged mildly. 'Just a guess.'

'Come on, Mark, I'm not that stupid. What's going on?' I said, frustration making me angry.

'Does it matter?' he said after a moment's awkward silence, joining me to gaze out over the lake vista. 'You looked pretty lonely standing there, and it's New Year's Day.'

'Well, it does matter that you keep popping up like this. It's a bit weird.'

'I did mention I might stop by and see you before I went north, and you sounded really disappointed on the phone the other day.'

I regarded him in exasperation. 'So how long have you got?'

'A couple of hours.'

'*Two hours?* You came all the way to Fiordland to spend two hours with me?' My voice squeaked with disbelief.

He shrugged again, still looking uncomfortable. I regarded him more closely. He didn't seem quite as well as usual. It was hard to put my finger on it, but there was a fragility about him I didn't like.

'Are you okay? You're not ill, are you?'

He shrugged. 'I've had better days.'

'What does that mean?'

'Ollie, do you want my company or not?' he asked, his own tone now uncharacteristically sharp.

I raked a hand through my hair, unconsciously imitating him. 'Yes, of course, but –'

'So shall we walk?'

'Are you up to it?'

'Hey, I'd have to be in a bad state if I couldn't go tramping.'

As we walked, I told him about a few jobs I'd applied for. 'I don't know what chance I have, but I thought it was worth a try.'

'Accounts receivable clerk?' he said, and grinned at me. 'Doesn't sound like *you*, somehow. I thought you used to work in a call centre.'

'Yeah, but before that I was in accounts. They got rid of the accounts section altogether, but some of us were offered jobs in the customer service department instead.'

'Did you like it? Accounts?'

I shook my head firmly. 'It was just a job.'

'Your dad's illness really messed you up, eh?'

I took a deep breath. 'Yeah, you could say that. I suppose if it hadn't happened, I'd have been more focused on my own life, thinking about a career. I'd rather have a job like yours.'

He gave me a sympathetic look. 'The DOC is only taking on New Zealand applicants right now.' He tilted his head sideways. 'Is that really what you want, then? To stay here?'

I nodded slowly. He already knew all about Niall.

'What is it you're looking for here, d'you think?'

I stared at him. It hadn't occurred to me that I was looking for anything.

'A job's just a job, in New Zealand or in the UK,' Mark said. 'There must be something else here that makes you want to stay.'

'Scenery, fewer people, different atmosphere,' I said.

'And that's it?'

'Isn't that enough?'

He shook his head slowly, his eyes on me as though he could see right inside me.

'Anyway, enough about me,' I said, feeling slightly uncomfortable. 'You're still far too much of a mystery man. Where on the West Coast do you work?'

'Fox Glacier,' he said, his gaze heading off in the direction of the lake.

'But you like it, though, being a ranger?'

He looked back at me. 'I love it,' he said. 'There's no other job I'd rather do.'

'So what's wrong? Why do I feel like there's something terribly wrong with you?'

He stopped walking and turned to stare intently at me. 'Do you?'

'Yeah, I do. It must be my intuition kicking in. Can't you talk about it?'

He sighed. 'It's not that simple, but I want you to know I've never met anyone else that I gelled with the way I do with you.'

'What, no girlfriend like that?'

He shrugged. 'Not quite, but this is different.'

'You mean we're just good friends.'

'Yeah, but it's… more than that. I can't really explain.'

'I get it,' I said gently. I felt the same way, that we were more than just friends but less than lovers. 'I just wish you could trust me with whatever it is,' I added.

We tramped the remainder of the trail companionably, and we discussed the dream, along with my intention to move on to Haast when the job in Manapouri came to an end. That kept us safely off any tricky topics, but when we arrived at the jetty where I'd left my boat, he refused to get in.

'Where are you going to go?' I asked, wanting to scream with frustration. 'How are you going to get back across?'

'I just want to be on my own for a while. I can get back by water taxi.'

'So this is it?'

'For today. I'll ring you when I'm in Wellington,' he said, and he surprised me with an affectionate peck on the cheek.

As I set off across the river, he wandered slowly back into the trees. I had the peculiar sense that he was far more lost and helpless than his cocky stride and ever-ready grin suggested.

Chapter Seven

I ground my hand into the grey sand and stared across the lake at its fringe of trees. There were tears on my cheeks. A slight breeze flickered across my face, and the drooping stem of a flax plant bobbed up and down, its large pods almost touching the beach. *How could she? Why did they? My best friend. Alan...*

I sat up in bed with a start. *The dream again.* My face really was wet with tears, just as it used to be when I was in my teens. I looked across at the bedside clock. It read 3.00am. I took deep breaths and went into the bathroom, where I splashed some water on my face. *My best friend.* Did it mean Alan was his best friend, or that *she* was? I stared at myself in the mirror, trying to see my dad's face in my own, but while I resembled him most in personality, I got my looks from my mum.

I switched the kettle on; I no longer felt even vaguely sleepy. There were new snippets of memory to the dream most nights now, and I'd spent the last few days thinking about my dad, trying to remember all I could. It was disappointing to discover how little I knew about him. Could he really have visited New Zealand, and if so, why had he never talked about it?

I'd brought up the subject obliquely with my mum when she rang the previous day.

'Did… um… I was wondering, why did Dad never want to go abroad?'

'That's a funny question.' To my relief, there was no hint of suspicion in her voice.

'I was just thinking about when I was a kid – I dunno, thinking about Dad a lot I suppose. He was a bit strong on it, I remember.'

'Yes, he always insisted that we had everything we could ever want in the UK. I didn't agree with him, but you couldn't move your dad once he'd made up his mind. Talk about stubborn – and you're just like him, you know, all this "I'm staying in New Zealand, no matter what".'

It wasn't the first time I'd heard that I was like my dad, and it had never been a compliment, coming from my mum.

'So he never went abroad in his whole life?' I pressed.

'No. Born and bred in Stratford, spent a couple of years in London just before we met. You know all this – what's really bothering you?'

'I suppose it's the dream; it keeps reminding me of him,' I said, knowing what I was letting myself in for but being unable to think up a better excuse.

'You're still having that dream? Oh Ollie, really. And you say you're *happy* in Manapouri?'

'I've got friends here now; even a bit of a social life.'

'I must say your new friend Ed sounds quite a good prospect. His own boat; these holiday homes he lets out. And he's only a few years older than you. You could do worse.'

I sighed. 'I'm trying not to encourage him. It's safer going out with Pastor.'

'Hmmm… a vicar who's lost his faith. You sure he's not some sort of pervert?'

Par for the course with my mum, I thought with a smile as I stirred my coffee. As for my dad, maybe those 'two years in London' hadn't been spent in London after all. But why would he lie? He was so straight and honest, not to mention religious. What did he have to hide, or maybe forget? If this thing happened before he met my mum, then surely he had no reason to be ashamed?

The Upper Waiau River curved around below us, shimmering with tiny wavelets. I'd never seen water so pristine and clear. I could look down to a depth of six feet or more and see brown trout swimming. It was a baking hot day, but surrounded as we were by lofty beech trees, the Kepler Track was quite comfortable.

'Penny for your thoughts?' Pastor asked from my side.

I grinned at him apologetically; I'd obviously been engrossed in my own worries for too long. 'Just the usual ones, going round in circles.'

'Your dad?'

I nodded silently.

'Want to talk about it?'

I shrugged. 'I just need to know – oh, I don't even know exactly what I need to know. Whether he was here, who this Alan was, who this woman was, whether he was in love with her, whether Alan betrayed him.'

'Just one or two things, then,' he said with a smile. 'What about whether Alan is still here?'

I turned sharply and stared at him.

'It's quite likely, don't you think? If your dad went home with a broken heart, maybe Alan stayed behind.'

'With "her",' I said.

'Uh huh, could be.'

I sighed. 'But even if he did, how do I find him? I'll be as bad as Mark, looking for an Alan in a haystack. Unless finding the beach equals, somehow, finding Alan.'

We passed a section of cliff edge that had fallen off, slipped, along with its attached trees. The path meandered around the gap.

'I've been thinking,' Pastor said slowly, 'that I might be able to help; at least with this trip to Haast you're fixing to take. If you like, I could take you, so long as you don't mind an old man for company.'

'Oh, that's really kind, but you don't need to do that. I mean, I'm used to being on my own.'

'I don't *need* to, but I know how troubled you are over this – I'm thinking maybe you shouldn't be on your own. I have the time, and in case you're wondering, I can afford it.'

I bit my lip. It wasn't as if Pastor wanted anything from me; I knew that, despite my mum's paranoia. 'Well, it would be nice to have company – and a car, to get to all these beaches,' I said with a cheeky smile.

'Exactly. So that's settled then.'

'I'll pay for my own accommodation though,' I added quickly.

'Sure. It's a deal.'

A small bunch of trampers passed us, all weighed down by enormous backpacks. They'd obviously walked a lot further than Pastor and I had in mind.

'I've been wondering,' I said as their chattering British accents faded into the far distance, 'about my Dad's religion. Did it make a difference to him, to how he felt about Alan, or to how he felt about his illness? It's weird, but now that I try to think about him, I can only remember scenes and events; I can't get a hold on him as a person. Maybe I was too young.'

'You want my advice on religion?' he asked with a lift of his eyebrows.

'I can't think of anyone better – unless you'd rather not talk about it.'

'No, I can talk about it. Guess everyone around here calls me Pastor for a reason – it's David, by the way. Was your dad still a believer to the end?'

I nodded. 'Definitely. The vicar came round quite often. My dad couldn't talk by then, but his eyes used to kind of light up, and he looked happier when the vicar had done his praying, or whatever it was.'

'Or whatever it was?' he said with a laugh in his voice. 'You weren't brought up in the faith then?'

I shook my head. 'I suppose he was a bit of an unusual believer. He never tried to push it on me; he thought I should make up my own mind. We used to discuss it intellectually, and I went to church with him a few times when I was little.'

'Okay, let's think about this,' Pastor said slowly. 'If we assume your dad came to New Zealand as a young man – you think he was in his early twenties?'

I nodded.

'So, he emigrated, looking for a new life. Who do we think Alan was?'

'His best friend.'

'And if Alan's his best friend, he probably came with him, don't you think? They emigrated together.'

'That makes sense,' I said with a feeling of rising anticipation.

'They'd have found jobs, or been allocated jobs together.'

'And met this woman together.'

'Seems likely. If your dad was very devout, he'd probably have had strong views about pre-marital sex. It could be that Alan didn't.'

'They could both have fallen for her…' I said, trailing off as a sudden thought occurred to me. 'Wouldn't there be immigration records for New Zealand? Emigration records from the UK? Maybe I could find something – Alan's surname at least. Where they went, even?'

'There could be some records online, I guess.'

I was shaking with excitement. At last, this might be the lead I needed. I sobered as I imagined finding Alan, and I reminded myself of the advice I'd given to Mark. What if Alan didn't want to know me? What if there had been bad blood between him and my dad? Just like Mark, I could be opening up a can of worms, and just like him, I didn't see any alternative.

***

Te Anau wasn't much fun in the rain, although it was still well filled with busloads of tourists busily scouring the shops. Once I'd parked and locked my bike, I dashed into an Internet café with the intention of catching up on my e-mail and chasing down immigration records. It had been a busy week out on the boat, and this was the first chance I'd had to get to Te Anau since my chat with Pastor the previous week.

I scanned happily through my pile of e-mail – it's amazing how much you can miss the Internet when you're without it for even a few days – including one from Niall, telling me he'd decided to go straight on to Australia and pretty well blaming our break-up on my choice to come to New Zealand. 'It just isn't my kind of place,' he said. 'I like the buzz of the big city. I can't wait to get to Sydney.' I was relieved to know there wasn't any chance of my running into him again. Suze had sent me a long description of events in her love life and in the call centre where she still worked. Reading about all the familiar office machinations just made me happier to be out of it and more determined than ever to stay that way.

Eventually, having replied to everyone, I settled in to search for a record of my dad's emigration. It turned out to be more difficult than I'd expected, and after a fruitless hour, I was getting ready to give up. Then, somehow, in skipping from link to link, I came across a website for ship passenger lists from the UK. I typed in my dad's name, put in a period that covered the two years he was supposed to have been in London and a destination of New Zealand and, with a frisson of excitement, clicked the mouse to search.

Another screen came up telling me I'd entered an incorrect time period. The site didn't cover any years post 1960. I gritted my teeth in frustration and spent another hour combing the net for passenger lists or emigration records for the early seventies, but I eventually discovered that these were not online, and the best place to search them was the

New Zealand archives in Wellington. I sat back in the chair, completely deflated. Could I afford to go to Wellington? It looked like a laborious process, trawling through countless ships' records. Hang on, though, what about Mark? He was still knocking about in the North Island, and he'd phoned me a couple of days earlier to say he was in Wellington. Not only that, but by now he must be an expert at searching records.

As I left the Internet café and headed to unlock my bike for what looked like a damp return ride back to Manapouri, I regretted yet again that Mark didn't have a mobile phone. I was just going to have to wait until he called me.

The week wore by with no word from him, and I became anxious and irritable, with the dream dominating both my days and my nights. As much as I loved Manapouri, I felt restless. Tramping trips with Pastor and fishing trips with Ed, who insisted he simply enjoyed my company, weren't quite enough to make up for the sense that I must uncover the story and rid myself of the dream. With Bob's wife expected to return to work in about two weeks, Pastor and I began our preparations for the trip to Haast, only there wasn't much point in us going there if I didn't even know what I was looking for.

My job search wasn't going too well, either, as I was forced to report to my mum when she rang me for her latest lecture about how much better off I'd be back at the call centre.

'It doesn't surprise me one bit that you've had so many rejections,' she said breezily. 'It's obvious they're going to want to employ their own if they can. That's why you should come home. There are plenty of call centres here, and I'm sure with all your skills you'd be snapped up in no time.'

All my skills, indeed! It was really skills I was lacking, or at least skills that I could put to good use. Skills and qualifications. Everyone seemed to have a degree but me. Even Mark had one, and he wasn't the intellectual type, whereas I was, at least according to Niall and Suze, and some of my other friends. Not for the first time in my life, I wondered if it was too late to study. Maybe I could go to Uni as a mature student? Back in the UK, there was the Open University, set up especially for people like me who had somehow missed the boat, but I still didn't want to go home, and it wasn't just to do with call centres and boredom. New Zealand had crept into my heart, and I was determined to find a way to stay.

Mark finally rang at the end of the week, catching me as I took an evening walk beside the lake. He hadn't been having any luck in the North Island, and he sounded dejected and, to my ears, unwell, although, as ever, he claimed to be fine. I told him about my latest discoveries and asked him if he could check out the Wellington records for me when he'd finished his own search.

'Yeah, no problem. I'll do it as soon as I've finished in New Plymouth. I can't be sure how long it'll take. Reckon you'll be in Haast by the time I get back down South.'

'Are you sure you don't mind?' I asked a little anxiously. 'Is all this okay with the DOC? I mean, you've been off work for such a long time – don't you have to get back?'

There was a moment's silence before he finally said in an unusually strained voice, 'No, no worries. It'll be right.'

I shook my head as I closed my phone. He still hadn't told me why he was off work. In fact, there were a lot of things he still hadn't told me.

Chapter Eight

My hands were clenched and damp with sweat as Pastor drove us into Haast, and it wasn't just because the temperature had climbed into the high twenties. The closer we got, the twitchier I became. This place felt *familiar*.

Haast was really a sort of nowhere-land. There was almost nothing there except a few motels, a small supermarket and a couple of cafés and restaurants. What could my dad have been doing there anyway? The good thing was that, given the size of the place, I imagined anyone local would be able to tell me right away if there was an Alan living in the area.

'Still feeling a bit peculiar?' Pastor asked, looking aside at me.

'Yeah. It's like I've been here before, but I know I haven't.'

He nodded slowly but said nothing. I pressed damp palms to my eyelids and then opened my eyes again as we pulled up outside a motel.

'Here we are,' Pastor said. 'Doesn't look too shabby, considering it's the cheapest place in town.'

We unloaded our stuff and booked into our separate rooms. I'd gone for a budget room, so it was very basic, but I really did need to eke out my last few hundred pounds.

On my last night in Manapouri, Bob had presented me with two hundred dollars – a hundred from himself and

Marion and a hundred from a local whip-round, stirred up, I think, by Pastor and Ed, so I was at least a bit better off than I expected.

I had a quick shower and picked up my mobile to text my mum to say we'd arrived safely, but the phone just burbled tetchily and advised me that there was no signal. Damn. I'd never thought of that. I'd assumed everywhere in New Zealand was covered, especially when a little place like Manapouri had a good signal. I supposed Haast really was the back of beyond, magnificently rugged and beautiful though it was.

It wouldn't have mattered so much if I weren't still waiting for news from Mark. He'd been chewing his way through the passenger list records in Wellington all week but hadn't found anything when he'd rung two days before.

I made a quick call to my mum from the payphone in the motel and then met up with Pastor at the door. We planned to eat at one of the restaurants in the township.

'You okay?' he asked, looking me over as we strolled down the road in the early evening sunlight.

'Yeah, I'm getting used to the strange feelings now,' I said, eyeing the dome-shaped mountain that dominated the township. 'It's weird, but it's not these roads and buildings that seem familiar, it's the backdrop. The shapes of the mountains and the way the waterfalls come down them like white veins in the green.'

'Maybe a lot of the other buildings weren't here in the seventies,' Pastor said thoughtfully.

'You really think it has to be down to my dad's memories?'

'Don't you?'

I sighed. 'Yes and no. I wish I had some real proof – I mean, it's all surmise until I know for certain that he was here. And now I'm cut off from Mark,' I said, and explained about the absence of a signal.

'Ah, a cellphone signal. I don't have one – never have gotten myself caught up with the modern age.'

'You're as bad as he is,' I said, grinning.

'He doesn't have a cellphone?'

I shook my head. 'And he's only twenty-seven. I mean, how many twenty-somethings don't have a mobile?'

'I wouldn't know, but I guess not too many. You're fond of him anyway, I gather?'

I nodded. 'He's just so mysterious all the time, and he's a big worry.' I chewed my lip, realizing I didn't want to go into details. Luckily, Pastor didn't press, and anyway, we'd just reached the restaurant.

Over the meal, he told me about his daughter Emily and her husband, Steve. It was the first time he'd even admitted to me that he had a child.

'She says she's coming over – or rather they both are. She's booked the flight already.'

'And is that bad?' I asked, wondering why he sounded so mournful.

'It ought to be good, but I know why they're coming. Steve's a pastor too. They see me as a lost sheep. They want me back in the fold, and that means back in the church, back in America and back in the family.'

'Do you have a lot of other family over there?' I asked, wondering why I'd always assumed he was childless.

He sighed. 'I have a son, too. He's in his mid-thirties, and we get along fine at this distance. It's Emily and Steve who just can't let it go. They're even leaving their kids with Steve's mom and dad for the duration.'

'So you have grandchildren?'

'Uh huh. Two girls. They're teenagers now, mind; they're getting real grown up.'

'Don't you miss them?'

He toyed with his chips. 'Sure, but I'm happy here. I just wish Emily could see that.'

After the meal, I asked the waitress if she knew of any Alans in the area. She shook her head slowly. 'Nope, don't know of a single one.'

Back at the motel, I asked the owner. 'No one by that name around here,' he said firmly.

I had the same lack of success everywhere else I asked: the supermarket, the café, and the other couple of restaurants. With such a common name, you'd think there would have been at least one. Then again, Haast *was* small.

The next morning, Pastor drove us down to Haast Beach, and I began to get excited as we jostled for space among the campervans before taking a look. My excitement didn't last long as I discovered that while the sand was the same approximate colour, it was a normal sea beach. There were some tree trunks and logs lying on the shore though, which was interesting. What had Mark said? Something about estuaries.

'Do you know if there are any beaches around here by estuaries?' I asked Pastor, shouting above the booming surf.

'I think there's one further down the road. You want to see it?'

I nodded, and wished I could phone Mark to check where I was supposed to look, but I'd resigned myself to him just turning up when he was finished, and the sooner the better.

We headed back down the road. I was unusually quiet because the feeling of déjà vu was increasing with every moment. Pastor had obviously decided to just let me be, and he stayed silent.

We reached a part of the road where the trees almost met overhead, and he turned suddenly into a muddy track which led us to the other side of the trees among sere grass and scrub. As I got out of the car, I was struck by the deafening singing of the cicadas in the trees. It was the first time I'd come across it – apparently they'd only just hatched. Pastor stayed in the car and left me to wander alone across the grass towards the shore. The dome-shaped mountain that dominates Haast was the backdrop to a large expanse of glassy estuary that slid between beaches littered with bits of branch and tree trunks. The sand on the opposite shore was slightly lighter than on this side, and there was the sound of breakers just out of view beyond the raised beach. It wasn't my dream beach, but it was frighteningly familiar. I could almost see shadow pictures here, of my dad and Alan and the mystery woman.

I was about to head back to the car when a voice called, 'Hey, Ollie!' and I turned to find Mark jogging towards me along the beach.

'Well, you pick your moments,' I said shakily, still trying to assimilate the host of peculiar sensations. Once again Mark had just turned up out of the blue in the exact right spot. 'How did you guess I'd be here?' I asked, just as I had on the track in Manapouri.

He shugged and grinned. 'Easy. I knew you'd be checking out all the beaches.'

I looked him over. He was unusually pale, but despite that, he seemed pleased about something.

'Did you have any luck? You've been so quiet I wondered what had happened, and there's no signal here.'

His grin broadened. 'I found your dad and his friend Alan.'

'What did you find?' I asked with a surge of excitement.

'They came out in 1972 on the assisted immigration scheme. They were assigned to work on a sheep station in Canterbury. Your dad's friend's name was Alan Jensen.'

'*Assigned* to work on a sheep station?'

'Yeah, that's how they did it, like a payment for getting into the country, do a job no Kiwi wanted to do for a couple of years.'

'But then what would they have been doing down here, on the West Coast?'

'You're sure that they were?' he said in some surprise.

I nodded. 'This beach, even.'

Mark looked around him. 'It's the dream beach?'

'No, worst luck, but it's painfully familiar. It's like… like… almost like my dad's ghost is here or something.'

Mark started oddly at that and gave me a strange look, but just said, 'What are you going to do now?'

'I've tried asking people with no luck, but maybe I'll do better with a surname. What about you? Are you going to stick around? Have you given up on finding your mum?'

'I don't know,' he replied thickly. 'I can't, really, but there doesn't seem to be anywhere else to look.' He forced a grin. 'So I guess that means I'll be hanging around for a bit, at least.'

'Come and meet Pastor,' I said. 'He's just over there.' I gestured in the general direction of the car, currently out of sight.

He glanced warily where I was pointing. 'Nah, I don't feel up to company right now. Look, I'll meet you again later, okay?'

He was already edging away down the beach, following the footprints I'd just made.

'Wait a minute,' I said in frustration. 'Do you have to go right now? How will I find you?'

He didn't stop, just carried on walking backwards. 'I need to be on my own for a while. Don't worry; I'll find you.' And he turned and headed towards the dome mountain, a solitary figure in an empty landscape.

What did he mean, he needed to be alone? Hadn't he been alone for the past few weeks, pretty much? I swallowed down my disappointment at his abrupt departure, and shored up my spirits with the information he'd just given me.

Pastor was still sitting in the car, waving his hand pointlessly at a couple of eager sandflies that had homed in on him. I told him about Mark turning up and giving me his news and he raised his eyebrows in surprise.

'Lucky he picked the right beach,' he said. 'And now he's just gone off on his own?'

I nodded slowly, easing myself into the passenger seat.

'He sounds like a bit of a troubled young man. You sure he's not… well, mentally sick?'

I bridled in Mark's defence. 'No, I'm sure he's not. No.' I thought back over all the times I'd met him: the cheery grin, the apparent self-assurance hiding a deeper insecurity, the sense of connection that I had with him. 'No,' I said again. 'He's weird and intense, but he's not mentally ill. I'm sure of that. Anyway,' I added brightly, 'I have Alan's full name now, and I know I'm on the right track. It's just... what were they doing here in Haast if they were assigned to Canterbury? And the feelings are so strong.' I paused in thought for a moment. 'Where does this road go to?'

'A small place called Jackson Bay. I never got down there when I was in the area last time. It's fifty kilometres – you want to go? This definitely wasn't the beach?'

I shook my head. 'There are too many things missing, and the water's the wrong colour. But there are indications that we're on the right track, so I'm thinking maybe it's at Jackson Bay or somewhere else en route.'

'Okay. We'll take a look. At least we can eat there – there's some sort of seafood restaurant.'

I agreed absently. Eating wasn't anywhere near the top of my list of priorities.

Two hours later, we turned a corner into the tiny township of Jackson Bay, which looked pretty much deserted. We'd made a few stops on the way, but none of them had yielded the dream beach, and oddly, none of them had generated the same peculiar sense of déjà vu that I'd had on the beach closer to Haast. This place, though, was setting off a number of jangling bells in my head.

Pastor pulled up beside the long curve of beach, and we got out to take a look. The sun was still shining in an intensely blue sky, although there were a few puffs of cloud on the horizon. There was a rough jetty going out to sea, and blue-green mountains framed a wild and deserted bay full of rocks and scree. It looked as though there had been a landslip, and the residue was still sitting on the beach, untouched. The beach itself was definitely not *my* beach. This place felt like the end of the world. Did anyone actually live here? How were we going to find anyone to ask? It might be the wrong beach, but I knew I was in the right place – or one of the right places – to find out something.

'Let's take a look at the café,' Pastor said, and we both walked speedily down the road, me flinging my arms around like a dervish as swarms of sandflies zeroed in on the only two warm bodies moving around. It looked like anyone with sense was staying inside their vehicles, I noted with a wry inward smile as I spotted a family observing the view from the cab of their campervan, and a couple doing the same from their car, windows tightly closed despite the heat.

The café was closed. 'Bad timing,' Pastor said with a grimace; by now it was mid afternoon. I looked around at the few houses, most of which looked empty. One had a fabulous view of the bay but sported a For Sale sign. Nothing moved except the sandflies. I was just starting to turn to Pastor in disappointment when there was a familiar screechy grind of a lawn mower off in the distance.

I didn't need to say anything; I smiled at Pastor, and he raised his eyebrows in response but followed along as I headed up the oddly named 'Pier Road' – there was no pier – in the direction of the sound that seemed so out of place there. We tracked it all the way up the road and down another, and then came to a slightly run-down house and a young woman in the garden who looked up at us with a momentarily wary expression, until she obviously decided we looked harmless.

'Can I help you?' she asked politely, with a strong Kiwi accent.

'Yes, I'm looking for someone called Alan Jensen, or anyone who might have heard of him. I think he might have lived here once.'

She shook her head slowly. 'No, never heard the name, but then I've only been living here for five years. Someone else might know, though. Try Barney at number seven.' She pointed down the road. 'He'll be in, just knock him up. He likes to talk.' She said this with a grin that suggested it was hard to persuade Barney to stop talking at times.

We thanked her and headed further down the road. All the houses looked deserted to the untrained eye, and Barney's was no exception. The timber it was built of looked like it wouldn't hold out for too many more years, and the garden around it was just a mass of weeds and grass. Even so, I knocked on the door with a jump of excitement.

A dog barked and a man coughed inside, and then there were slow, steady footsteps before an elderly man opened the door and stared at us through his insect screen. I was still waving my hand against the sandflies and eyed the screen greedily as a possible sanctuary.

The man tilted his grizzled head sideways as I told him who I was looking for. 'Alan Jensen,' he repeated slowly, looking us both up and down.

'He might have been here with a Paul Kimpton,' I added eagerly. 'Paul was my dad.'

The man's bushy grey eyebrows shot up, and then his expression softened from wariness to interest. 'Come on in,' he said, opening the screen door. 'You both look like you could do with a bit of shade and a nice cool beer.'

The house was as worn and faded on the inside as it was on the outside, but Barney, whilst obviously pretty old, didn't seem to be infirm. He took us into his kitchen and handed us each a cold can of beer out of his fridge. I'd never seen Pastor drink alcohol yet, but he took the can without complaint. Barney led us to a veranda overlooking his weedy back garden. It was all screened in, so we sat on old sofas and enjoyed the breeze. I took a gulp of beer. It tasted good.

'So what're you looking for, exactly?' Barney asked, his rheumy grey eyes alert in his lined face.

'I want to find Alan Jensen if I can,' I said. 'My dad died fifteen years ago.'

'And if you find him?'

'I'm hoping he'll be able to explain some… unusual things about my dad.'

Barney took a sip of his own beer. 'Well, as it happens, I did know them. It was a long time ago, but they were here all right. Early seventies it was, a right hippy time, and that's what they were see, a bunch of hippies taking a holiday. They camped out down there by the beach for a few weeks. Likely I wouldn't have remembered if I hadn't seen Alan since, him and his missus and the kids. He brought them down here to show 'em the place – the kids I mean.'

'Did anything odd happen when they were here? I mean, with my dad?'

'Nah, not that I know of. They were the best of pals, those two. Emigrated from England together, didn't they? They were just travelling around in an old campervan, them and two other blokes and a couple of girls, all having the time of their lives.'

'What were the girls like?' I asked.

He sat back, considering. 'One of 'em was dark and dumpy, nice enough, but the other one, Jenny, was a real wild 'un. You know, the sort that doesn't want to be tied down to anything, wears all those floaty clothes and long beads and things. Changed a bit by the time she came back here with the three kids, mind.'

'Alan married her?'

He nodded. 'She was plenty tied down by then.'

'And the other girl? Do you know either of their surnames?'

He shook his head slowly. 'Can't say as I do. Mind, didn't that Jenny have a funny surname, now I come to think of it?'

I was almost tapping my fingers with impatience as he pondered in silence for a minute, taking slow, deliberate sips of his beer.

'Moody! That was it. Jenny Moody. Suited her well, if you ask me.'

I took some deep breaths to calm myself down. This was going far better than I had ever expected. 'And did… did Alan say where he was living now, with his wife and children?'

Barney leaned back on his sofa again. 'Westport, I think. Somewhere up that way. Said they were all doing really well. Of course, that was a long time ago. I reckon those kids are around your age by now. The oldest was about fourteen. The other two were girls.'

He went on to reminisce about Alan's visit, which, if he'd got his dates right, had happened about twenty years ago. I listened with half an ear, my mind whirling with both excitement and disappointment. I supposed it would have been too good to be true to have found Alan that easily. I just hoped he hadn't moved too far from Westport in those twenty years.

We finished our beers – even Pastor – and left Barney's house to be confronted by even bigger clouds of sandflies. I'd never seen so many. We rushed back to the car, swatting around our heads as they droned at our ears.

'I guess that was a case of good news and bad news, huh?' Pastor said as he started up the car.

'Mmm. I suppose my next stop has to be Westport. I wonder whether there are any lakes nearby.'

***

We got back to the motel in the early evening, and Pastor headed off to his room for a nap. I was still feeling restless and over-stimulated and couldn't settle to anything, so I decided to walk down to Haast Beach, partly in the hope of running into Mark. It was a relief to take a brisk walk after spending most of the day cooped up in a car. No matter how handy they were, I could never really enjoy travelling in them.

At the beach, I was pleased to find that there weren't a host of motor homes keeping me company, but disappointed that there was no sign of the elusive Mr Juniper either. Somehow I expected him to just pop up, like he usually had of late. I was keen to tell him my news, and I was already itching to get going up the West Coast.

I walked back to the township as it was winding down in the sunset, and I was on a quiet road that led to the motel when I spotted Mark heading my way unusually slowly, for him. It was almost as though he were walking through treacle. He was very pale and seemed distracted, but he listened eagerly as I told him all about our discoveries at Jackson Bay.

'So now I have to get to Westport,' I said. 'I don't think Pastor will be able to go any further with me. How d'you fancy tagging along?'

A shadow passed over his face and the closed-in look returned. 'I… can't right now, Ollie. I thought I would be able to but… things have just got… difficult. I'm not sure how much longer I can… be around.' Even his voice sounded more faint than usual.

I put my hands on my hips. 'Mark, what's going on? Why can't you confide in me? I hate seeing you like this. You're so pale. Have you seen a doctor? Is that what this is about – you're really ill or something? Is that why you're trying to find some relatives?'

He laughed hollowly, humourlessly, which was completely unlike him. 'It's… something like that, yeah.'

I stared at him, stricken. 'You're not dying or something? It's not some horrible terminal illness?'

He struggled to speak. 'Ollie, I… look, I…' He glanced at something behind me, and his expression altered. 'I have to go. I'll find you again if I can.'

He started edging away just as he had that morning, and I turned to see Pastor coming towards me. When I looked back, Mark was heading off down the street. 'Mark!' I shouted after him. 'Don't go yet. I need to –'

He didn't even look back, and then Pastor was at my side, staring down the road with a peculiar expression on his face.

'Are you all right?' he asked, his voice full of concern.

'I'm okay. It's just Mark. I don't know what to do, how to help him. He's just pretty much said goodbye to me.' I'll find you again *if I can.* What did he mean? I looked back at his diminishing figure, feeling close to tears. 'Mark!' I shouted again.

Pastor put a hand on my arm. 'Olivia,' he said gently, 'there's no one there.'

I jerked my gaze up to him. 'What do you mean? He was just –' I looked down the road again. Mark was heading out of sight around the corner. 'You must need your eyes testing,' I said, forcing a teasing tone I didn't feel.

He shook his head sadly. 'No. You were standing here talking to yourself. There never was anyone here.'

The whole world seemed to turn inside out. A cold wash of icy sweat suffused my skin, I felt as though I was going to choke, and my legs began to buckle.

'That's not true,' I whispered hoarsely, clinging on to Pastor's arm as though I'd fall down without it. 'He was just here.'

Pastor just shook his head again, regarding me sadly, even pityingly. The look in his eyes roused me a little, and I pulled my arm away.

'I've lost my marbles and invented an invisible friend for myself, is that what you think?' I said in a tremulous voice.

'I don't know, but I guess it kinda makes sense,' he said, failing to hide a disappointed tone.

'What do you mean, it makes sense?' I asked, my hurt increasing as his withdrawal became more tangible.

'You were here in New Zealand on your own, getting short of money, having this dream that was really bothering you, losing lots of sleep because of it. Maybe Mark filled a need. You wanted help, a friend, someone to talk to, and there he was.'

When he put it like that, it sounded completely plausible. When had I first seen Mark? *In Alexandra, just after I left Niall.* Then he just seemed to turn up at all sorts of convenient moments. And he never ate or drank anything or spoke to anyone else in my presence. But what about his endless search for family? What about all the time he'd been away, all the times when I'd wanted him to be around and he wasn't? And what about the information he'd found for me?

I enumerated all this to Pastor as we headed back towards the motel. We had been intending to eat out, but I felt more like vomiting than eating right then.

'Most of all, what about Alan's surname?' I said. 'Mark found that out for me in Wellington.'

He shrugged and sighed slightly. 'The name was probably in your head somewhere, and you just remembered it yourself.'

I was getting angry. 'So you really think I'm a nutcase now, is that it? Do you even believe the dream is a true one any more?'

'Of course I don't think you're a nut,' he said unconvincingly. 'I do think maybe you need help, like that psychiatrist told you. I think chasing your dream has brought all this on. I kinda blame myself as well – I got caught up in it, got you more caught up in it, too.'

Tears were stinging my eyes, but I didn't want Pastor to see them. How could he lose confidence in me so quickly? I thought he was my friend, and here he was, virtually consigning me to the psychiatric ward.

'But there is something in it,' I persisted, forcing my voice to remain even. 'What we learned today about the hippy camp and about Alan.'

'Uh huh, but all that proves is that your dad was here.' His tone was becoming more dismissive and distant.

We were back at the motel by then, and I desperately wanted to be alone. I was starting to shiver – my teeth were even trying to chatter.

'Olivia, maybe you ought to go back to England after all, forget all about this. Why don't you call your mom, make some arrangements?'

He just wants to wash his hands of me. I turned away, towards my room, so that he couldn't see my face. 'I'm going to have a rest now,' I said through clenched teeth.

'Good idea. Get some sleep. You know where I am if you need anything.' I could tell by the way he said it that he hoped I wouldn't call on him.

I bolted into my room and locked the door before heading to the bathroom and throwing up all my stomach contents. Between sessions of vomiting bitter bile, I sat on the bathroom floor, shivering and crying. Earlier in the evening, I'd had two good friends and now, it seemed, one never existed, and the other wanted to abandon me.

Eventually I staggered to my feet and ran the shower as hot as I could, stepping into it with a sense of relief as my shivers began to abate. I didn't believe Mark was a figment of my imagination, but if he wasn't, what was he? Why would I make up a whole quest for someone called Juniper? I'd never met anyone else with that name in my life. The things Pastor said *could* be true, and I supposed it might seem that I was seriously deluded, driven to it by loneliness and lack of sleep, but I hadn't had the dream since we'd arrived in Haast. I wasn't tired, and I wasn't lonely either.

I stepped out of the shower and dried off, realizing with a wry grimace that I felt lonelier than I had since entering the country. I dressed quickly in comfortable jeans and a t-shirt and started packing. I didn't want to hang around, and I certainly didn't want to talk to Pastor again. I knew what I had to do to prove this thing one way or another, and obviously I'd have to do it alone. I'd go to Fox Glacier and find the DOC office. If Mark were real, or ever had been real, then they'd surely be able to tell me.

I wrote a short note for Pastor and headed down the corridor to the reception area of the motel, where the male side of the husband and wife team dragged himself grumpily out of their private back room. The sound of their TV blared out. I told him I was checking out early, and when he insisted on my paying for both nights, I just handed over the money without complaint. I passed him the note for Pastor and asked if he'd give it to him tomorrow morning. He gave me an odd look but agreed.

As I exited the motel into the cool night, I realized that my actions were only going to confirm Pastor's opinion of my mental state. I'd never hitchhiked before, but I wanted to get away as quickly as possible: cut my losses and escape from the source of the hurt.

I started walking northwards. I was fit and strong; I'd damned well walk all the way if I had to, but I hoped it wouldn't come to that.

There weren't many cars passing at that time of night, and it was only the residue of anger that kept me making the hitchhiker's hand signal, despite my fears. If my mum knew what I was doing, she'd be horrified. I just hoped I was right in believing that New Zealand had fewer 'perverts' than the UK.

I'd reached the long, single-lane bridge over the Haast River and was walking along the edge beside the narrow stretch of road when a lorry pulled up in the next passing bay. Once I reached it, I noted with relief that it was a woman driver. She was middle-aged, weather-beaten and plump. She looked down at me from her cab and wrinkled her nose.

'*What* are you doing? Are you crazy, thumbing a lift at this time of night, looking the way you do? Where you headed, anyway?'

'Fox Glacier,' I said in a small voice, feeling a complete fool.

She sighed. 'Well, get in then, 'cos I'm going all the way to Greymouth, so I guess it's your lucky night.'

Chapter Nine

I woke up feeling as hollow as a chocolate egg, and just as fragile. I was in yet another anonymous motel room, and a luxury one at that, with satellite TV, phone, full kitchen and spa bath. The motel owner was a friend of the lorry driver, and this was all they had. It had been so late and I had been so tired that I just agreed, despite the cost.

I got out of bed and twitched back the curtain. Outside, water was drumming on the roof, cascading out of the gutters, streaming down channels and ditches clearly built for this very purpose. This was the West Coast, after all, where it was meant to rain more often than not, but I'd rarely seen rain quite like this: so consistently heavy. It was early, only seven, but someone had already left my complimentary newspaper by the sliding door. I brought it in and noticed it was *The Press*, which reminded me of Diana. I wondered what she'd make of all this: probably agree profoundly with Pastor and phone Greg to get the men in white coats out to me.

I made myself a cup of tea using the carton of milk provided in the fridge and then picked up the local phone directory which was next to the phone, looking for the address of the DOC. Of course, if Mark weren't real, there might not be a DOC office here at all. I ran my finger down the listings and didn't realize I was holding my breath until I found it: Main Road, Fox Glacier.

My mobile phone burbled, making me jump. It was just a text saying I was running out of credit, but it indicated the return of a signal. I ought to ring my mum, but what was I going to say? *Hey Mum, guess what, this friend I haven't even told you about was never real in the first place, and Pastor thinks I need psychiatric help. He thinks I should come home to the safety of your maternal bosom, because I'm clearly too deranged to manage on my own, having been unhinged by just being alone in New Zealand.*

I had overreacted last night; I could see that now. But Pastor's sudden withdrawal of support, his obvious backing off, made things so much worse.

I went back to the window and watched a couple from the room next door packing up their car to leave. Was Mark *dead*? Had I suddenly become one of those 'I see dead people' psychics? Between that and the dream and the déjà vu, I was beginning to wonder. Intuition, I'd always called it. Knowing things I couldn't know, sensing things that others didn't. Like when my dad was getting close to the end, and he couldn't talk or move or eat: I used to *know* when he wanted something, or if he were uncomfortable, or if he were really sad. He couldn't make facial expressions by then, but I could feel it. That made it harder for me in a way; empathising with him like that, *feeling* for him. That's why everyone said the dream was down to the stress. Now I was wondering whether this empathy we had then was deeper than I'd ever imagined.

But what about Mark? If he were a ghost, why had he found *me*? Why would a ghost be looking for his relatives anyway, and why would a ghost start to look ill?

***

I couldn't bear to sit in my room waiting for the rain to stop, but I was the only fool out on the streets of Fox Glacier, which were deserted under the deluge. I was soaked to the skin long before I found the DOC office.

'Mark Juniper?' the receptionist said blankly.

'Yes, he works – worked – here. I'm... um... a relative of his, and I really need to find him. I'm wondering if anyone here can help.'

My lying skills were appalling, but she looked at me impartially and said, 'I'll just go and check with someone else, if you'll wait a minute.'

While she was gone I dragged off my sodden jacket and tried to tease my hair into something other than rats' tails. There was a muffled exclamation from the room she'd entered, and then a muscular, bronzed man of about forty came out, giving me the once-over with more than casual interest.

'You're looking for Mark Juniper, you say?' he asked.

'That's right. It's really important. Do – did – you know him?'

He pressed his lips together and gestured me over to a quiet corner of the reception area, where we sat down.

'You say you're a relative?'

I nodded and then realized that this man must know Mark to be taking such an interest. I just hoped my lying talents were about to improve. 'I... um, I've found out he's my brother,' I said. 'You know he was adopted?'

He nodded, his eyes fixed on my face, but his expression became more mournful by the second.

'I've managed to track him this far, but I gather he doesn't work here anymore?' I said as brightly as I could with a million warning bells going off in my head.

'He hasn't worked here for some time, Miss... um?'

'Olivia. Olivia Kimpton.'

'Well look, Olivia, Mark did work here for a few years. We were rangers together.' He bit his lip. 'The thing is... he got ill.'

It wasn't a surprise, not after yesterday, but I still felt cold sweat begin to sheath my body.

'He had to leave, eventually,' the man continued. 'That was five years ago, I'm afraid. I know he went north, to be closer to Grey Base Hospital, but that's the last I heard.'

'What was… what was wrong with him?' I asked, my voice trembling.

'I don't think it's my place to say. We were friends when he worked here, and I know he'd be delighted to have a sister, to find any relatives, but it's really up to him to tell you himself.'

'So this illness,' I swallowed, 'wasn't terminal? Mark's still alive?'

He sighed. 'I don't know. He cut himself off after he went away.' He looked at me again as though he guessed how I was feeling. 'I'm sorry, but I think it's highly unlikely that he's still with us. I wish I could say otherwise.'

I trailed back to the motel through drenched streets. The rain had eased off slightly, but I was glad to get back into my dry room and have a hot shower. Afterwards, I curled up on the bed and very reluctantly picked up the phone again.

'Grey Base Hospital,' the receptionist intoned.

'Um, yes, I'm wondering if you can tell me if you have a patient with the name Mark Juniper,' I said.

'May I ask who's calling?'

'I'm his sister. He's missing, and I'm worried he's been in an accident or something. It's really urgent.'

'Just a moment…' There was a clacking of a computer keyboard, 'No, we don't have any patient here by that name.'

When I put the phone down I wasn't sure whether to be relieved or not. Surely my leads couldn't end there. Should I go and check graveyards or death records? Was I really ready to believe Mark was a ghost?

Whatever he was, there was no need for me to stay in Fox Glacier any longer. I'd head to Greymouth and see if I could find any trace of Mark before moving on up to Westport to look for Alan Jensen. It struck me as a little odd that I was now engaged in two quests that converged on the West Coast.

The clack of a helicopter overhead roused me from the bed. The sun was out at last; helicopter rides over the glaciers must have resumed. It was one of the activities even Niall had been enthusiastic about when we'd originally planned our itinerary. A helicopter flight was too expensive for me now, but there was a small lake nearby that surely had to be worth a look. I couldn't do Mark any good by moping in my room, and there were hours of daylight left. I headed to the motel office to ask how to get to Lake Matheson. I usually found being active an excellent means of keeping my spirits up.

***

The next day I was almost dozing on the bus to Greymouth, thinking about my tramp around Lake Matheson – which was definitely not the dream lake – the previous afternoon and gazing idly out of the window, when something by the side of the road caught my eye, and I suddenly sat bolt upright.

'You all right, dear?' asked the older lady sitting next to me.

'I'm not sure,' I said, staring at the passing scene while new sensations of déjà vu crashed into my mind. 'Where is this?' I asked, as the bus began to cross an enormously long bridge over an estuary.

'We're just coming into Hokitika. This is the bridge over the Hokitika River.'

Hokitika. A place no one had mentioned. I hadn't even glanced at it on the map; it looked small and insignificant. I gripped the armrest of my seat as the bus drove through the long, wide streets. Small or not, it was the biggest place I'd seen for a while, and I knew before the bus even pulled up that I was going to get out there.

It wasn't difficult to find a motel room near the centre, and once I'd dumped my stuff, I set out to explore the town, with the side aim of seeking work, if there were any to be found. Looking for work in a strange town had been a lot easier when Mark was on the case. How *had* he found out about those jobs? I'd never really questioned it, just assumed he'd had more local knowledge and knew more people, but the way he'd come up with the one in Manapouri never did make sense.

One bar offered me a few casual hours as a barmaid if I could start at that very moment, so I spent what was left of my first day and evening serving drinks and food. I came away with a few dollars, just enough to buy myself some provisions.

Over the course of the next day I fell in love with Hokitika. I walked for miles along the sea beach strewn with tree trunks and branches, tripped around the shops, had a meal in a café, and discovered my first proper supermarket since Dunedin. A visit to the tourist information centre revealed that there were two lakes nearby, although sadly not nearby enough for me to get to them on foot.

I found a library and remembered Mark's mentions of the electoral roll. When the assistant handed it over I was surprised but pleased to find that it covered the entire West Coast. My hands trembled as I worked down the Js. I sank into a chair with relief when I saw that there *was* an Alan Jensen listed in the Westport area, but I was excited and intrigued to note that there was also a Ewan Jensen in Hokitika. A hard ache formed in my chest when I found no Mark Juniper listed at all, but surely all that proved was that he wasn't living in the West Coast. Could he have moved somewhere else?

I checked through the local phone book for either Alan or Ewan Jensen but they weren't listed. Ewan's address was apparently quite a way out of town – again, too far to walk. It had been so much easier with Pastor's company – and transport – but I still didn't want to think too much about Pastor. Nor did I want to analyse in any depth why I was so keen to seek out Ewan Jensen. After all, I had no proof that he was any relation. Except that New Zealand is quite a small place, compared with the UK, especially the South Island, and my intuition was telling me it wasn't a coincidence. If I were right, he should be around my age and able to give me more of an idea of what to expect from his dad.

The next morning I hired a bike for the ride out to Ewan Jensen's. The roads around Hokitika were good for cycling, being mostly straight and flat, but even so I was inevitably red-faced and perspiring in the hot sun by the time I'd cycled the fifteen miles or so to what looked like the middle of nowhere. As it turned out, he lived in the bush, well off any main roads. I eventually pedalled down a dirt track through native trees and shrub and into a clearing beside a fast-flowing stretch of river.

Off to one side was a small, prefabricated cabin similar to Pastor's, but closer to the river there was a far larger half-built wooden structure. Two men were lugging planks about, and another stood nearby, frowning over a clipboard he was holding. He turned around as I jumped off the bike and leaned it against a tree. An expression of irritation crossed his features before he came over. He was tall like Mark and dark like Niall, with wavy and obviously unruly hair cropped short. He wore casual jeans and a T-shirt and had to be in his mid-thirties. I would have found him quite attractive if he weren't scowling at me through his gold-rimmed glasses.

'Can I help you?' he asked brusquely, impatiently, glancing back at the men as they plonked down their planks. 'Are you lost?'

'Um no, I-I'm not lost,' I stuttered, taken aback at this unfriendly attitude. 'I'm looking for Ewan Jensen.'

He frowned even more and looked at me closely, his mouth twisting as though he didn't like what he saw. 'You've found him,' he said, with obvious reluctance. 'What can I do for you?'

‘I –’ His whole manner was making me nervous. ‘Are you related to Alan Jensen?’ I finally said in a rush.

He looked surprised, but then shrugged. ‘My dad’s name *is* Alan, yes. Is it him you want? He lives in Westport.’

This was hard going, but at least I knew I was on the right track. ‘Well yes and no. I just, well, wanted to meet you, while I was in Hokitika. I think my dad and your dad were friends when…’ I quailed slightly as his expression remained politely quizzical, ‘when they were young. My name’s Olivia Kimpton.’

He exhaled sharply and looked back at the workmen again before turning to me. ‘Well look, I don’t know anything about that, and as you can see, I’m pretty busy right now. Maybe I can call you later. How long are you going to be in town?’

Clearly the last thing he wanted to do was call me, but his antagonism made no sense. ‘I’m, um, here for a couple of days, at least,’ I said.

‘Okay, if you give me your number, I’ll check with my dad and get back to you.’

As soon as he’d noted the number on his mobile, he turned away. ‘No, not that way, Joe. It needs to be at a right angle,’ he said to one of the men, and he strode back to the half-built structure without a backward glance.

This didn’t augur too well, if Alan Jensen was anything like his son. I stood watching for a minute as he rapped out orders like an army major. I sighed in sympathy with the poor workmen. As for me, I was hot, tired and disheartened, but I had no choice but to pick up my bike and cycle back to town with my tail between my legs.

I arrived back at my motel with a very sore backside for the want of a decent break in my journey. My phone rang just as I turned on the bath taps.

‘Why has it been almost a week since I heard from you?’ my mum said.

‘It’s just been… well there’s been a few things going on.’ I really hadn’t felt up to it.

‘What sort of things?’ she asked. ‘Are you all right? Are you still in Haast? Has that Pastor friend of yours done something?’

‘I’m fine,’ I said quickly, explaining where I was, and that I’d found a little bar work. A very little, actually, but she didn’t need to know that.

‘Aren’t you tired of all this gallivanting about yet?’ she asked. ‘Ron and I are really worried about you, and you don’t sound very happy to me. You must be getting low on money, too.’

Mums, eh? Doesn’t matter how hard you try, they can usually see through it. Even though I’d put on a bright and cheerful manner, the despondency that had come over me since Haast must have crept into my voice somehow. I attempted to divert her, waffling on about how much I loved Hokitika, but by the time we hung up, the anxious tone still hadn’t left her voice.

Chapter Ten

It had been a toss-up, Ewan or one of the lakes, and after yesterday's debacle I was sorry Ewan had won. My stomach cramped oddly as I set off to Lake Mahinapua on a bright blue morning. My sore backside also protested at another long bike ride after only a few hours respite. I'd lain awake worrying for most of those hours, and when I'd finally drifted into sleep, the dream had woken me with its usual jolt at dawn.

I was feeling tired, tetchy and emotional when I eventually turned into a rough, dusty road through the trees. It was almost midday and hot and sunny. The shade came as some relief after the ten-kilometre bike ride. Excitement and dejection vied for supremacy in my mind. On the one hand, I was sure this place was significant; it was at around the point where I'd sat up and taken notice on the bus, for one thing. On the other hand, although I'd hoped that my phone would ring, it had remained stubbornly silent. Ewan Jensen had probably forgotten I existed already. I should have just asked him for his dad's phone number.

I parked the bike near the lake shore with every antenna of intuition twitching madly. There were a few people around, lying on the grass sunbathing, or paddling at the shingle beach. I walked towards a nearby jetty on slightly shaky legs.

Yes, this lake was the familiar reddish colour and surely *there* was the fringe of trees! Even the sky looked right, *and* the distant mountains drowsy through a blue haze. Everything fitted except the beach. There *had* to be another beach here.

Cicadas chorused loudly around me as I investigated a couple of paths that led off from the main parking area. The first one came to a dead end, but the second, far longer, led me through trees and clearings to a small gap fringed by vegetation. I was trembling as I stepped through the opening and *there* was the grey sand, the tree stumps in the water and even a drooping flax plant, although it wasn't at quite the same angle. I sat down on a fallen tree trunk as a gentle breeze passed across my face. Just as in the dream, the beach was empty.

I stared across the lake at the trees that were so achingly familiar. *Here I am, Dad,* I wanted to shout, as my dad's memories began to coalesce with my own feelings of sadness. Everything had reached a crisis point. The situation with Mark, Ewan Jensen's dismissive manner, Pastor's betrayal, the fact that I'd had to lie to my mum only last night and tell her everything was great, and the fact that I was here at last but there were still no answers. I put my head in my hands in despair.

'Ollie… what is it? What's wrong?' a familiar voice scratched faintly from nearby, and I looked up to see Mark, but this time he even *looked* ghostly, and he wasn't moving. He was like a holographic image of himself.

I jumped up from the log. 'Mark, where are you, *really*? Are you alive? How do I find you?'

His eyeballs flicked from side to side but he still didn't move. 'Is this the beach?'

I nodded impatiently. 'But –'

'That's good. You found it.'

'I went to the DOC office in Fox Glacier. The man there said you left because you were ill. He said that was five years ago. Where are you *now*?'

'I just wish I could have found her,' he said wistfully. 'I wish…'

He faded out. He just *faded out* right in front of me. I collapsed back onto the sand and burst into tears.

My mobile phone went just as I was reaching the hiccupping stage. I wiped my eyes and tried desperately to control my sobbing breaths before I flipped it open and quavered, 'Hello.'

'Is that Olivia Kimpton?' a strange man's voice asked.

'Yes it is,' I croaked, still sniffling.

'This is Alan Jensen. My son gave me your number. Are you all right? You sound a bit upset.'

'I'm… um… I'm okay. It's good to hear from you. I've been trying to find you.'

'I was surprised when Ewan told me you'd called round, but I'd love to see you. How long are you in New Zealand? You know I live in Westport?'

'I'm here for at least another couple of months,' I said.

'That's great. Do you have transport? Ewan said you were on a bike. I told him he should have invited you in if you'd cycled all the way out from Hokitika, but he claims he was too busy with the lodge. Anyway if you don't have a car, I'll get him to bring you up here, and that way you won't have any trouble finding the place. Can I ask – what's happened with Paul?'

Alan didn't pause too much for breath, but he certainly sounded keen. 'My dad died in 1995,' I said as gently as I could.

There was a brief silence. 'I'm really sorry to hear that. We lost touch – I gather you know that – but we grew up together. I've never had another friend like him.'

I had my sobbing hiccups under control by the time Alan had extracted the information from me about how I was travelling around and why I was visiting New Zealand. I didn't let on that all I seemed to have ended up doing was look for people and places, or that now I'd found him, I'd still have to try to find Mark, because no matter how it looked, I didn't believe he was dead.

'So I'll get on to Ewan and tell him to come and pick you up tomorrow, and you can stay here – there's plenty of room – if you're sure you're finished in Hokitika? He needs to take a break from the building work anyway; it's all he thinks about since the divorce.'

I was tempted to say I'd be fine going on the bus, as the prospect of two hours or more in Ewan's constant company was more than a little daunting, but I didn't want to hurt his feelings. By the time I flipped my phone shut, it was all apparently arranged. Ewan would pick me up from the motel tomorrow at nine. I wondered how he was going to feel about that.

I lingered for a while longer on the beach, paddling in the rusty red water. An eel writhed away towards the half-submerged tree trunks, and I looked down into the water and spotted a trout swimming close to my bare legs. Peace stole slowly into my thoughts as the flax stem bobbed up and down in the breeze and a small dinghy sailed past on the opposite shore. I could only imagine my dad went there in his pain because it was that kind of place: somewhere soothing that you'd probably have to yourself. I'd been there for hours and not seen a soul, even though there had been quite a few people back at the main beach area.

I was feeling a lot better as I dried my feet and pulled my trainers back on. I was just getting up to leave when my mobile phone rang again.

'Ewan Jensen here,' said the abrupt, businesslike voice. 'I gather you've spoken to my dad. He seems to think you're upset and I should come to your rescue and take you out or something. "She's all on her own in a strange town" were his exact words.'

'Oh. No, I'm all right; he just caught me at a bad moment,' I said, wondering how Alan imagined Ewan might be in any way a welcome rescuer.

'Well, whether or not, I've had my orders. I'm in town right now, as it happens. Are you at the motel?'

'No, I'm out at Lake Mahinapua, but you don't –'

'You cycled out there?' he asked sharply.

'Yes –'

'Okay, I can be there in a few minutes. I'm in the pick-up, so the bike isn't a problem. Wait in the main parking lot for me.'

He'd cut off before I had the chance to protest again, or to mention that I had to tramp back to the car park first. I wondered what he did for a living. Maybe he was a company director or something, used to having his orders obeyed.

Sure enough, a tetchy text arrived ten minutes later, when I was still only halfway back to the car park, and when I finally emerged and went to unlock my hire bike from its post, Ewan was there, grabbing it from me impatiently.

'Look, you don't need to do anything, really. I'm fine on my own,' I said, watching him heft the bike into the back of the pick up.

He turned to look at me and that same strangely irritated look I'd noted before passed over his face before he said, 'No, my dad seems very concerned about you, and to be honest, it's the most interest he's taken in anything much for a couple of years. Get in.'

I gave up and jumped meekly into the passenger seat. As I was buckling up, he added, 'This is all news to me. He's never mentioned a Paul Kimpton before. Now he tells me they emigrated here together.'

'Same here. I mean, my dad never told either my mum or me about it. I found out by chance after I got here.' I hoped he wasn't going to ask for details, as I didn't relish revealing all about the dream.

He looked aside at me as he pulled out of the car park. 'Doesn't that seem strange to you? If they were such friends, why keep it to themselves like that? Why lose touch at all?'

'Your dad didn't say why?'

'Nope. Very cagey on that point.'

I was reluctant to tell him my theory about a love triangle. Apart from Ewan's somewhat unfriendly attitude, I'd learned my lesson from Pastor. I didn't want anyone else giving me that pitying look, ever again. Besides, how was he going to feel if, as I strongly suspected, his own mother was the apex of that triangle?

'Do you remember going to Haast when you were a teenager?' I asked.

'Uh huh. How'd you know about that?'

I told him about Jackson Bay and that Barney had remembered the name Kimpton.

'So your dad was with my mum and dad down there in the hippy campervan,' he mused. 'We heard a lot about that when we were growing up, that's for sure. It's where they fell in love, so they told us. Bit odd that they never mentioned your dad though.' He glanced over at me, for once without a frown or look of irritation. 'What if this is something we don't really want to know?'

'I'd like to know, I think. My dad died of motor neurone disease, and by the end, he couldn't talk even if he'd wanted to. I'd like to know about those times and why he never mentioned them.'

He nodded slowly, his eyes on the road. We were already approaching the Hokitika Bridge. 'My mum died two years ago, so I suppose there's not much stopping my dad from telling all, if he wants to.'

I bit my lip. He was obviously starting to reach the same sort of conclusion that I had.

'And to be honest, I think he wants to. He was quite insistent on my taking you up there, even though he knows I've got a lot on.'

'He said something about a lodge. Is that what you're building?'

'Yep. It's going to be a tourist lodge. We got the land cheap because of the recession. So do you fancy eating out somewhere? There's a couple of good restaurants here.'

I swallowed so hard I was afraid he'd hear the gulp. A candlelit dinner for two with him scowling across the table at me?

'Or I guess you could come back to the house. I'm not much of a cook, mind you. I tend to exist on beans on toast.'

I laughed in spite of myself. 'Me too.'

He started to smile, and then somehow a frown managed to take over, so I added quickly, 'I'd be interested in seeing what you're building. It looked like a gorgeous spot.'

His expression lightened again. 'Okay, let's go out there. I could do with getting a couple of things done before it gets dark, in any case.'

Great, so he was proposing to get down to work while I was there? On the other hand, at least it would spare us from too many awkward silences.

We made desultory conversation on the way – about the weather, what I thought of the lake, how I was finding New Zealand, but I knew he was only going through the motions for his dad's sake.

I was still going over the Mark situation in the back of my mind. I wished I had someone to talk to about that. The thought kept recurring that he was passing the baton to me. *Find her because I can't.* But where could I possibly look that he hadn't already?

Ewan pulled up outside the cabin and led the way across to the half-built lodge. I followed him around as he expounded on what he was trying to build. 'It's going to be an eco-lodge. We'll be taking our water from the creek, and all our energy will be supplied by sustainable sources. There are a couple of great swimming holes upstream, and we're creating some tramping trails through the bush. It'll be a peaceful haven for people to escape to.'

I looked around appreciatively at the creek and the jungle of native trees and ferns and wondered who else he meant when he said 'we'. I wanted to ask, but I was reluctant to say anything that might bring the frown back onto his not-unattractive features. Did it have anything to do with the divorce Alan had mentioned? Perhaps he now hated all women, or just those of us with long auburn hair.

He asked me to help him hold some lengths of wood while he did a bit of hammering. I could have done more than hold them if he'd asked, but like most men, he'd automatically assumed I was a girly girl, and at that moment I couldn't be bothered to disabuse him of the idea. Eventually he led the way back to the prefab cabin. 'It's not much, but it's home for now,' he said, apologetically.

It was virtually a carbon copy of Pastor's house, and very much a single man's habitat. I guessed the 'we' didn't include a woman.

'So, d'you fancy some beans on toast, or something else?' he said, leaning against his fridge in a relaxed pose and actually smiling in a normal manner.

My breath caught for a second, because he was surprisingly good-looking when he wasn't scowling.

I tried to smile back and said, 'Maybe we could make something more elaborate between us? It's worth a try.' I was calculating that it would keep us safely and innocuously occupied for quite a while.

'Okay, let's see what I have in the cupboard.' He started calling out the contents of various tins and we eventually cobbled together some meat, potatoes and veg. It was surprisingly companionable until we had the food on the plates and were forced to make conversation again.

'So what brought you to New Zealand?' he asked. It should have been a simple question to answer, but somehow I didn't want to mention Niall or our break up. Nor did I want to tell him about looking for work, even though he might have been able to help. His brusque manner suggested that he wouldn't look too kindly on someone working on a tourist visa.

'I've always been interested in seeing it,' I said lamely, but at least it wasn't a lie.

‘Uh huh. Which parts have you visited so far?’

Phew. I was able to spend the remainder of the meal expounding on the joys of the Otago Rail Trail and various other places around Dunedin and Manapouri.

‘Do you… um… work in Hokitika?’ I asked, as we did the washing up together.

‘Only on the lodge,’ he said. ‘It’s a joint project between my dad and me. He’s planning to move down here, once it’s built. He’s got a good job up in Westport, or he’d be down here already, but he’s taking early retirement next year, and we’re going to run the place together.’

He looked up at me then, fully engaging in eye contact, which we both seemed to have been avoiding all evening. ‘So what about you, what do you do in England?’

‘Did,’ I said firmly. ‘I worked in a call centre.’

‘So you’ve no job to go back to?’

‘I don’t plan to go back if I can get a job here.’

‘Not so easy in a recession.’

I forgot myself and told him about the jobs I’d applied for while I was in Manapouri, but when I looked up at him again I could see the look of irritation was back on his face, although he was trying a bit harder to hide it. What had I said wrong this time?

‘I suppose you’ll be wanting to get back to your motel now?’ he asked, and I nodded in agreement, thinking I’d be glad to stop walking on eggshells.

After he’d dropped me at the motel, I watched him drive off with mixed feelings. We’d managed, somehow, to make conversation on the way back, but I could *feel* his withdrawal. It was as if he realized he’d let his guard down and was now overcompensating by pulling right back inside the hard carapace. Did I look like his ex-wife or something? He certainly hadn’t mentioned her, and there were no photos of her, or of any children, scattered around the cabin.

I went down to the beach and walked up and down, watching the breakers as the sun set, my loneliness almost a physical ache. Eventually I sat on one of the ubiquitous tree trunks and phoned my mum. She was surprised to hear from me again so soon, to say the least.

'Has anything happened – are you all right?' she asked anxiously.

'Everything's fine,' I said. 'I just thought I'd let you know I'm moving on to Westport tomorrow. I'm going to stay with someone there for a while, so I won't be paying out for a motel.'

'What do you mean, "someone"? Who is this person?'

I thought quickly. 'He's an old friend of Pastor's,' I said, adding to my tally of lies. Obviously my lying skills were improving.

'So he's another clergyman?'

'No, he's, um…' I realized too late that I had no idea what Alan did for a living. 'He's a businessman,' I said.

'I see, and he's just going to let you stay there and want nothing in return, is he? That seems rather unlikely.' I could imagine my mum pressing her lips together while all sorts of suspicions passed through her mind. 'Ollie, please be careful. You've always been far too naïve where men are concerned.'

I sighed inwardly, wishing I could tell her the whole story, but I didn't want to hurt her, and I still didn't know the conclusion. One thing I did know, though, at long last, was that finding the dream beach hadn't revealed anything wrong at her end.

Chapter Eleven

Damn, my breath caught again at the sight of Ewan the next morning. He jumped out of an ordinary family Toyota with a surprising smile and a 'G'day,' that reminded me of Mark. I found myself noticing, reluctantly, how good he looked in his tight jeans, and how some chest hair was visible at the apex of his crisp white cotton shirt. I'd always been a sucker for a hairy chest.

He threw my backpack into the boot, and I hopped into the passenger seat, wondering if I was becoming too accustomed to the convenience of cars, which were still, in my opinion, the scourge of the world. Cycling might be hard work at times, but at least I didn't feel like a big hypocrite as I pedalled along.

I was sorry to see Hokitika falling behind me. I couldn't know whether my dad just stopped off there when he was passing through, or whether he liked the place as much as I already did. I preferred to believe the latter.

As we headed northwards, with the sun glinting off the sea to our left, I tried to make conversation with Ewan and get back to the comfortable footing of our meal last night. I struck gold in asking about his eco-lodge. He'd got it all worked out, from how to treat the river water to where to put the solar panels. I was impressed.

'Will you really be able to generate enough power though?' I asked. I may not have gone to university and studied it, but I'd read a lot about green energy over the years.

He nodded firmly. 'It's just a case of attention to detail; it's all in the design.'

'Did you design it yourself?'

'Dad and I did it between us. He's an architect – green design is his speciality.'

'Ah. So when it's built, you and your dad will both live there and run it?'

'That's the plan,' he said, and the frown was back, as though his thoughts had just turned dark again.

Fortunately, we were coming into Westport by then, and he was distracted by pointing out various places of interest in what was really his home town. He'd lived there from when he was six, he told me.

It was a bit bigger than Hokitika but had the same kind of wide, straight streets, and a large number of shops. There was a kind of steamy, tropical feel to the place, reflected in the palm trees growing by the roadside, but I wasn't getting any sense of familiarity at all, which was a relief.

Eventually, Ewan pulled into the drive of an ordinary but fairly large suburban house in an older style than the cabins and prefabs I'd seen a lot of to date. No sooner had he turned off the engine than a man rocketed out of the front door and dashed over to the car. Alan was short, slightly plump and in his late fifties. His balding hair was still dark like Ewan's, although the benign and jovial expression on his face as he opened my door for me was a complete contrast to Ewan's usual scowl.

'Olivia,' he said warmly as I got out and returned his smile. 'Good to have you here.' He stepped back slightly and regarded me. 'I can see Paul in you. Same eyes; same hair colour.'

'It's great to meet you at last,' I said, feeling relaxed with him, as if I knew him already.

Ewan was getting my backpack out of the car, but at least he wasn't frowning. He even smiled a bit as he looked at his dad. 'You're all right then, old codger?' he asked.

Alan just laughed and flicked his eyes upwards in amused exasperation. 'Come on in, the pair of you.'

The house was cool and airy, with large rooms artistically decorated and furnished. It was distinctly not a bachelor pad. I could see a woman's touch everywhere, despite having no such feminine homemaking talents myself. If Ewan's mum had died two years ago, Alan had clearly had no desire to alter her tasteful decorative scheme since.

Alan showed me into a large, bright bedroom that he told me used to belong to his daughter, Carol. 'She won't be making use of it anytime soon,' he said. 'She's been in Australia for six years.'

Ewan dumped my backpack on the floral carpet. 'Wow, Dad, you've actually made the room up. What came over you?' he said. He looked at me. 'I keep telling him to get a housekeeper, but he won't have it.'

'I don't need some busybody ordering me around. Now let's have some coffee, shall we?'

I followed them into a big, country-style kitchen. Large windows offered views over a garden jostling with roses in full, blowsy bloom.

'So you mentioned you'd always wanted to visit New Zealand, Olivia.' Alan said, as he busied himself getting mugs out of cupboards. 'Was it because of Paul? Did he ever talk about me? About Jenny?'

'No, he didn't tell me anything,' I said, somewhat sadly.

Alan had his back to me, and his shoulders slumped slightly.

'So what's all this about then, Dad?' Ewan asked with slight impatience, seating himself at the kitchen table and stretching out his long legs. 'You never mentioned a Paul Kimpton to any of *us* either, nor did Mum.'

Alan sighed as he handed over the mugs and joined us at the table. 'We never wanted to talk about it. We put it behind us, decided to forget it, I suppose. Not that we ever could, not really. I never stopped wondering what had happened to Paul. We were best friends, grew up together, emigrated together, worked here together.' He looked at me. 'Did you know all that?'

I nodded silently, well aware that any explanation of how I knew some things would involve revealing the dream.

'Ollie says he was with you at Jackson Bay, in the hippy campervan,' Ewan prompted.

Alan sipped his coffee slowly, and then said, 'Yes, he was. The six of us travelled cross-country, just like we told you, and we decided to hang around the Haast area for a while. It was so untamed down there: empty, even more so than today. We had a great time, but things started to go wrong at Jackson Bay.'

He gazed apologetically at Ewan. 'You have to try and imagine the times. We were so young, and Paul and me had been working on that sheep station for months so we were desperate for a break, a bit of freedom. We were all just a bit wild, and your mum was probably the wildest of us all.' He paused and looked at each of us in turn. 'When we set off on the trip, she was Paul's girlfriend.'

Ewan raised his eyebrows but stayed silent. I was almost holding my breath.

'By the time we got to Jackson Bay he was crazy about her, but she...' he glanced at Ewan again, 'she wasn't as committed. She didn't want to be tied down. She cared for him, but not the way he did about her.' He looked down at his coffee cup, his genial expression pulled down momentarily into sadness. 'Then, I don't know how it happened, really – it just happened. She was... I loved her too... I didn't want to hurt Paul but...' he exhaled sharply. 'It wasn't like in films; he didn't walk in on us, or anything like that. In the end, I couldn't stand to deceive him, so I told him.' He passed a hand over his face. 'I don't know what I expected – understanding, forgiveness maybe, but he just looked at me as if I'd broken his heart. Then he went to find Jenny, get the story from her.'

The clock on the wall ticked steadily, and a bird called outside in the momentary silence. Neither Ewan nor I moved or spoke.

'That was the end of the holiday. We'd moved on up to Haast by then and camped out beside an estuary. Paul was missing all that night and came back looking like a ghost. I tried to talk to him but he ignored me and started packing. I kept on trying… he was my best friend; I'd never wanted to hurt him. Anyway, he just walked away all stony faced, without even saying goodbye.' He paused and took a shaky breath. It was obviously very emotional for him to recount, even thirty-seven years later. 'I never saw or heard from him again. I guessed he'd have gone home. He wouldn't have been allowed to stay in the country, as he'd quit his job. As for Jenny, she went really quiet and would hardly talk to me either. When we got back to Canterbury, she said she was leaving to stay with her aunt for a while, and she wanted a clean break from me as well as Paul. I thought that was that. I went back to my job on the sheep station pretty depressed, wondering how everything could have gone so wrong, so fast.'

He took another slow sip of coffee, gazing out of the window at the roses. Ewan glanced over at me and raised his eyebrows but said nothing.

Alan sighed and put down his cup. 'Jenny turned back up out of the blue a year later. She was a bit different: more subdued, more grown up, I suppose. I guess we both were. She asked me if I knew how to find Paul, but I had no idea; I'd tried writing to him at his parents' address back in England but had no reply. Then… the two of us ended up spending a lot of time together, getting to know one another properly, and… well,' he looked at Ewan and smiled, 'the rest is history.'

I had tears in my eyes, and my voice croaked a little as I asked, 'Did she say why she wanted to find my dad?'

'She felt really bad about how she treated him. She wanted to know that he was okay,' Alan said. 'I'd like to know that, too. Tell me about him, what happened after he got back to the UK. How he died…'

I told him what I knew, a little shaken to have had all my intuitions about places and events proved right. No wonder I was besieged by so many sensations on the estuary beach near Haast, if that's where it had all come to a head.

Alan was visibly upset when I told him about my dad's illness. 'Motor neurone disease,' he repeated. 'That's a terrible thing. I had a friend die of that a few years ago. You remember, Ewan, Debbie Finch?' He gazed at me sympathetically. 'Hard for you to watch, and you were so young, too. But your mum's happy with her new husband?'

I nodded. 'They're inseparable.'

'So how did you know about me? Did Paul tell your mum?'

I hesitated, and then said reluctantly, 'I'm almost certain he never told my mum about you, or Jenny, or even New Zealand.'

Alan looked disappointed again. I could almost feel his sadness at the prospect that my dad never forgave him. *But maybe that wasn't true.*

'I know about you because of the dream,' I forced myself to say, and I tried to avoid Ewan's scorching gaze as I explained.

'I first had it when my dad was dying,' I began and went on to tell them about the beach, and how the dream had returned with full intensity here in New Zealand. 'I found the dream beach yesterday at Lake Mahinapua. I think…' I gulped, feeling the emotion all over again. 'I think my dad went there after it happened.'

'Is that why you sounded so upset when I called?' Alan asked.

'Well, that was part of it.' I paused, and added, 'I had started to catch more background to the dream, and the name Alan and that you were his best friend. That's when I realized it wasn't me I was dreaming about.' I explained the odd series of events that had led me to Westport. 'And then a friend checked the archives in Wellington for me and found my dad's name and yours on the passenger lists – and, well… here I am.'

I finally risked looking over at Ewan, but to my relief he just looked stunned, rather than sceptical. Alan sat back in his chair and relaxed slightly.

'I think…' I said quickly, 'I think my dad must have been dwelling on it all in his last few weeks. He didn't have one of those Stephen Hawking sorts of talking gadgets, so he couldn't communicate in any way. His intellect stayed the same, but he was trapped in a helpless body. He and I had a sort of connection…' I exhaled sharply. 'I used to know what he wanted, how he was feeling, and maybe, somehow, he managed to get it across to me.' I looked directly at Alan. 'I think he wanted me to find you. At the end, it was you he was thinking about.'

CHAPTER TWELVE

'Well you've made him happy, anyway; I can't complain about that,' Ewan said, as he drove through the wide Westport streets the following day. We were on our way to the supermarket, because when Ewan had checked the contents of Alan's fridge and cupboards, they'd been devoid of much in the way of food.

'I thought you were going to start eating better, Dad,' Ewan had said, frowning over the couple of tins of beans and the loaf of bread.

Alan had shrugged and then looked at me apologetically. 'I just get takeaways most of the time, or have snacks,' he'd explained.

I was deputed to help Ewan do a proper shop, which seemed ironic when my own eating habits weren't that much different. Alan appeared to harbour the quaint, old-fashioned idea that as a woman I would know best what to buy.

'Are you okay about what your dad told us? Were you shocked?' I asked, a bit boldly.

Ewan glanced aside at me. 'I'm surprised. I didn't know my mum and dad had such a torrid past.' He shrugged. 'Then again, it's nothing compared with these days. I should know.' He said the last part in a bitter tone, and his expression hardened. After a minute of contemplative silence, he added, 'It's hard to think of my mum like that, to be honest. Yeah, we all grew up hearing the stories about their wilder, younger days, and an obviously expurgated version of their travels in the campervan, and I've seen all the photos from those times, but when it comes down to it, your mum's your mum. You can't really imagine how she was as a person before that, if you see what I mean.'

I nodded slowly, thinking about my own mum. How well did I know her, really? We'd never been close because we were so different. Even though we should have got closer after Dad died, we'd actually drifted apart. As for Ewan's mum, I longed to know what she was really like: what my dad loved about her, whether she regretted what she'd done, and why she'd gone back. I'd noticed a couple of pictures of her in the house but hadn't had an opportunity to look more closely at them.

Ewan and I trawled the supermarket, looking for tasty food that was easy to cook. We laughed together as we threw in tin after tin and packet after packet. The only things we bought that weren't pre-packed were half a dozen eggs and a joint of New Zealand lamb. While Alan wanted to celebrate my news, and my presence, with a decent meal, he seemed oblivious of the fact that none of us could cook. Free spirit Jenny had apparently spoiled the entire family with her culinary expertise over the years, but none of them had followed in her footsteps. Anyway, Ewan's sisters were both in Australia, so they couldn't help. I'd decided to try roasting a joint, since to the best of my knowledge you just put it in the oven in a bit of fat for an hour or two, turned it over a couple of times and it was done.

'You've never been married, then?' Ewan asked suddenly as we walked back to the car, laden with bags.

We'd been so relaxed together all day that I didn't hesitate. 'No. Just a couple of attempts at living together that didn't last long. What about you?'

'I got divorced a year ago. She'd been playing around big time.'

'Sorry to hear that,' I said as I lumbered a couple of bags into his capacious boot.

He shrugged, and the scowl had returned to his features. 'Yeah well, beautiful is as beautiful does, eh?' he said, looking at me significantly.

I was too taken aback to react right away. Did I assume he thought I was beautiful? It was hardly a compliment though, was it? It made more sense of his attitude towards me, at least, but it was rather unfair of him to draw the conclusion that all attractive women would be unfaithful.

I settled back in the passenger seat with the feeling that I couldn't win with men. All they ever seemed to do was make assumptions. That I was a high maintenance girly girl, that I'd had a boob job, that I must be in a constant battle for the elusive size zero, that my interests must naturally include hours spent grooming, and now that I must automatically be a two-timer, or even worse than a two-timer. Where was the man who was going to see the real me? Well maybe that was Mark. *Where was Mark*?

'You've gone quiet,' Ewan said, dragging me back to the moment. 'I suppose I shouldn't have said that, but you can't deny that looking the way you do, you can pretty much take your pick.'

I eyed him coldly. 'I can't alter my looks,' I said. 'But I haven't come across any research that indicates a woman's looks have any bearing on her fidelity.'

He raised his eyebrows and then gave me a second glance, as though trying to size me up. 'You're not quite what you seem, are you?' he said.

'Depends what I seem. I'm not a two-timing man-eater, if that's what you were thinking.'

He sighed. 'Okay, I admit I'm prejudiced, but I've got good reason.'

He didn't elaborate, and the frown stayed on his features for the remainder of our return journey. I was relieved to be greeted by Alan's cheery smile when we got back.

I stuck the joint in the oven surrounded by a stack of potatoes and some kumara, the New Zealand sweet potato that had been growing on me. The whole lot came out of packets. It was strange to be in charge of any cooking activity after all the years of being considered a liability by my mum. I only ever cooked the most basic of meals for myself as a singleton.

While the house filled with delicious aromas, Alan broke out the photo albums. I was all too happy to take a look at them, although Ewan seemed a little uneasy, knowing, I suppose, that it wasn't just images of Alan and Jenny's lives that were about to be revealed, but his as well.

The oldest album contained pictures from Alan's childhood, and he pointed to one of two boys aged about twelve, one dark and one ginger and said, 'That's us, Paul and me, when we were at school together.'

'I've seen this photo,' I said. 'We have one just like it.'

There were a few others of them together as boys and teenagers, and a couple more that were identical to the ones in my dad's albums. I'd never thought about the identity of the other boy when I'd looked at them before. It was another aspect of your parents' pasts being like a long lost world when you're a kid. I remembered being told off by my mum for calling any time before I was born 'the olden days'.

When we reached the post-emigration period, there was one of Alan and my dad in the shearing shed and one of the whole gang on the beach at Jackson Bay. It wasn't a close shot, so it was hard for me to get a better idea of what Jenny looked like until Alan turned to the next photo with a sad sigh.

'I took this one at Haast,' he said, and a startling surge of familiarity passed through me at the sight of Jenny on the estuary beach: a very pretty girl with a wide smile and long, flowing blonde hair, a beaded necklace hanging over a billowing blouse and an Indian cotton skirt just touching the sand. She was posing in a sort of ballet position and looked as though she was about to topple over.

Jenny's face became very familiar as we moved through Ewan's birth – a cute, smiling baby, somewhat to my surprise – to those of his sisters and their ensuing childhoods. Ewan became restless as we approached his adolescence.

'Off to Uni in Wellington,' Alan said, while Ewan squirmed, and then: 'Fully fledged teacher – that was the first school he taught at.' I looked over at Ewan in surprise. I hadn't pictured him as a teacher. He raised his eyebrows at me, and his lips turned upwards slightly, as if my reaction amused him.

'You've given up teaching now?' I asked.

He nodded. 'Since I came back south. I'm concentrating on the lodge.'

So he used to live in the North Island, taught there even. Maybe the lodge was all part of a new life he was trying to forge, one that didn't include his ex-wife.

Alan skimmed over Ewan's wedding fairly swiftly, probably to spare him any more discomfort, but I took note that his wife was absolutely gorgeous and far more glamorous than I'd ever been – or desired to be.

Finally we reached the last album, in which Jenny, still looking good in her fifties, smiled sweetly in a family shot containing all three children, all of their spouses and three grandchildren.

'She was already dying then,' Alan said. 'It hadn't quite taken hold, so you can't tell, but we all knew.'

My eye was drawn to Ewan, standing with his wife and looking, in my estimation, profoundly miserable. Was his marriage already on the rocks? How long ago was this? Three years?

It was hard to lift the miasma of sadness and revive the good mood once Alan had put away the albums, but I got them both helping with the final touches of the meal, and by the time it was ready even Ewan was smiling again.

To my surprise, my tactic with the meat actually worked. Maybe there wasn't so much to this cooking lark as I'd always thought. In fact, the whole meal looked pretty good, considering our combined ineptitude.

We ate on the deck overlooking the back garden and what Alan told me were Jenny's roses. I hadn't seen many sandflies since Haast, but he assured me they weren't exactly an unfamiliar sight in Westport. 'They often come with a change in the weather,' he said.

When we sat back after the meal, sated, sipping cold beer, Ewan said, 'So what are you going to do next, Ollie? Now that you've found Dad? Are you going to carry on looking for work?'

Alan interjected before I could reply. 'You could stay here for a while,' he said eagerly. 'I'd like to get to know you better. You're a real chip off the old block; I can tell that much.'

'That would be great, if you're sure,' I said, thinking that maybe I could look for work in Westport, at least while I decided what to do about Mark. If there really were anything I could do about Mark.

'I'll have to get back home tomorrow,' Ewan said abruptly. 'I'll be getting behind schedule if I don't.'

'That's okay,' Alan said. 'I'm sure Ollie and I can manage. I'll show her around the area – all the sights. Plenty of good stuff to see around here.'

I was about to say something in response when my mobile phone chirruped in my pocket. It was the early hours of the morning at home, so it couldn't be my mum. I gave Alan and Ewan an apologetic look and headed to my room as I flipped it open. It was a New Zealand number, but not one I recognised. Maybe Mark had reverted back to this means of communication?

'Olivia, it's David – it's Pastor.'

I closed the door to my room and leaned against the frame. I was silent for a minute, while all the emotions of last week came back to oppress me. 'Why are you ringing?' I eventually said coldly. 'How did you get my number?'

'Bob gave it to me. I was worried about you. Where are you?'

'What difference does that make? You wanted to wash your hands of me. You're free of my lunatic presence now.' I realized as I spoke that I sounded childish, but my hurt and anger hadn't diminished.

He sighed heavily at the other end. 'I know I messed up. I just couldn't handle it – I was so shocked to see you talking to thin air.'

I didn't want to think about what a fool I must have looked. The nausea and panic of that night were starting to fill my mind again.

'*Are* you okay?' Pastor said into the silence.

'I'm fine,' I replied, in a voice like ice chips.

'Are you going back to England?'

'No, I'm not. I still have things to do here.' I relented a little and added, 'I've found Alan.'

'That's great. And he's okay about the situation with your dad?'

'More than that: he's thrilled that I've found him.'

'And... Mark?' he said slowly, doubtfully.

'I've had it confirmed he *was* a real person – I just don't know what happened to him yet. Whether he's... alive... or not.'

'You're thinking he might be a ghost?'

He sounded a least willing to consider that as a possibility, and I allowed myself to unbend a bit more. 'I don't know what he is, but I do know he needs my help, if only I knew how to help him. If only I could *find* him.'

'Sounds like you're setting yourself a new quest.'

I didn't detect disapproval in his voice, but I couldn't help bridling. 'If you'd been made to feel like a total madwoman, it's likely you'd want to understand why.'

'I really am sorry, Olivia. I realized… well, I've realized a lot of things since that night. When I got your note, I knew I'd made a big mistake.'

My note had been the epitome of furious brevity – all I'd written was: *I'll carry on the search alone. Thanks for your help to date.*

'I went looking for you, drove back down to Jackson Bay, and then up to Fox Glacier and Franz Josef, but there was no sign of you.'

I softened. 'I really am okay. I found the dream beach in Hokitika; I've found Alan, and he's great. I'm just worried about Mark.'

'How did you find out he was a real person?'

I sat on the edge of my bed and told him about my visit to the DOC office.

'He said Mark was sick?'

'He thought Mark was probably dead,' I said sadly.

'But you don't believe him?'

I sighed. 'I don't know what to believe. It would make more sense, in a way, if he were a ghost. I mean, a lost soul, looking for his mother…' I choked up with emotion. 'But whatever he is, or was, I have to know.'

'Well I want to help if I can, if you'll forgive me for letting you down. I guess you can tell I'm back home in Manapouri, but if you need anything, any more help, just let me know.'

When we cut off, I was left wondering at such a complete change of heart. He certainly sounded genuine enough, but I didn't want to be hurt again.

'So you're happy to stay here with my dad for a bit?' Ewan asked doubtfully. 'You'll be on your own for most of the day.'

'I'll be okay,' I said, scrubbing at the roasting tin in the washing up bowl. One disadvantage of doing actual cooking was the clearing up afterwards. Still, at least Ewan was willing to muck in and dry up and was standing by with the tea towel.

'I'll take a look around the town, do some exploring. Unless you think I shouldn't stay?' I added, in case he thought I was a freeloader on top of all my other apparent failings.

He shrugged. 'No, I think you're probably good for him. Like I said, this is the most animated I've seen him since my mum died.' He paused and then said, 'Look, I'm sorry about what I said earlier. I guess I did judge you by the way you look, but Natalie gave me a pretty rough time of it.'

I nodded. 'Being good looking isn't all it's cracked up to be, you know.'

He stared at me, a reluctant smile starting to form on his lips. 'Good looking isn't a term I'd use. You must know you're stunning. I know you don't… well, *do* anything to emphasize it, but you'd stand out a mile in any room.'

I stared back at him solemnly. 'That can cause its own problems,' I said, thinking of Niall and his expectations.

'You could have any man you fancy, make a pile as a model, travel the world,' he said in a slightly bitter tone.

I laughed humourlessly. 'And be forced to keep up with every nuance of fashion, worry about every hair out of place, every wrinkle? That's just not me. I'm *not* about how I look. People tend to make assumptions; it can get annoying.'

'I'd never thought of it that way,' he said, looking slightly chastened.

There was a lot more I could have added, but it wasn't the time. I put a pan on the draining board and tried a change of subject. 'Do you miss teaching?'

'Yes and no. I used to love it, back at the beginning, but...' He shrugged. 'Maybe fifteen years was enough. The lodge is a complete change of direction: a bit of a risk, in a way.' He looked at me. 'Are you going to look for work here in Westport?'

'I don't know,' I said hesitantly. 'I still have some… unfinished business.'

He raised his eyebrows. 'Something else to do with your dad?'

I shook my head. 'Someone I met here in New Zealand. He's in trouble, but I'm not sure how to help him.'

I'd barely got the words out before his expression altered.

'The guy who rang you earlier?' he asked, his voice tight.

'No, that was Pastor – I met him in Manapouri. He's in his late sixties,' I tried to smile, wishing I'd never mentioned it. I hated to see him withdraw, just as we were starting to get comfortable with each other.

'For someone who doesn't want to trade on her looks, you seem to have a lot of admirers,' he said roughly.

Here we go again. I clanged the last pan on to the draining board and tipped out the washing-up water with an angry flourish. 'The old-fashioned term is *friends*,' I said, and turned my back on him to stalk to my room.

Chapter Thirteen

'Ollie,' a voice scratched. 'Ollie, wake up.'

I pried my eyes open. The room was almost dark, but standing by my bed was a ghostly figure. I jumped in momentary fright and turned on the bedside light.

'Mark!' I cried out, and I put a hand to my mouth at the sight of him. He was even less substantial than last time; there was almost no colour to his form.

'Yeah,' he whispered. 'Listen, I'm out of...' His voice faded off and then came back. 'Wairau... Come to Wairau…'

He was gone. Just like at the beach, he'd disappeared.

I got up, shaking, and went to the window. It was nearly dawn; the bedside clock said 6.10am. I pulled on an old dressing gown that had once belonged to Alan's daughter Carol and headed to the kitchen to make myself a coffee, then took the steaming mug out onto the deck that I'd been helping Alan repair over the last few days. The scent of roses filled my nostrils as I paced up and down.

Ever since I'd been in Westport, I'd had a sense of impending doom, with Mark at its centre. I hadn't known if it was real or not, nor what I could do about it. Now this. *Wairau*. What or where was Wairau?

'You look awful,' Alan said when he came into the kitchen for breakfast an hour later, dressed for work. 'What's up?'

I put his bacon and eggs on a plate. I'd got into the habit of cooking for us both since I'd been staying with him, and my culinary skills had distinctly improved.

'I... um... had a strange dream.' I paused. 'There's this word or name I haven't been able to get out of my mind. Have you heard of somewhere called Wairau?'

He was about to start eating but stopped with his knife and fork poised above this plate. 'There *is* a Wairau River. Have you ever been to Blenheim?'

I started and stared at him, shaking my head. 'It's in *Blenheim*?'

He nodded. 'Mean something?'

'My friend Mark is from there,' I said. 'Or at least he was born there.' I sat down and started picking at my own scrambled eggs. 'It feels like he needs my help.'

'You don't know where he is?'

'He's been out of touch since Hokitika. I've been quite worried about him.'

'So that's what was wrong. You should have said. I thought maybe you were getting tired of hanging out with this old fogey. You reckon your dream was some sort of message?'

I smiled wryly. 'Well, as to that, you turned out to be real, so...'

He grinned across the table at me and then sobered again. 'What do you want to do?'

I shrugged hopelessly. 'I suppose I'll have to go to Blenheim and see if I can find him.'

Alan nodded. 'Shouldn't be that hard if he's on the electoral roll. I'll miss you, though. I've been seriously spoilt since you've been around, you know.'

'I'll miss you as well.' I'd become very fond of him over the past couple of weeks and begun to see him as a sort of surrogate dad. As for Ewan, he hadn't been back, but he did ring Alan every few days.

'Do you want me to drive you over there tomorrow?' Alan asked.

'It's a long way – are you sure you don't mind giving up your Saturday?'

He shook his head. 'Of course not. Plus I think I might be able to help out with some accommodation. Lisa lives in Blenheim, and what's more, I'm sure she runs a Bed and Breakfast.'

'Lisa?'

'Jenny's best friend from the campervan days. I met her by chance when I was on holiday in Picton last year, and she gave me her address and phone number. I'll see if I can look them up tonight. I'm sure she'll put you up.'

It was a hot, humid afternoon when we pulled into the drive of an elegant house surrounded by pretty gardens, which were in turn bounded by vineyards stretching in every direction. A short, plump woman emerged from the house to meet us. I recognised her from the pictures in Alan's album, but she looked far more sophisticated now.

'Alan, it's good to see you again,' she said with a warm smile, before turning to me. 'You must be Olivia. Welcome to The Cedars. I've got Rose Cottage all ready for you. It's only small, but I think you'll be comfortable.'

'I'm sure I shall, and thanks so much for letting me stay,' I said as we followed her into the cool house. It was very elegant, even luxurious. Obviously an up-market B&B compared with the ones I'd stayed in back in the UK.

We sat down on squashy sofas, and Lisa poured us some cold juice.

'I've got just one couple staying in the bigger cottage at the other side of the house, so I think you're going to find it very peaceful around here. Alan says you're looking for a friend?'

'That's right. I need to find the library and take a look at the electoral roll.'

She nodded. 'It's five kilometres into Blenheim, but the library will be closed now until Monday morning anyway.

Never mind,' she said, obviously noting my disappointment. 'You can take a day out and ride around the vineyards. I have bikes for my guests' use.'

'It's a big thing here,' Alan explained. 'It's nice and flat for cycling, and you can even call in at the wineries and try out the wines.'

It would have sounded great if I weren't so on edge. 'How close is the Wairau River?' I asked.

'A couple of Ks east of here,' Lisa said. 'Did you want to see it?'

I shook my head. 'I was just wondering,' I murmured. I'd asked Alan not to tell Lisa anything about my dream.

When we'd cooled down a little, Lisa took us to the little single-storey cottage she was letting me stay in rent-free. It was cute, with beds of flowers in bloom all around it and a table and chairs in a tiny lawned area. It was similar in size and design to my Manapouri loft, consisting of one room with a kitchen area and a separate shower room.

'I'll leave you to settle in,' Lisa said, 'but don't hesitate to come up to the house if there's anything you need, or even if you just want a bit of company.'

'She seems very nice,' I said to Alan when she'd left.

'Yes, she was always really good natured,' he replied. 'I never did get to the bottom of why she and Jenny fell out. She's probably lonely herself, since her divorce. You sure you're going to be all right here on your own? You know you can come back as soon as you like, don't you?'

I grinned. 'You've told me enough times. I'll be fine.'

Alan looked at his watch. 'Guess I'd better be getting back, or I'll never make it in daylight.' He gave me a hug. 'Be sure to tell me how it goes. I'm really going to miss you, you know.'

After he left, I fought off sudden loneliness by taking a long walk around the gardens and closest vineyards. When I got back, I found Lisa lying on a sun lounger beside the swimming pool. She lifted her sunglasses to look at me. 'Do you like swimming? Feel free to use the pool whenever you like.'

I grinned. 'I do, thanks. It looks really inviting.' I sat down on the adjacent lounger. 'Um, I was wondering… Do you remember much about my dad?'

Just for a second an odd look passed over her face. Anxiety? Fear? It was gone so fast I wondered whether I'd imagined it.

'I was really sorry to hear he'd died,' she said slowly. 'As for what I remember – I assume Alan's told you all about it?'

I nodded. 'He's told me my dad left because of him and Jenny. I just wondered if you could tell me anything else about those times. I never knew anything about them. He didn't even tell us – my mum and me – that he'd ever been to New Zealand.'

She pursed her lips slightly. 'He was very hurt; I know that. Thing is, we were friends, but we weren't close. It was all just about having fun – or it was until Paul left.'

'And Jenny? You and she were close, weren't you?' I took the risk of asking. 'How did she feel about my dad leaving?'

She was silent for a moment. I wondered if I'd gone too far. 'To be honest, she didn't really care, not at first. Later yes, but not at first.' She jumped up with a brisk air. 'Now, that's enough of all this reminiscing. I've got a nice meal on the go for your first night. You can help me finish it off, if you like.'

I returned to the cottage three hours later, full and a little tipsy. The conversation throughout the meal, which we'd shared with the couple staying in the other cottage, had been confined to New Zealand and its many attractions. I had the feeling Lisa really didn't want to talk about the hippy campervan at all.

The following day, which was hot with a bright blue sky, Lisa provided me with a packed lunch, a bike, and a proposed cycle route through a few wineries. 'You can take a look at the river, too, if you want to, although it's a bit of a detour,' she said.

I tried to relax and enjoy my time in the vineyards, but after visiting two wineries and consuming my lunch, I paused at a crossroads. The map was telling me to turn left, but something else, something I couldn't even understand myself, was drawing me straight ahead. According to the map, the Wairau River was in that direction too. I didn't hesitate for long. Apart from anything else, Mark's voice saying 'Wairau' kept recurring in my mind. I pedalled straight across the intersection.

More vineyards stretched out on either side of the long, straight, deserted road. Cars passed me at the rate of about one every half hour. My internal compass continued to urge me to stay on the road, but I kept stopping to consult the map, a little worried when it turned from tarmac to stony track and the rather monotonous vineyards gave way to stark green-brown farm fields. What was more, the whole area seemed totally deserted, with hardly a house in view. I carried on over the rough track for about a mile, and at last there was a sign of life: a house with protective dogs barking at the gate. I moved on quickly towards a clump of trees in the distance. There was something odd about those trees. Apart from the fact that they looked like an oasis in a very dry landscape, they seemed familiar. I had no intense, emotional sensation of déjà vu, such as at Haast and Hokitika, but rather a warm recognition, like a homecoming. I bounced along the dusty road, gazing at the grove of trees as though it was a beacon guiding me onwards.

The afternoon had worn on into evening, and I was feeling pretty tired by the time I arrived at a gate that led into a tree-fringed drive. A white notice nailed to the gate read 'Private'. I tried the gate, but it didn't budge; only then did I spot the padlock and chain. Damn. I had a compelling need to see what was down that drive that I couldn't even explain to myself, plus according to the map, the river was right here. I shaded my eyes and looked along the track I'd just turned off. There were no other houses or even trees coming up. The road petered out a few hundred yards away beside a gate into what was obviously a farm.

A tall, grassy bank bordered the track, and I clambered up over the short, sere grass hoping to gain a better view towards the trees. To my surprise, there on the other side of the bank was a wide, blue river: surely the Wairau. I guessed the bank was a flood defence. Unfortunately, although I had a view for what seemed like miles over the parched brown grass and grey dusty roads, no matter how hard I peered into the trees from my lofty vantage point, I could see nothing through them. Apart from the warm wind whipping around my clothing and the water birds in the river, there was no sound. A car threw up a wake of dust on a track about a mile away. Was there a house among the trees? I had to get in there somehow and find out.

A look at the position of the sun in the sky reminded me I couldn't hang around too long. Lisa would wonder where I was if I got back too late, and she'd promised me another delicious dinner. I could see no alternative but to break all my own rules on manners and politeness and climb over that gate.

I ran back down the levee and took a closer look: it was steel rather than wood, there were no handy toeholds and it was topped by barbed wire, but the wooden gatepost, while plastered with electrified wire, looked a bit easier. I put my foot on one of the electrified wires: nothing happened, so I lifted my other leg and tried to get it over the top of the post. A small, uncomfortable shock made me jump; I caught my leg on the barbed wire, and a sharp point tore into my thigh.

'Damn!' I said aloud as I dropped to the ground on the other side with blood seeping through my jeans. I pulled some tissues out of my backpack and pressed them against the wound before limping down the track. After a couple of hundred yards, the path opened out to reveal a wooden house with a corrugated iron roof and a veranda. All continued to be quiet, although there was a car in a garage to the side. I headed for the front door and knocked, with no idea how I was going to explain myself if someone answered. I seemed to be on autopilot. After knocking twice more and waiting several minutes, I resorted to peering in through the windows. The inside of the house looked as though it had been adapted for a disabled person – there was a hoist in the living room and a wheelchair lying askew in another room. It was a fairly large house with an upstairs, which was unusual in my experience of New Zealand, except in Dunedin.

Despite poking my face rudely at every window, no one came to tell me off or shoo me away; obviously there was no one in. Maybe my intuition had let me down this time: everything pointed to this being the home of an elderly person. I sat on one of the chairs on the veranda and delved deeper into my backpack for a plaster to cover the gash in my thigh – it was deeper than I liked with a long bike ride to get through, but there was nothing else for it. I peered around among the trees on my way back out, but apart from a large number of twittering birds I was still alone.

I managed to get over the gate without any further injury, but the gash was so uncomfortable I decided to walk rather than ride until I got off the bumpy track onto proper tarmac. When I reached the house with the barking dogs, there was no sign of them. Instead there was a woman outside watering her plants with a sprinkler. I limped over and called out.

She turned off her sprinkler and came over. 'You okay? Not lost?' She was about my age and very skinny. She was dressed in the New Zealand national costume: T-shirt, shorts and sandals.

'I'm fine, thanks,' I assured her. 'I was just wondering if you know your neighbour?' I indicated the clump of woods.

Her face immediately formed itself into a sorrowful expression. 'Oh yes, such a shame; poor man.'

'Something's happened to him?' I asked.

'Well, he's had to go into the hospice for good now, of course. Just couldn't stay at home any more. Wasn't safe.'

'Hospice?' I said. So my instincts had been correct about an elderly and infirm person.

'Yes, and so young, too. Tragic. I said to Dave – that's my husband – I said, you just never know what's coming. You need to live every day as if it's your last.'

'Young?' I said, staring at her. Surely not? But I had to know – I *had* to ask. 'Is he… is his name…' I swallowed. 'Is it Mark Juniper?'

'That's right. Poor thing.' She seemed to realize that I was upset and came closer to peer into my face. 'You a friend of his? Didn't you know?'

I shook my head silently.

'Oh look, you'd better come in and sit down, you've gone really pale. Dave!' she shouted in the direction of the house, 'Put the kettle on, will you?'

She opened the gate to let me in and guided me into her living room. The two ferocious dogs sniffed around me while the TV blasted out an episode of *Emmerdale*. Her husband got up reluctantly as she explained my situation, and headed to the kitchen as ordered.

'I'm Miriam,' she said as we sat down. 'So you didn't know Mark was ill?'

'He was fine the last time I saw him.'

'Well, you're from England eh? Not been over here long?'

I shook my head silently.

'Over five years ago it started, but it's a terrible thing: takes everything away, bit by bit. We went to see him last week and he looked pretty poorly. He's just picking up from the pneumonia now.'

'Pneumonia? You said he was in the hospice – what's actually wrong with him? He's not… dying?'

She nodded. 'They reckon it's a matter of weeks, couple of months at the most. I'm sorry love – it's motor neurone disease.'

There are moments in life when everything seems to freeze, when you remember every sensation with total clarity.

I stared at Miriam and noticed how she twisted her wedding ring. It was a gold ring with an embossed pattern, and it was loose on her finger. She was holding her hand near her face and unconsciously twisting the ring back and forth and up and down. I was almost mesmerised until Dave shambled back into the room with two cups of tea. The theme tune of *Emmerdale* filled the silence, and I glanced over at the credits going up before taking the proffered cup from Dave.

'You've gone white. It's a big shock, eh?' Miriam said.

I nodded, took a large gulp of tea and swallowed, blinking my eyes to prevent any tears from flowing. 'So he's gone into a hospice? What hospice is it?' I asked in a slightly wobbly voice.

'Marlborough hospice – it's at Wairau Hospital; well, it's in the same grounds.'

'Wairau Hospital? That's in Blenheim?'

Miriam nodded. 'Where are you staying? I could write down the directions for you.'

She made a note while I finished the tea, which was a bit strong for my taste.

'You cycled out here?' she asked as she handed me the piece of paper. 'You've got a few kilometres to go to get back, and you were limping, weren't you?'

'It's just a bit of a graze,' I fibbed.

'All the same, I don't think you should cycle five or six Ks after a shock like this. Dave, you could give Olivia a lift to her B&B couldn't you? Wouldn't take more than half an hour.'

Dave agreed without demur, and within a few minutes we were crunching down the dirt road, the bike poking out of the boot of his estate car.

'Good bloke, Mark,' he said. 'We used to know his mum and dad. It was their house, but when they died, he moved away and left it empty. He came back three years ago. They've been on at him lately to go into a care home, but he wouldn't have it. It's only because of this bout of pneumonia that they've got him in the hospice now. To be honest, if they have their way, I don't think he's going to come home.'

I didn't need to ask who 'they' were. My dad had been able to stay at home because he had us, his family, to look after him, but who did Mark have, right out here? Maybe carers to come in and wash him, get him in and out of bed and make his meals, but that's not enough with MND once your breathing or swallowing are affected.

'Can he still talk?' I asked.

'Oh yes, and he can still swallow semi-solids, but since the pneumonia he's been trying the machine to help him breathe. I don't think he likes it too much.'

Dave dropped me at The Cedars and told me I knew where they were if I wanted anything, which seemed very kind of complete strangers. I leaned the bike against the wall and nipped rapidly into the cottage, hoping to avoid Lisa until I'd calmed down. I ran the shower, turned it to full blast and tried to think of nothing at all. I was glad of the noise of the water as it drowned out my desolate sobs.

Chapter Fourteen

'What's wrong?' Lisa asked, peering closely into my face as I picked at the local green-lipped mussels she'd prepared. 'Your eyes are red. Have you been crying? Are you homesick?'

'I'm all right,' I said, trying to keep my voice steady.

'You've been away from home for quite a while, haven't you? You must miss your family and friends in England.'

I took a deep breath. 'Yes, a bit, but I'm fine, really.'

'You don't look fine. Don't forget I've got two kids of my own, similar age to you. Sure you don't want to talk about it?'

I shook my head, and she let it drop, asking me what I thought of the wineries instead.

She obviously hadn't really let it drop though, as after I'd gone back to the cottage and snuggled under the duvet, Alan phoned me on my mobile.

'What's this I hear about you being homesick?' he asked.

'I'm really not,' I protested. 'I just didn't want to tell Lisa what was wrong.'

'Which is?'

I swallowed. 'I found out that Mark is… dying of motor neurone disease.'

'Like your dad?'

'Yeah. Sounds like it.'

'You've seen him?'

'No, I met his neighbours, and they told me he's in the hospice at Wairau Hospital.'

'So your dream was right again. Wow, Ollie, you really must have some sort of… I don't know… psychic ability or something.'

'Yeah,' I said in a small voice. 'Only I don't like to think of it that way.'

Everything that had happened that afternoon had scared me. The way I knew the house and the trees, even. The whole thing was surreal.

'Guess not. Anyway, are you going to see him?'

'Yes, tomorrow. I'm not looking forward to it.'

'I bet. Damn, I wish I could help, but there's no way I can get away from work this week; I've got a project I have to finish. The boss is breathing down my neck. I don't like to think of you dealing with this on your own, though, not with your memories of your dad and everything. How close are you to Mark? I mean, are you more than… you know, friends?'

I sighed softly, hoping he wouldn't hear. 'No, we really are just friends, but he's sort of special somehow. I don't want to watch him die, too.' I choked back a sob.

'Damn, Ollie, I feel so helpless. Is there anyone there who can help? You sure you can't talk to Lisa? She sounded quite worried about you. Have you told your mum?'

'I like Lisa, but it's too personal. As for my mum, no, I don't think I can tell her just yet.' I didn't like to admit that she still knew nothing about Mark. 'Don't worry; I'll be fine,' I lied.

We talked for a while longer and just talking made me feel calmer. When we eventually said goodnight and hung up, I curled up in the bed and fell asleep from sheer emotional exhaustion.

***

It was my mobile phone ringing that woke me the next morning. I hadn't set the alarm, and it was nine already. I jumped when I flipped open the phone. *Ewan* was ringing me? Surely nothing had happened to Alan since last night?

'Where are you? Still at the B&B?' Ewan asked as soon as I answered.

'Yes. Why? What's wrong? Alan's okay, isn't he?'

'He's fine, but he insisted I come on a mission of mercy. I'll be at The Cedars in an hour. Wait for me, and I'll take you to the hospice.'

'Er… you're driving all the way from Hokitika because of me?' I asked in an astonished tone.

'Dad wouldn't let it rest until I did.'

'But… I told him I'd be okay, and –'

'He didn't believe you. Anyway, I've been on the road since five, so it's too late to protest. Dad seems to have got quite fond of you,' he said, in a manner that suggested he couldn't understand why. 'I'll see you later,' he said as abruptly as usual, and cut off.

I closed the phone slowly. *Why* did Alan think Ewan could help? He must see things in Ewan that I didn't. Mission of mercy indeed! Had Alan actually told Ewan the whole story? It was hard to believe he'd made all that effort considering his reaction the last time I'd mentioned Mark to him.

I forced myself to get up, drank a cup of coffee and tried to engross myself in the paper. My appetite was non-existent. Once I'd gone through every page of *The Press,* I heaved a huge sigh and got dressed slowly. The gash in my thigh felt sore, and I put another plaster over it before donning my jeans.

I was just peering out of the door at the drizzle when Ewan's blue Toyota pulled up outside. He jumped out and came over, giving me a look up and down and then frowning.

'You're a bit pale, I have to say,' he said. 'Dad said it had been a big shock to you.' He actually sounded sympathetic.

'It's just – MND,' I said, my voice cracking.

He nodded. 'Are you ready? You can visit any time, I gather.'

'As ready as I can be,' I said.

As we headed towards Blenheim, he asked me about Mark.

'So this is the guy you were worried about? The one you met here?'

'Yes.'

'He didn't tell you about the MND?'

I shook my head silently.

'It's come on pretty quickly then,' he commented, looking puzzled.

I didn't know how to answer him, so just nodded. I could see him out of the corner of my eye, glancing my way as if he was concerned, but he didn't say any more until we arrived at the hospice.

'I'm guessing you won't want me to come in with you,' he said. 'I'll wait in the car. Take as long as you need.'

I met his gaze. 'Ewan, thanks for coming,' I said. 'You really don't need to wait, though. I'll be all right. You must have lots to do at the lodge, and it's such a long drive –'

'I'm staying, so you needn't bother trying to persuade me otherwise. Dad's already texted, asking if you're okay. I don't think he'll be too impressed if I go off and leave you now, do you?'

I gave him a small smile. 'I suppose not.' I turned reluctantly towards the hospice.

'Ollie,' he called, and I looked back. 'Good luck.'

Once inside the building, having collared a nurse who pointed me in the direction of Mark's room, I plodded down the corridor feeling like there was a stone in my guts. I was completely torn: I wanted to see him badly, but I dreaded seeing him with MND.

The door was slightly ajar. I tapped softly and pushed it open. Mark was sitting up in bed with a breathing mask covering his face. His eyes opened slowly as I approached, and then they widened in surprise.

'Ollie!' he said, his speech slightly obscured by the mask and the gurgle of the machine. 'You found me.' His hair was still blonde and his eyes bright blue, but he looked a few years older.

I eased myself into the chair next to him, my legs trembling.

'Yeah, I found you. And in the weirdest way,' I said, surprised at how calm and normal my voice sounded. I explained about finding his house and meeting his neighbours. 'They said you've had pneumonia?'

'Yeah. I'm just getting over it.' He spoke between gasps as the ventilator forced air into his lungs.

'You look older – you must be a bit older than me,' I said.

'Thirty-six.'

My dad had also developed MND when he was in his thirties.

'Why twenty-seven?' I asked, just as I realized what the answer must be. 'That was before this ever happened, wasn't it? Back when you were healthy?'

'Yeah. It started – the first signs – when I was thirty-one. Can you take off the mask for me?'

When I'd obliged and turned off the ventilation machine, he said, in a voice with far less power behind it, 'I hate to use it, but I'm practising a couple of times a day, in case.'

'In case you have to go on it full-time?'

'Yeah. Or I just don't, and I let nature take its course.'

I was a little surprised. My dad had taken every treatment available to delay death.

'So what was all that with the ghost thing?' I asked, in an attempt to avoid that uncomfortable topic.

'The out-of-body? It's something I've always been able to do. I call it my gift. You're the first person that's ever been able to see me; I don't know why.'

‘So you can just leave your body and swan around anywhere you like?’

‘Yep.’

I breathed out sharply. ‘And that’s how you could just turn up wherever I was – but hang on, that means you didn’t have to stay in the North Island all those weeks. You could have just… popped out to visit me.’

‘Yeah, but you were already getting suspicious enough. I didn’t want to spoil it, partly because of your dad, and partly because it was so great to be almost normal again, with you.’

‘I thought you might be dead, after Haast, when Pastor told me you weren’t really there. You could have spared me that, you know.’

‘How would you have felt though, if I’d just come out with it: oh, by the way, I’m not really here; I’m a sort of ghost and my body’s sitting in my house, dead to the world, and just so you know, I’ve got MND?’

I smiled weakly. ‘Okay, I suppose there wasn’t an easy way of coming out with it,’ I agreed.

‘As for being dead, I got pretty close with the pneumonia – it all kicked off that day at Haast, although I’d been getting weaker all along. I thought I was a goner, to be honest, and then I had no energy to get *out* again until two days ago. Anyway, if I had told you, would you have believed me?’

‘I suppose not,’ I replied with a sigh. ‘So it’s because of the MND that you’re so driven to find your mum?’

‘Yeah.’ His eyelids drooped momentarily. ‘It’s always bothered me, not knowing, but after my diagnosis five years ago, I couldn’t let it go.’

‘Have they said… how long?’

He grinned, and despite everything, the grin was the real Mark. ‘Don’t beat about the bush, Ollie; we both know I’m gonna die. Breathing is hard now, and like I said, I nearly died of pneumonia. I can try the non-invasive ventilation for a while, but even so, could be any time.’

He sounded so resigned to it all. I knew that his swallow and his speech would be next, and then... My dad had lingered in the twilight world of ventilation, peg feeding and complete paralysis for a few weeks. Now that I was with Mark, I realized how much I'd missed him, and, just as with my dad, he was still the same person inside the faltering body.

We talked for an hour or so longer. I wanted to know anything he could tell me about his out of body trick. It seemed incredible, and I couldn't imagine how someone could be born with such a talent, as he said he had been, pretty much. According to him, he'd been able to travel that way since he was six years old. Once he became immobile with MND it became an even more valuable gift. 'It saved me, really. You know how I am about being cooped up,' he said. When he began to show obvious signs of weariness, I promised I'd be back the following day, and left him beginning to doze off.

Ewan was waiting in the car, listening to the radio. He turned it off as I got in.

'Okay? How was he?'

'Not too bad, considering. He's mostly over the pneumonia, but obviously he's still… terminal.'

'Do they say how long?'

'I asked – he says any time. He seems to have accepted it. If only…' I trailed off, not sure whether to tell Ewan about Mark's quest.

'If only?'

'He was adopted, and his parents died a few years ago. He wants to find his real parents – his real mum, mainly. He's tried everything, without success.'

Ewan drove us into town, and we had lunch in a café. I ended up telling him all about Mark's search – or at least the expurgated version – over omelette and coffee. He listened sympathetically, so I encouraged him as casually as I could to talk about himself and his dad.

'It's a shame about the girls – my sisters,' he said, drinking his coffee and looking as relaxed as I'd ever seen him. 'I guess I was always closest to Dad, but why they both moved away as soon as they got the chance, I don't know.

Since Mum died I've felt… well, quite protective of him. He's been so lost and lonely. Your turning up was a big boost. Obviously this business with your dad had been preying on his mind as well, even though he'd never told us about it.'

'I've grown really fond of him,' I said. 'It's been so long since my dad died that I'd forgotten what it was like, but, well, he's become a sort of second dad to me.'

He nodded and didn't look offended, as I'd feared. 'If there was any way he could help you to stay in the country, he would,' he said. 'I know for a fact he's asked around at his firm, but they don't need anyone right now.'

'That was good of him,' I said. I'd been in New Zealand for almost three months, so I had a further three months before I'd have to return home, unless I found a permanent job.

'He's a great guy. Mum spoiled him though – did everything for him, so that now he's pretty hopeless at doing things for himself.' He sighed. 'I did try to persuade Carol or Julia to come home to help out, but they're both too settled where they are.'

'So that's why the lodge?' I hesitated. 'You didn't give up teaching because of your divorce?'

He smiled – a rare event, at least in my direction. 'You've sussed me out. Just don't tell Dad. He was getting so down I was worried he might… you know… do something. He wouldn't go to the docs for the depression either. I thought us doing the lodge together would give him something new to aim for.'

'And it's worked. He doesn't seem depressed now.'

He nodded slowly. 'Yes, it was working, and then you came along and somehow put the icing on the cake. I have to thank you for that. I don't think he'll sink back down now.'

'What about you, though?' I felt bold enough to ask. 'Will you be happy if you can't teach?'

For a moment it looked like he was going to respond honestly, but then he collected himself. 'I'll be happy enough,' he said in his usual brusque manner. He looked at his watch. 'I'll have to be heading home before too long. Do you want to go back to The Cedars, or is there anywhere else I can take you before I go?'

I had him take me back to The Cedars and tried unsuccessfully to persuade him to stay there overnight. He and Alan seemed to be forever driving hundreds of miles for my sake, although in this instance Ewan had actually done it for his dad's sake.

'Thanks for coming,' I said as he prepared to leave. 'It did help.'

Another rare smile crossed his features. 'No worries. I'm glad,' he said, and luckily for me, he turned to get into his car. I'd managed to wipe the astonished expression from my features by the time he looked my way again, waved briefly and drove off.

I watched his car exit the grounds of The Cedars with an unexpected sense of disappointment. He was chippy company, but I liked being around him.

Back in my cottage, I made a call to Pastor. Whatever else, he was the one person who knew all about Mark. Besides, when he'd rung me last week, he'd seemed genuinely repentant.

I poured the whole story out to him and awaited his response, which was silence.

'What's wrong? You're not going to say you don't believe me, are you?' I said, steeling myself.

'No, no, nothing like that,' he assured me hastily. 'It's just that I don't see how it can be down to chance.'

'Neither do I. Why can I see him when he's doing his out of body thing, and according to him, only me?'

'I guess it could have something to do with that intuition of yours,' he said. 'All this is giving me some food for thought,' he added in a slightly absent tone before becoming brisk again and saying, 'Anyway, are y'all going to be okay on your own? I'll be up there myself soon – Emily and Steve are touring the North Island right now, but they're due to arrive in Picton in a couple of weeks, and I promised to meet their ferry.'

'I'm okay for now. I'm staying at The Cedars for a while longer.'

'Well, if you do get too lonely, you know where I am, and you know how sorry I am about what happened. I want to make amends – ring me any time if you need me.'

CHAPTER FIFTEEN

Summer was at its height in Blenheim. There was barely a green blade of grass to be seen outside people's well-watered gardens. The Wither Hills off in the distance were brown, and there was no sign of rain after a week of sunshine and clear blue skies.

I cycled through the now-familiar landscape of endless vineyards and pulled up on the driveway of The Cedars. I'd been staying there for a week, feeling bad that Lisa wouldn't let me pay her anything for the use of my little cottage. Alan had promised to visit this weekend, and I was pleased to see his car already parked outside the main house. He didn't like to think of me spending all my time just cycling back and forth to the hospice every day, so he'd promised to show me more of Marlborough. 'You need a break from all that sick visiting,' he'd said.

I found him talking quietly with Lisa in her lounge. I noted with a slight jolt that they looked surprisingly close.

'So how's Mark today?' he asked as I joined them. I wondered whether I'd interrupted something, especially as Lisa headed straight off to her kitchen to finish the evening meal.

I shrugged slightly. 'He's over the pneumonia, but his breathing's still no stronger. He's started asking about going home, but I don't think the medical staff are too keen. They're having a big discussion with his social worker and who knows who else about how feasible it is. How are things going with the lodge?'

'Slowly – poor old Ewan's tearing his hair out. His workers keep on letting him down: going off sick or the like. I'm going down there next weekend to help him out. Have you heard from him?'

'He's texted me a couple of times.' They'd only been courtesy texts though, cool and polite. As ever, after showing a little of his real self, he'd withdrawn into his shell.

Alan frowned. 'He's got a one-track mind at the moment. Listen, if you fancy a break, you could come and help us out. I've told him you're a dab hand with a hammer.'

I chuckled. 'What did he say to that?'

'You know Ewan. He thinks if you're good looking, you're good for nothing except sucking the life out of men. And I thought you two had hit it off at last.'

'We had, sort of,' I said. 'He was fine when he came on Monday. In fact he was fine at your house too, until I mentioned a couple of male friends.'

He shook his head slowly. 'Sorry you keep getting the sharp end. It's all down to the way Natalie treated him. I sometimes wonder if he'll ever get over it. Would you rather not come, then? I could drive over here next Friday afternoon and pick you up.'

I gave him a doubtful look. 'Don't you get tired of the drive? I feel bad about your coming over here so much on my account.'

He patted my arm. 'Of course I don't mind the drive. I enjoy driving, and we're used to it here – most places are a lot further apart than you're used to in England.'

I bit my lip thoughtfully. It would make a pleasant change, as long as Mark was still stable. 'Okay,' I said. 'After all, how can I resist a weekend being bossed about at the lodge?' I didn't allow myself to consider that my ready acceptance might have something to do with seeing Ewan again.

Up until then I hadn't felt able to leave Blenheim, although Mark assured me I didn't need to spend as much time with him as I was doing. I was concerned that he didn't get many visitors; he was paying the price for moving away from the West Coast and cutting himself off. Besides me, his only visitors were his neighbours and a couple of old friends.

I found out why Lisa had been so keen to return to the kitchen when she produced Alan's favourite, bangers and mash, but done in her own special style with herbs and onion gravy. He was obviously touched that she'd remembered and gone to the trouble especially for him. There were no other guests that night, so I just kept my head down and listened as they reminisced about the hippy campervan, missing out the awkward parts and concentrating on the fun moments they'd all had together before everything went wrong. Alan seemed relaxed in her company, and she was more vivacious than I'd seen her yet.

The following day, Alan drove me on a sightseeing tour of Marlborough, including a boat trip through the Sounds. Afterwards we went to the hospice, and I introduced him to Mark. They seemed to get on well, so just as on the previous night with Lisa, I sat back and listened. They had more in common than I'd expected, and they shared anecdotes about tramping trips to various parts of the country. I was pleased to note that Mark had a little more colour, but his voice was weak, and he was still reluctantly trying out the NIV.

I made a tactical withdrawal that evening at The Cedars and announced my intention of heading out on a long bike ride, citing a dire need of exercise after all that sitting around in cars and boats. I wasn't sure whether there was any chance of anything happening between Alan and Lisa, but if there were, I didn't want to play gooseberry. Lisa flashed me a brief look of gratitude and understanding, but Alan seemed a little bemused. Still, he didn't put up a lot of resistance, and I left him happily ensconced in Lisa's lounge with a glass of wine in his hand.

I headed through the vineyards to Mark's house. He'd given me the keys a few days ago, and it seemed like a good time to check everything was in order there. Plus I'd have the opportunity to call in on Dave and Miriam.

This time there was no need for me to clamber over the gate, and I shut it behind me and bumped down the track to the house. Everything looked the same as I leaned the bike against the veranda and hopped up the steps to unlock the front door.

The house smelt musty and unlived-in, and I went from room to room vacuuming, dusting and tidying. As I worked my way through the house, I became slowly aware of another presence. It felt as though someone were watching me, but every time I looked in their direction they just slipped out of view. Had I *really* become 'psychic'? Mark hadn't mentioned that his house was haunted, and I was definitely in denial of anything along those lines. I tried to ignore it, and the house was certainly silent. There were no odd bangs or bumps to add to my fancy. 'Your imagination's running away with you,' I said out loud to myself as I opened a window in one of the upstairs bedrooms and leaned out to admire the view over the Wairau.

A slight gulp of laughter made me pull back and turn sharply, but the room was empty. 'Who's there?' I called out. No answer. I took a deep breath. 'Okay, look,' I said to the silent room, 'if there's someone here, why don't you just show yourself?' I laughed to myself at the absurdity of what I was doing. 'I'm supposed to be psychic, you know, so if you want to pass on a message from the other side, now's your chance.'

Silence.

I sighed and finished my cleaning before closing the window. Just as I pushed the latch to, I thought I saw a flash of yellow out of the corner of my eye. I turned again, but it was gone.

I returned downstairs wondering what on earth was going on. There was no way Mark would play games with me like that. Or would he?

***

'So what was that all about last night?' Alan asked the next morning as he dropped me in Blenheim on his way back to Westport.

'I don't know what you mean,' I replied, trying and failing to keep a straight face.

He glanced aside at me, his own lips curving in a smile. 'Are you playing matchmaker now?'

I shrugged. '*Do* you like her?'

'Well, she's quite good company,' he said thoughtfully. 'I find her soothing to be around. She's got that sort of way with her.'

'You mean she looks after you?' I teased, grinning.

He laughed. 'I hadn't thought of it that way, but I suppose there is that aspect to it. So anyway,' he added, quickly changing the subject, 'I'll be back next Friday morning to pick you up, okay?'

'Okay. I'm looking forward to it.' And I was; it would be a welcome change of scene and the chance to see Ewan again, even if I was deliberately closing my mind to the reasons *why* I was keen to see Ewan again.

After I'd waved Alan off, I headed to Mark's now-familiar hospice room. He was lying back in his bed with his eyes shut and his mouth open. I went over and touched his shoulder, but he didn't stir.

''Hey, sleepy, wake up!' I said, and there was still no response. I started to panic and turned to the door to call a nurse, but before I'd moved two steps he said, a little weakly, 'It's all right. I'm here.'

I turned back and gazed into the bright blue eyes that were now open. 'Damn, you were trying to get *out*, weren't you? You could have warned me! Did you succeed?'

He smiled weakly. 'A bit, but it was the same as when I saw you on the beach at Lake Mahinapua. It's like pulling open a heavy gate but being too tired to go through it.'

'Where did you go?'

'One of my favourite tramping tracks at Fox Glacier, but I was stuck just looking, not moving.' He gave a small sigh. 'Maybe it won't come back,' he added sadly.

'You're still improving though,' I said, attempting encouragement.

'Temporarily.'

'Anyway, if you try to get *out* here they might start carrying out CPR or something – I was about to get a nurse, you know.'

He grinned. 'I've got caught out before – there were a couple of panics at home when the care workers came in and couldn't wake me up. And when I was a kid, I scared my parents a few times until I learned how to keep a little bit of me aware in this body. Guess I've got too weary lately to do that properly.'

'So your real body is almost unaware of anything that's going on?'

'Suppose so. The carers even called an ambulance once – thought I was in a coma! I nearly woke up in the ICU.'

'I still don't understand it. Do you feel like a real, living person when you're *out*?'

'Yep. I can do some ghostly things, like walk through walls, but I can't float in mid-air. I did make the attempt, more than once,' he said wryly and tried to laugh, but it turned into a cough.

When he'd settled back down, I mentioned my strange experiences at his house the previous evening. 'In view of what you just said, it couldn't have been you playing a trick on me. Have you ever heard or seen anything strange there before?'

'Nope.' He narrowed his eyes and stared at me in mock-seriousness. 'Maybe you were right about being psychic. Hey, this could be your chance to make a fortune as a medium. I can see it all now: Madame Olivia and her crystal ball.'

'Crystal ball indeed,' I retorted. 'Anyway, who could it have been?'

'My mum or dad – grandparents?'

'The laugh sounded female, somehow.'

'You're really convinced there was someone there?'

'It's hard to believe I imagined it all. Anyway,' I added, changing the subject, 'Are you all right with me heading to Hokitika next weekend?'

'Hey, I'm not going to croak that soon, okay? And speaking of croaking, I'm working out my "advance directive". When it gets to the point that I can't swallow, I'm going to let nature take its course.'

'You're sure?' I asked, watching him closely.

He gave me the sincere look that had to take the place of a nod. 'It's hard enough to talk right now, with or without the ventilator going, but once I can't swallow or speak, I reckon that should be the end of it.'

My own throat tightened as I tried to avoid thinking of that end, but I was glad at the same time that he wouldn't have to go through the final agony that my dad endured.

It was late afternoon and sultry when I arrived back at The Cedars. Lisa waved to me from the window. As she'd been so kind, letting me stay on free of charge, I'd taken to helping out with cleaning the rooms in the mornings to try to repay her.

I entered the cool of the main house, and she called to me from the kitchen. I found her surrounded by heaps of lemons. 'I'm making some real lemonade,' she explained. 'I grow them in the garden, and there's a big crop this year.'

Wow, growing your own lemons. I was impressed.

'Ollie, I know what you were up to yesterday, but thanks anyway.'

I shrugged. 'No problem. You two seem to have really hit it off.'

'Well, I... it's not...' she blushed.

I stared at her, and she reddened even more. Now I was really intrigued. 'It's not...?' I prompted gently.

She squashed a lemon rather fiercely into the juicer. 'I always was fond of him,' she said finally.

My mouth dropped open until I snapped it firmly shut. 'You mean, back in the campervan?'

She nodded, her face bright red. She lifted out the pulverised half of lemon and picked up a fresh one. 'I admit I was pretty jealous of Jenny. She was my best friend, but it seemed a bit unfair that she had *all* the attention – and she didn't even appreciate it.'

'Did Alan know, back then?'

She shook her head. 'He just saw me as a mate; they all did. Heck, I wasn't that bad looking, just a lot less fascinating than Jenny, I suppose.'

'And now? Alan likes you. Do you think you might... you know... get together?'

She looked me in the eye then. 'He said he likes me?'

I nodded silently, unwilling to break any more confidences by going into detail.

She rinsed her hands under the tap and stared out of the window. 'I don't know about our getting together.' She smiled suddenly. 'We'll just have to wait and see, eh?'

I helped her to finish the lemonade, and she didn't refer to the subject again, but it gave me plenty to think about.

I was still pondering the situation a while later in my cottage when my mobile rang. To my own surprise, I felt a jump of pleasure on seeing that it was Ewan.

'My dad said you were thinking of coming down at the weekend? He reckons you're good at DIY.' His tone was more than a little sceptical.

Funnily enough, Alan was right about my practical expertise. My dad had taught me carpentry, building and even some electrician skills in the years before the MND struck, and I'd relished it all, soaking it up in what my mum considered a most unfeminine manner. She used to stand on the sidelines offering tea and biscuits while Dad and I built variously a shed, a garage and a conservatory extension. I felt very close to him during those times, although our companionable days weren't marked by any great confidences on his part. He was always a quiet man, never a big talker.

'Would you rather I *didn't* come?' I asked, bristling slightly.

'I could do with the help – as long as you're really going to be up to it.'

'You obviously don't think I am,' I said, somewhat coldly.

He gave an exasperated sigh. 'You don't look as though you've ever held a hammer in your life.'

'As I've told you before, appearances can be deceptive,' I said.

'I hope you're right. I don't need you just getting in the way, looking pretty.'

I gasped at his deliberately unkind tone, but he'd said goodbye before I could retort. I closed my mobile phone thoughtfully. Despite our seeming to gel on our day together in Blenheim, Ewan wasn't mellowing one bit. Did I really want to place myself back under his scornful gaze?

Chapter Sixteen

'You don't have to worry about camping out at Ewan's,' Alan said as we headed cross-country towards Hokitika the following Friday. 'A friend's letting us stay in his bach for the weekend. Luckily for us, he's had a last-minute cancellation.'

'His *bach*?'

'Haven't come across that word yet, eh? It's a holiday home. This one's a bit of a beaut, too, on Lake Kaniere.'

'Really? Sounds great!'

'So it won't be all work. You can have a bit of fun.'

'I'm not sure Ewan sees it that way,' I said.

Alan looked over at me. 'Gave you a hard time on the phone, did he?'

I laughed dryly. 'When doesn't he give me a hard time?'

He frowned. 'I keep hoping he'll get over it.'

'Can I ask what happened with his wife?'

He sighed. 'She hurt him more than he'll ever admit. They met when he was a young teacher, and she'd just started up her own business making and selling jewellery. She seemed to be a real arty type, a bit like his mum. Maybe that was what drew him to her, I don't know. She and Jenny got on so well back then.' He shook his head sadly.

'He kept them both going on his teaching salary for the first couple of years. They seemed like the ideal couple; we all thought they were happy. Then her business picked up, started to be a bigger thing, and she changed. She was always a looker, but she started to really do herself up, dress to impress and all that, and she had to be away from home a lot.' He paused, negotiating a sharp corner, and then continued quietly, 'The first couple of times he forgave her. She swore she still loved him, and he tried to carry on, but whenever she was away on business, he'd fret that she was being unfaithful. He's a one-woman man, and when it happened again, he just couldn't take it; he couldn't trust her any more.' He paused for a moment, sighing again. 'To cap it all, when he finally broke it off, she accused him of being too boring for her. He's never been able to forget that.'

I stared out of the window at the rugged and mountainous landscape we were passing through. 'Otira', a sign read as we flashed by.

'I can see why he might have taken against women in general after that,' I said, 'but he seems to be determined to see me in particular in the worst possible light.'

Alan glanced across at me. 'And you can't work out why?'

'What do you mean?'

'He likes you, Ollie, but he really doesn't want to.'

We arrived at the bach in the early evening. At first I was a little taken aback by what Alan had described as 'a beaut'. It was a rough wooden cabin with a corrugated iron roof, but it was literally next to the lake, and there was a beach with a dinghy moored nearby. The sky was cloudy and the light murky, but the lake was magnificent: crystal clear water surrounded by ranks of native grey-green trees.

The bach had two bedrooms, so I dumped my stuff in one of them and then followed Alan out on to the shingle beach. 'Fancy a trip out in it?' he asked, indicating first the dinghy, then the lake. I was all too quick to agree, and we headed out on to the lake for a companionable couple of hours, during which the sun began to peep out from behind the grey cloud. By the time we returned to shore the sun had reached the horizon. We built a large driftwood fire and sat on the beach eating baked potatoes, watching the sunset and sipping glasses of wine.

'Hey, have you ever had a bush bath?' Alan said as the embers were dying down and we prepared to head back to the cabin.

'I'm not even sure what a bush bath is,' I said.

He took me around the side of the bach and extended his arm with a flourish. 'Your bath awaits,' he said with a smile.

I stared at what looked to me like an abandoned bathtub sitting in the small garden area. 'It's plumbed in?' I asked.

'Of course. It's a Kiwi tradition to have a bath under the stars every now and again. Now's your chance,' he looked up at the sky, in which a few stars were becoming visible, 'and you know I won't peek.'

I couldn't resist, and before long I was lying in a tub of hot water in my swimsuit, watching the stars pass slowly overhead and listening to the gentle slap of the lake waters against the dinghy moored nearby. I closed my eyes for a moment, feeling more relaxed than I had since Manapouri.

'Everything all right out here?' Alan's voice called from a distance, and I opened my eyes suddenly. I must have drifted off to sleep. The water felt decidedly cool, so I turned on the hot tap and sloshed it around a bit.

'Fine,' I called out. 'Sorry, I must have dozed off.'

'No problem. By the way, Ewan rang. He's expecting us at seven sharp tomorrow, so you need all the sleep you can get.' There was a laugh in Alan's voice. He obviously understood his son's most irritating foibles.

Half an hour later, I joined Alan in the small living room of the bach, feeling warm and glowing and full of bonhomie, to which I was quite happy to add with some more wine. It was getting late, but we talked about my dad and about Jenny, and Alan told me again how glad he was that I'd come to find him, and how fond he'd become of me.

We were both more than a little tipsy when he took out his wallet and handed over a picture of Jenny I'd never seen before. She was sitting among some tall, dry grasses and waving a couple of fronds in front of her face. She was smiling: an open, serene smile.

'That was taken at Jackson Bay, before…' He sighed wistfully. 'That's how she was when I fell for her. Jennifer Juniper your dad always called her, after the song, you know.'

I jumped slightly and stared at him. 'Jennifer *Juniper*?'

He nodded. 'Your dad thought it suited her, "hair of golden flax" and all that. He loved that song.'

I shook my head. I didn't know the song, or at least it only rang a vague bell. 'Jennifer Juniper,' I repeated in a whisper. I shook my head, trying to clear it, to remove the befuddlement brought on by excess alcohol. It was just a pet name, surely. I was clutching at straws.

***

When my alarm shrilled the next morning, I sat up in bed and stared out of the window at the lake, which was shrouded in mist at this early hour. The idea that Jenny might be Mark's mother seemed even more preposterous now that I was sober. My thoughts seesawed from one end of the spectrum to the other. It *must* be chance. If my dad had known she was pregnant, he'd never have abandoned the child, and surely Alan would have known if she'd given birth to a child before they married. On the other hand it would make at least a little sense of why I could see Mark, and why I felt a connection with him, and MND… it's sometimes genetic. It would fit. *It would fit all too well.*

I was lost in my own thoughts over breakfast. It was the coincidence of the MND that kept recurring. My dad's was never diagnosed as familial, but I'd always known it was a possibility. We couldn't identify a family history because my granddad had died in an accident when he was only in his late twenties. My dad had been just a baby then, and my nan brought him up on her own. I'd thought occasionally about getting tested, but there was only one gene they could test for – the appropriately named SOD1 gene – and without proof that my dad had the familial form *and* a mutation of the gene, there was no point. Besides, most MND is sporadic, not genetic. Mark wouldn't have been tested for the SOD1 mutation either, without a family history of MND. He might legitimately have wondered whether either of his real parents had MND, though.

'What's up?' Alan asked finally. 'Not worried about Ewan, are you?'

I started and forced myself to smile. 'No, Ewan is the least of my worries right now,' I said.

When we arrived at the lodge site half an hour later, Ewan was already at work, busily sawing lumber. He was wearing a worn-out shirt and tatty jeans and still managed to look sexy. He seemed to be unable to meet my gaze and addressed himself to his dad.

'Right on time, I see,' he said, grinning. I found myself comparing his grin, and his overall appearance, with Mark's; after all, they could be half brothers. But Ewan was as dark as Mark was fair. They seemed seriously unalike. Surely it all had to be a fantasy of my fevered imagination? All the same, if by any chance there *was* anything to it, I needed to find out right away, because Mark's days were distinctly numbered, particularly as he was about to draw up that advance directive.

Ewan turned to me at last and looked me up and down – like him, I was dressed in scruffy jeans and an old T-shirt – clearly seeking some sign of inappropriate girly gear. 'Are you sure you can handle it?' he asked in a slightly awkward tone.

'Just tell me what you want done and show me the tools,' I said airily. Alan gurgled slightly with laughter, but Ewan just raised his eyebrows and gave me a resigned look and a shrug before leading the way back over to the half-built lodge.

After a lot of unnecessary explanation – I understood the point the first time – the pair of them left me happily lugging wooden planks around and hammering them into place to create a big deck overlooking the river. They got on with putting walls up in the part of the lodge that already had floors. The familiarity of working with wood, the smell and feel of it and the curiously satisfying rhythm of the work were all enough to send my mind spooling back in time to the late eighties. I could almost see my dad working alongside me and hear his cheery whistle, so much so that when Ewan appeared in front of me with a mug of tea, I was momentarily surprised that it wasn't my mum.

'You *are* allowed a break, you know,' Alan said, from his position lounging on the grass near the river.

I took the mug from Ewan with a quick smile and joined him and Alan at the water's edge. I was pleased to note that it didn't seem to be a bad sandfly day.

'You're a good worker, I'll give you that,' Ewan said grudgingly.

'What did I tell you? A chip off the old block,' Alan said.

This reminder of my dad had me comparing faces again. Did Mark look like him? Certainly not in hair colour with my dad having been the proverbial ginger nut. No, Mark definitely shared 'hair of golden flax' with Jenny. He had my dad's height, build and brilliant blue eye colour, but his cheery grin and light-hearted manner were the opposite of my dad's quiet smile and serious nature.

'You sure you're all right, Ollie? You've been a bit subdued since last night. What is it – are you worried about Mark?' Alan asked.

I looked up into his genial, open features and wondered how I could possibly ask him about Jenny. 'Yes, a bit,' I replied. 'Although he assured me he had no intention of dying this weekend,' I added lightly, hoping to deflect his concern.

'Have they said how long?' he asked.

I shook my head. 'Not to me. I don't think they like to put time limits on lives. They won't let him go home, though. They say he's not safe there, even with care workers coming in. There's a bit of a debate between the hospice staff and Mark's social worker about what to do. He can't stay in the hospice indefinitely if he's still got months to live, but he doesn't want to go into a care home. I don't think he has months myself.' There was a real sense of urgency in my mind. If I were going to find out about his parentage, I'd better hurry up about it.

Once we'd returned to work, I drifted back into my circular thoughts to such an extent that I didn't notice Alan and Ewan had stopped. The silence penetrated only slowly, and I looked up sharply to see their work boots standing squarely on my new decking. I sat back on my heels and gave them a patient look while they both smirked.

'I reckon it's time we called it a day,' Ewan said, and to my surprise he put out a hand to help me up.

I removed my work gloves and put my grubby and greasy hand into his, starting a little at the contact. He seemed to feel it too and pulled back as soon as I was upright, looking discomfited and a little red in the face.

'We've been talking,' Alan said, 'and we think you deserve a night out, so we're taking you to Don's.'

I laughed lightly. 'Okay, if you say so. What's Don's?'

'The best restaurant in town. Don knows how to serve up a great plate of fish and chips.' He looked around at the lodge. They'd put a wall up, and I'd nearly finished the deck. 'I think we got a lot done today, don't you?'

Ewan nodded and glanced my way briefly before saying, 'It's a shame my casual workers don't have the same work ethic. I'm lucky if they turn up most days.'

'I enjoyed it,' I said. 'It's great to have a visible result to your labours, something that will be used and even lived in.'

Back at the bach, I got ready for my date. Ewan seemed to have softened towards me again, but for how long? I opened my backpack and took out the simple white cotton dress I'd bought off a bargain rail in Blenheim just yesterday. Tonight seemed a good time to wear it, and I slipped it on with a pair of flat sandals. I viewed myself in the mirror and decided that I looked okay, although obviously not girly or 'done up' enough by Niall's (or my mum's) standards, what with my hair loose and curly and my face as devoid of make-up as ever. I grinned to myself at the thought of Niall. Whatever had I been thinking of when I got engaged to him? I tried to get back inside the skin of the oppressed customer service adviser I used to be and failed dismally.

Ewan and Alan were talking quietly in the living room as I entered. Ewan greeted my appearance with an expression of surprise followed just as swiftly by a frown of irritation. He'd cleaned up very nicely and was wearing a casual black jacket over a dark blue shirt and smart jeans. Damn, why was I so attracted to this man who found me a repugnant reminder of his ex-wife?

Don's was a small, unpretentious restaurant with a limited seafood menu. I ordered the blue cod and chips as advised by Alan and wasn't disappointed. It amused me to be on the other side of the world and still eating fish and chips regularly.

Ewan made an effort to be sociable throughout the meal, regaling us with anecdotes from his days as a teacher. Once again I wondered if he'd really be happy running a tourist lodge. Just as in the café in Blenheim, an interesting and caring person emerged from the spiky exterior. What with that and a couple of glasses of white wine, I let down my own guard and talked about my customer service days. I even mentioned that it was because I was so sick of listening to complaints that I agreed to Niall's proposed year abroad. I realized my mistake when Ewan's face froze. 'Who's Niall?'

'He was my fiancé. We came out here together.' I said, wishing I'd drunk less wine and remained more circumspect. Not that it ought to matter, but with Ewan *everything* mattered.

'So where is he now? You've never mentioned him before,' he asked with slight belligerence.

'They've obviously broken up,' Alan said, trying to ease the sudden tension.

'Yes,' I said. 'Not long after we got here. Being together twenty-four hours a day was too much.'

'So *you* broke it off?'

I took a deep gulp of wine. 'I broke it off,' I said, nodding, 'and I haven't regretted it yet.'

'So where does Mark come in – I mean he's a New Zealander, right?'

'I met him in Alexandra,' I said and added swiftly, 'but he and I are just friends… more like…' the words caught in my throat, '…like brother and sister.'

Ewan gave me a sceptical look. 'Like moths to a candle flame,' he muttered bitterly.

'*Ewan*,' Alan said quietly in a warning tone. 'Not all women are like Natalie.'

Ewan stared at me, and I held his gaze until his taut shoulders slumped and he exhaled sharply. 'No, I suppose you're right. I'm sorry, Ollie. It's not your fault.'

After that we tried to regain the previous mood, with only partial success. Even so, when I headed for bed later, I hoped this was the start of a real thaw in the atmosphere between us.

Chapter Seventeen

I woke up the next morning to bright sunlight and bird calls and took a stroll along the beach, trying to clear my mind and decide how to approach Alan about Jenny. If it weren't for Mark's desperate situation, I would dismiss the whole idea as merely my own fancy, but if there were *any* possibility that it could be true, then I owed it to him to check it out.

When I eventually returned to the bach, Alan was preparing breakfast for *me* for a change.

'I noticed you'd gone for a walk and thought it was about time I made an attempt,' he said, flipping an egg in the frying pan before turning back to me. 'Are you okay? I'm sorry about the way Ewan acted last night.'

I shrugged. 'I'm fine. I understand… I think.'

'I told you, he likes you a lot more than he lets on.'

I settled down at the table and looked at him enquiringly.

'Seriously. And he can't keep his eyes off you.'

I laughed, slightly embarrassed. 'Should you be telling me this?'

He slipped the egg on to a plate already piled with bacon and passed it over to me. 'Probably not, but I don't think you're going to give me away. I suppose I've been hoping the two of you might get it together. Don't think I haven't noticed the way you look at him, either.'

I opened my mouth to respond, but I was momentarily speechless.

'C'mon, Ollie, I'm in my fifties, not in my dotage. I know sexual tension when I see it.'

Alan set his own plate on the table and sat down. His pile of healthy fried bacon was even higher than mine.

'Well, even if there is – and I'm admitting nothing – there's not much sign of Ewan and me getting together. I only have to mention male friends, and he assumes I'm a scarlet woman. I couldn't cope with that in a relationship any more than I could stand Niall's attempts to control me. And what's more,' I added, waving my knife in the air, 'I decided after Niall that I was going to stay single for good.'

Alan laughed quietly. 'Sounds to me like one of those best laid plans that's bound to go awry.'

'We'll see about that,' I said, lifting my eyebrows at him in challenge.

True to form, Ewan was awkward with me again when we arrived at the lodge. He seemed to have decided that businesslike mode was best, and he issued brisk orders about what needed doing 'because we only have half a day left'. Alan and I intended to leave at three in the afternoon to head across to Blenheim.

I obeyed my orders meekly and spent the rest of the morning completing the deck. It was a blazing hot day, and when I went for a toilet break at lunchtime I swilled water over my face and neck in an attempt to cool down. As I headed back out of Ewan's cabin I started at the sight of a blond head in the trees closer to the road. I glanced furtively across at the lodge and noted that Alan and Ewan were just out of sight behind one of the new walls, and then I hurried down the track and into the woods.

Mark was leaning against a tree in his usual casual manner. It was such a pleasure to see the Mark I knew best, to see him healthy and whole and without a ventilator or oxygen mask that tears started in my eyes. I blinked them away quickly, hoping he wouldn't notice. 'Are you okay?' I asked in a low voice.

He grinned. 'I've finally got *out,* so I thought I'd come and take a look at this place – and this guy Ewan. It's strange – if I want to find you, I just think of you, and I'm wherever you are. I've been watching you slave away for a while. Never would've thought you were so good with a hammer. Nearly as good as a man,' he said, widening his eyes provocatively.

'Oh, only *nearly*, eh?'

He gestured towards the lodge with a tilt of his head. 'Your friend Ewan's not bad looking. He fancies you rotten, you know.'

'Oh yeah? What makes you think that?'

'Keeps on looking at you all the time. Even when he's meant to be concentrating on his work, his eyes keep straying over.'

I sighed. Everyone seemed to be telling me the same thing.

Mark looked distracted suddenly, as though he were looking at me but not seeing me. 'Oh-oh. Nurses shaking me, or something. I'll have to go.'

'Mark…' I began.

He regarded me questioningly.

I threw my arms around him. I didn't want to say the words, but I was so afraid I'd never see him again like this. He hugged me back, and to me he had substance. It must have been all in my head, but he felt totally real.

'Oh-oh,' he said again as we pulled apart.

'What's wrong?'

'Your friend Ewan coming over with a face like thunder. Must be time to get your nose back to the grindstone or something. Good luck!'

He headed off through the trees and disappeared from view, and I turned to see Ewan staring at me from beside the cabin. Alan was still out of sight over at the lodge, and there was the sound of energetic sawing. Was this going to be another Pastor moment? Had Ewan seen me talking to thin air?

He didn't move as I approached, but the familiar look of scorn was back on his features. 'Another *friend*, was it?' he said.

I started. 'Sorry?'

'Some sort of secret assignation in the bushes? No need to be shy. You should have introduced him.'

He turned sharply and headed into the cabin. I watched him go in stunned silence. *He'd seen Mark,* and now he was even more convinced I was some sort of deceitful slut. I felt a slightly hysterical giggle rise up and scooted over to the lodge, where I could let it out amid the sound of Alan's loud sawing. There was no way Ewan would believe me if I told him who it really was, but why could he see him? Unless he really *was* his half brother.

I choked back my amusement and went to help Alan with the sawing. By the time Ewan returned, I was innocently engaged in helping Alan with the next bit of wall. Ewan joined us but remained taciturn for our last couple of hours. For whatever reason he failed to mention my 'assignation' to his dad.

By the time three o'clock arrived, I was feeling so tense at Ewan's cold-shoulder that it was a relief to be leaving. Despite his attitude though, he did have the grace to thank me for my help.

'Things are getting back on target – I appreciate it,' he said and even granted me a small smile. 'I'll phone you later in the week, then, old codger,' he said to his dad.

'Make sure you do, young whippersnapper,' Alan replied. Ewan's smile for his dad held genuine warmth and affection. I fought down a desire for him to look at me with that kind of fondness.

'So, what happened this afternoon?' Alan asked as soon as we were heading back up the coast.

'Happened?' I asked innocently.

'Come on. You and Ewan fell out yet again. What was it about this time?'

'He's always on the lookout for new ways to brand me a brazen hussy.' I looked over at him with a wry grin. 'It doesn't take much.'

After about two hours' drive in the blazing heat, we decided to stop at a roadside café. We sat outside drinking Cokes, and I decided I couldn't put it off any longer.

'Alan,' I said hesitantly. 'I have to ask you something… well… awkward.'

He looked at me enquiringly, and I sighed. I didn't want to trigger any depression, but I had to ask, for Mark's sake.

'There's a couple of things making me wonder… um… when you told me about Jenny and my dad, you said she went away for almost a year. I'm wondering… well… is it possible that she… had a child? You'd have known, when she came back. I mean, you couldn't avoid knowing.'

His whole face sagged, and he just gazed at me in silence for a minute before nodding slowly.

'She did lose a child,' he said and passed a hand over his eyes. 'It was stillborn. A boy.'

'Was it… yours?'

'No. She was pregnant by Paul before we even got to Jackson Bay.' He regarded me seriously. 'I don't know what made you suspect – I said you were psychic – but I admit I missed that bit out. I couldn't bring myself to tell Ewan about it. I was afraid it would ruin his memory of his mother.'

'It's okay. I won't mention it to him if you'd rather I didn't.'

He nodded. 'Please. Jenny would hate it if any of the kids knew.'

He paused and took a big breath before he said: 'She told Paul that night – the same night I told him what she and I had... done. I don't think she was planning to, but they had this big row. He'd already been on at her to get married, but that only made it worse. Paul was so religious; he'd wanted to make it official. He couldn't stand it any longer – you know, sex outside of wedlock and all that. An illegitimate child was totally out of the question. He told her he'd forgive her for being unfaithful with me, begged her to marry him, but the more he pressed, the more trapped she felt. She insisted she was going to have an abortion as soon as she got back to Canterbury. She was angry and wanted him off her back, so she was pretty adamant about it.'

He put his head in his hands suddenly. 'I wish he'd talked to me, but of course he didn't feel able to; she didn't tell him I had no idea about the pregnancy. I can only guess what he was feeling, but knowing him so well and how hurt he must have been, I think he just wanted to get away from the source of pain as soon as possible. Jenny told me he pleaded with her half the night not to have an abortion, but she was so stubborn back then, and she wanted to be free of him.' He lifted his head to meet my gaze. 'I didn't know anything about it until a few months after she came back and found me on the sheep station.' He paused thoughtfully. 'In a sense, she never really got over losing the baby. Sometimes I'd catch her crying when she thought there was no one around. She was always worse in November, because it was the anniversary of his death.'

'Where did she go – when she was away?' I asked, hoping I didn't sound too intrusive.

'Oh, up to Kaikoura apparently. She and Lisa shared a flat together. She didn't want to go back to her parents' house – too close to Paul and me for comfort I suppose – and the story about staying with an aunt wasn't true. She was sure Paul would come back once he'd worked it out of his system. She didn't imagine he'd take it so badly.'

My throat was tight with emotion. 'Why do you think she wanted to know where my dad was? Did she want to tell him?'

He nodded slowly. 'Like I said, by then she'd grown up a lot. She wanted to tell him she hadn't had an abortion, make up for how she'd treated him.'

I was trembling. What if she hadn't had a stillbirth either? What if she'd abandoned the baby in Blenheim? It *was* possible; even the year was right. Could she have been intending to tell my dad when she went looking for him at the sheep station? She might have hoped he'd go to Blenheim and be a father to Mark. And he would have, wouldn't he? *If he'd known.* I fought to keep tears at bay, biting my lip to try to stem them. It was still all mere speculation, and how could I help Mark without hurting Alan?

'What are the words of that song?' I asked. 'You know, the one you mentioned the other day: Jennifer Juniper.'

He smiled and began singing softly. I realized that I did know it vaguely. *Jennifer Juniper, hair of golden flax. Jennifer Juniper, longs for what she lacks*. Mark looked like Jenny, far more than Ewan did. The more I learned, the more convinced I became. But how could I prove it?

As we took the last lap towards Blenheim a thought suddenly occurred to me. *Lisa*. Of all people, surely she must know. She'd already shown signs of unease when I'd asked her about my dad, yet she was so kind and considerate about everything else.

'Did Lisa know about Jenny's pregnancy?' I asked Alan.

'Of course,' he said with a nod. 'They were best friends back then, and they shared a flat. They fell out afterwards, I gather, or their friendship just grew cold, you know, the way it can go sometimes.'

I leaned back in my seat. Lisa knew *something* all right.

***

I broached the subject as I helped her to clean the larger cottage the next morning.

'You and Jenny were really close friends, weren't you?' I asked, looking up at her from the happy position of cleaning the toilet.

She gave me a curious look as she scrubbed the shower. 'We were, before she went away. Why do you ask?'

'Alan told me yesterday she had a child,' I said slowly.

'Did he?' She dropped her scrubbing pad and stared at me.

'He said you shared a flat, so you must have been with her then.'

'Well yes, we did. I was. But we lost touch after it was born.'

'Was it really stillborn?' I asked baldly.

'What makes you ask that?' she said on a slight gulp.

'I have reason to believe I have a half-brother,' I said quietly.

'What reason? I mean, how could you possibly…? Unless she told Alan, but I'm sure she… I don't think she would have.'

I flushed the now sparkling toilet and turned to her earnestly. 'Please, Lisa. I really need to know for his sake. Jenny told Alan the baby was stillborn, but that's not true, is it?'

She sighed. 'I promised her I'd keep her secret, even though I've never been happy about it.' Her eyes met mine, and she seemed to come to a sudden decision. 'No, it wasn't stillborn. It was a boy, and it was your dad's baby all right, although I never saw him. She'd told Paul she was having an abortion, but after a couple of months, she felt differently, started to care about the baby and wanted to keep it. Trouble was, she was too scared to even tell her mum and dad she was pregnant. We were only eighteen, and it was still shameful back in those days to have a baby outside marriage.

'She hid away in the flat and told her parents she was too ill to visit them, but one day they turned up unexpectedly, and there was quite a scene. By then, it was too late for an abortion anyway, but they tried to persuade her to have it adopted. They didn't want anyone to know about it.' She shook her head sadly. 'To be honest, Jenny didn't know what to do. Eventually she said she was going to keep the baby, no matter what, and that's when her parents pretty well disowned her, they were so ashamed. She was under enormous pressure, and she was scared. How was she going to care for it, especially without parental support? I couldn't help, as I had a full-time job of my own.

'When she was eight months, I went to visit my own parents for a couple of weeks, and while I was gone she went into premature labour. I didn't know anything about it until I got back to find her in a heck of a state. "I've left him behind," she said. "I didn't know what to do. I didn't know what was best. He'll be better off without me; I'm sure he will." She'd gone to the hospital on her own, and it seems the staff had kept on asking questions, and the nurses were really disapproving, giving her a hard time. She felt really alone and helpless and just couldn't cope with it all, so she ran away.'

'Did she say what she'd called the baby?' I asked, holding my breath.

She nodded. 'Mark, after her dad. But she didn't give her real surname at the hospital. She gave the pet name Paul had for her. Juniper. He used to call her Jennifer Juniper, after the song.'

A huge wash of relief went through me; I'd been right. 'So she never went back – never had second thoughts?'

'Oh, she had lots of second thoughts, but…' she sighed. 'She was really confused, felt guilty as hell one minute and sure he'd have a better life without her the next. And as soon as she'd told everyone he was stillborn, she couldn't go back on it.'

'She didn't tell her parents the truth?'

'No, them least of all. She was mortified about running away, and they never questioned her story. Maybe it was easier for them to accept it at face value. She never really got over what she'd done, and she never forgot him. I tried to persuade her to go back to the hospital and confess, but she couldn't face it. I think that's why our friendship faded – I was the only one who knew the secret. I agreed to keep it to myself, but she promised to tell Paul. Of course, in the end, she never did, because he'd already left the country.'

She checked her watch and returned to her scrubbing. 'We'd better get this finished. They'll be arriving soon. Anyway, I'm glad I've told you now, as Paul's daughter. But how *did* you know?'

I started polishing the washbasin taps. 'I met Mark – he calls himself Mark Juniper – by chance after I came to New Zealand. He was desperately searching for her, or for any relatives. He's the one I'm visiting at the hospice.'

'The one who's dying of MND?' She looked at me with sympathy and then with dawning realization. 'Of *course*; that's what happened to your dad.'

'That's one of the things made me wonder – that and when Alan told me about the song.'

'To think he's been searching all this time. Feeling unwanted and wondering if Jenny ever cared about him. Which of course she did, a lot more than she ever wanted to let on.'

I nodded. 'Alan said she used to cry about him. He said she never forgot his birthday.'

'No, I don't suppose she did.' She paused, then asked, 'Do you plan to tell Mark all this?'

'Yes. He needs to know he has a half sister.' I bit my lip. 'But Ewan's his half brother. And there are Ewan's sisters as well. I don't see how I can tell Ewan without telling Alan.'

Lisa looked alarmed. 'You can't tell him,' she said in a panicked voice. 'Think how he's going to feel. Jenny lied to him all those years, and him still grieving for her. You *can't* tell him.'

We finished the cleaning as speedily as we could and left the cottage looking spotless. Just as we entered the cool main house from the back, the doorbell went at the front. 'That'll be the new guests. Can you go and welcome them, Ollie? I'll get this put away.' Lisa said, taking all the cleaning equipment with her.

I opened the door with a smile of greeting ready-pinned to my face, but my jaw dropped in astonishment as I saw who was standing there.

'Well, Ollie, aren't you going to give me a hug?' my mum said, with a self-satisfied smirk.

'And one for your old stepdad as well,' Ron added.

CHAPTER EIGHTEEN

'What… I mean… why… I mean… how come you're here?' I asked, once we were safely alone in their cottage.

'You were obviously holding out on me,' my mum said crisply as she unpacked a large suitcase. Evidently they weren't planning a short stay. 'You've hardly phoned me in the past couple of weeks, and even then you were very evasive. I know you, Ollie. Something's going on.'

'So we thought we'd have a little holiday and find out for ourselves,' Ron added.

'This is a nice place, I have to say,' my mum remarked, looking around the bedroom of the cottage. 'Lisa seemed very pleasant, if a little distracted. What I don't understand is why she's letting you live here rent-free. A bit of help with the cleaning is hardly enough to pay for everything, is it?'

'I told you on the phone; she's a friend of Alan's.'

'Oh yes, the man who let you stay at his house in exchange for a bit of cooking and housekeeping. I wasn't born yesterday; something's going on here.'

'You could at least have told me you were coming,' I protested.

'We thought it'd be a nice surprise, didn't we Ron? As you know, your father never would go abroad, and you've been telling us so much about how great it is here. We decided a few weeks in the sun would do us good.'

'A few weeks?' I squeaked.

'No need to sound quite so horrified. You would have found out sooner if you'd actually phoned in the last few days. We arrived four days ago – had a lovely time in Christchurch.'

'Well,' I began, feeling guilty, 'I would have, but there's been a lot going on.'

My mum raised her delicately plucked eyebrows. 'Has there indeed? What sort of "goings on" might that be, then? And there was me being led to believe you were just having a lovely time enjoying the sunshine and the swimming pool.'

'I *have* been enjoying the sunshine and the swimming pool,' I said, feeling like a little girl again.

'You can enjoy it now, then, with us,' she said. 'Lisa mentioned that we could use the pool at any time, and I could certainly do with a swim. Couldn't you, Ron?'

My stepdad answered in the affirmative, and Mum gazed at me with challenge in her eye.

I looked at my watch. 'I… um… can't right now. I have to get into town, to…' I floundered under my mum's sharp stare. 'I have to visit someone in the hospice,' I said finally, giving in. There was just no point in trying to make up a story.

My mum looked surprised. 'Hospice? You know someone here who's terminally ill?'

I nodded. There was no way I was going to be able to keep this from my mum now. I was assailed from every angle. I couldn't tell Ewan because Alan didn't want him to know about Jenny; couldn't tell Alan because it might tip him back into depression; couldn't tell my mum because… well… I had no idea how she'd react, but just like Alan, she'd been lied to by omission.

'Who is it that's dying? Someone you met here?' my mum pressed.

'Yes. His name's Mark. He has MND.'

She just stared at me. 'So how did you meet this Mark? I'm sure I don't need to remind you that you've never mentioned him at all.'

I glanced at my watch again. 'Look, Mum, I'll have to go. It takes half an hour to cycle up there.'

'You're cycling? Oh for goodness' sake, Ollie, we can take you. I'd like to meet this Mark. That is unless there's some reason why we shouldn't?'

I shook my head. 'Not really. But, Mum, he's bad. I mean, it's like with Dad near the end.'

She pressed her lips together. 'I think I can cope with that,' she said firmly.

'So, are you going to tell me what's going on?' she persisted once we were in their hire car, with Ron driving.

'Mark's a friend I met here,' I said.

'But failed to mention to me. I seem to recall Pastor, Ed, Alan and Ewan, but no Mark,' she said repetitively.

'It was difficult.'

'Because of the MND?'

I sighed. 'Partly.'

'Oh Ollie, stop being so mysterious.'

'*Mum*. Can we talk about it later?'

'All right,' she agreed with obvious reluctance. 'But my instincts were obviously correct – something very fishy is going on here.'

Mark was sitting up in bed with his eyes closed. He wasn't wearing the NIV mask. My mum hesitated for a moment before entering, and he opened his eyes to gaze in surprise at the unusual number of visitors.

'This is my mum, and my stepdad. They arrived *unexpectedly*,' I emphasized with a small smile.

'Pleased to meet you, Mrs Lewis, Mr Lewis,' Mark said with admirable composure.

'Ah, so Ollie's told you about us, then,' my mum said.

'*All* about you,' Mark said with a grin.

'Well that's nice to know,' she replied. 'I wish I could say the same about you.'

'What would you like to know?' he asked.

'Where did you two meet?' my mum asked, settling into a chair.

'Oh, that would be Alexandra,' he said without hesitation.

'Alexandra! But that's where… that was *months* ago!'

'Yes. She'd just split up with Niall at the time.'

I was getting a bit fed up with this. Mark was being no help at all.

My mum turned to me with a frown, just as Mark said, 'But of course, we *are* just friends. Ollie has other fish to fry.'

'*Mark!*' I said. My mum gave me a speculative look. 'Can I just have a word with Mark on his own?' I said to her. 'There's something important I have to talk to him about.'

'Of course,' she answered, still giving me *that* look. 'We'll wait in the car. Take as long as you need.'

Once we were alone, I turned to Mark. 'What are you trying to do to me? Other fish to fry indeed! Who would that be, exactly?'

He gulped with laughter. 'Ewan, of course. You like him as much as he likes you. I could tell that yesterday.'

'Oh yeah? Well, you missed the next bit, where he assumed you and I had an *assignation* in the bushes. I think that's put paid to any romance between us, don't you?'

'You and me? He *saw* me?'

'Saw you, thought you were some lover I'd just had tag along, apparently.'

He looked puzzled. 'I don't get it. No one could ever see me. Then there was you, and I thought that was because you're a bit psychic. But Ewan – not the psychic type, is he?'

I laughed. 'I don't think so somehow. But there is an answer. Are you ready for a big shock?'

His eyes widened. 'As I'll ever be, I guess.'

I perched on his bed. 'Okay. Ewan is your half-brother.' I let that percolate for a second and added, 'I'm your half-sister.'

He grinned lopsidedly. 'Aw come on, Ol, don't mess around.'

'I'm not messing around. Ewan's mum was *your* mum. Jennifer Jensen, born Jennifer Moody, called herself Jennifer Juniper in the hospital after the song, because that was my dad's pet name for her.'

He gaped at me, speechless. After a minute or two, he finally said, 'Juniper wasn't even her surname? My real name should be Mark *Moody*?'

I laughed. 'Doesn't quite have the same ring to it, does it? I don't even want to think about how you'd have got on at school.'

He allowed himself a small smile. 'So come on, spill. How d'you know all this? Does Ewan know?'

'He certainly doesn't, and I don't know how to tell him, or even if I should.'

I regaled him with the whole story, from how my dream fitted in to Lisa's revelation. When I'd finished, he was silent for a while. The only sounds were a murmur of voices from outside in the corridor. I folded my arms, widened my eyes and waited.

'So that's why I have MND. Like your dad. *My* dad.'

I nodded slowly. 'Probably, but there weren't any tests back then, and there was no reason to think it was hereditary.'

'I want to know all about him. Everything you can tell me. And everything about Jenny. *My mum.*'

'I'll have to get Alan to tell you about Jenny – but first I need to find a way to break this to him.'

'And Ewan… hard to believe he's my half-brother. He's pretty grim, isn't he? Doesn't seem like we have much in common. How's he going to feel when he knows you're sort of related?'

I laughed. 'I dread to think.'

'You must have pictures of your dad. I'd love to see what he looked like.'

'Thing is, I don't have any with me. They're all at home. Alan has some though, and maybe my mum has one with her. Speaking of my mum, I have to tell her, too.'

'She seems like a game old bird. I reckon she can take it.'

'A *game old bird*? Don't ever say that in her hearing.'

'Get her back in here and introduce me properly,' he said.

He was obviously on such a high that he felt nothing could go wrong, and just then I wanted to go along with it. I texted my mum, and she and Ron reappeared within minutes.

'Everything all right?' she asked, looking from me to Mark.

'Um, Mum, I think you should sit down. I've got something to tell you.'

She seated herself and raised her eyebrows.

'It's about Dad,' I said, abruptly.

'Dad?' she said, startled. 'What does your father have to do with anything?'

I couldn't help laughing slightly. 'It's more a case of my father having everything to do with everything. You remember my dream?'

'Of course.'

'Well it was about Dad, and it was about New Zealand.'

'Ollie, your dad never left the UK. He wouldn't even go on holiday to France. God knows I asked him enough times.'

'I know he never told you, but he did. He emigrated to New Zealand in 1972 with his friend Alan Jensen. They worked together at a sheep station in Canterbury.'

'Alan Jensen? That's this Alan you've been telling me about? I do remember your dad mentioning an Alan Jensen. They were childhood friends. There are some pictures of him in the albums.'

'Yes, that's the same Alan. Only… they both fell for the same girl, Jenny Moody. She got pregnant by Dad –'

'*Pregnant?*' She jumped up from her chair momentarily, and Ron came rushing over from his post near the door.

I nodded. 'I know it's a shock –'

'A shock?' she repeated, as she subsided into the chair, Ron's hand over hers. 'You've got a gift for understatement, my girl. How exactly do you know all this?'

I sighed and gently outlined the whole convoluted tale. 'Thing is, Jenny told everyone except her closest friend that the baby was stillborn, but he wasn't.'

My mum has never been slow on the uptake. She turned with a gasp to stare at Mark. 'MND,' she whispered. 'My God.'

'Mark is my half-brother,' I said unnecessarily. 'Ewan is *his* half-brother, and he has two half-sisters too.'

'My God,' she said again, shaking her head slowly. 'No wonder your dad never wanted to hear anything about New Zealand. He even used to switch off the TV if it was mentioned. How on earth did he keep that to himself all those years? He was just so *closed* in some ways.' She dragged her gaze from Mark for long enough to give me a stern look. 'I don't want you to end up like that, Ollie.'

'I don't think there's much chance of that.'

'You were so obviously keeping things from me all these weeks that I was starting to wonder.'

'Do you have the picture of Dad with you?' I asked, changing the subject.

'Of course. Never without it, even after all these years.' She rummaged in her bag and took out the familiar snapshot. I didn't even need to look at it to know what it showed. It was a head and shoulders shot of my dad and me, side by side. He was in his late twenties, and I was seven. Our matching ginger nuts shone out in bright haloes. We both looked happy, smiling.

Mark pored over the picture in silence and then looked at me. 'Lucky for you your hair toned down as you got older, eh?' he said.

***

'So, I'm wondering what exactly you plan to do with your life now,' Mum said, as she sat on the bed in her cottage brushing her hair. Ron was in the other room, watching *The Vicar of Dibley* on the telly. 'You've had your New Zealand adventure, dug out these amazing secrets, but now you need to think about your future. You can't just bum around here for the rest of your days. You have to be sensible.'

'I've got unfinished business here, and I'm still looking for work,' I said, gritting my teeth with the effort to be patient.

'I know you won't want to leave until Mark… well, until he's… passed, but *after that*, what then? This looking for work business isn't very realistic, is it? You've told me yourself they won't take someone on from abroad unless they have special skills, and you don't, do you?'

'Thanks. You really know how to make me feel good.'

'I'm just trying to get you to see sense. In that way you're just like your father. A dreamer.'

'How was he a dreamer, exactly?' I asked, still trying to get a fuller picture.

'Oh, he always wanted things to be better than they were, thought there should be more to life. He wanted to go and be an organic crofter in Scotland one day, or set up his own business making some sort of gadget or another the next. He could never settle down.' She turned to look at me and emphasised her words with waves of her hairbrush. 'Just like you, Ollie.'

'But he never did any of those things. He stayed an electrical engineer until the MND got too bad for him to work.'

'Too right he did. I made sure of that. All that other stuff was just castles in the air.'

'Well, I'm not so sure that castles in the air are a bad thing, and I'm staying here until I decide otherwise,' I said firmly.

My mum pressed her lips together but remained silent for once.

'Anyway, I'm more interested in how you feel about Dad's past. You haven't said much.'

She put down her hairbrush. 'I'm still taking it in, but it certainly explains a few things. I'm not sure how I feel about something that happened before we met. It hurts that he never told me, yes, but if he were as devastated as you say, then I suppose he wanted to close the door on it completely. I would like to talk to Alan, hear what he can tell me.'

I sighed inwardly. How was I going to tell Alan?

'You've got to tell him, Ol. He's my half-brother, even if he is a miserable bugger.' Mark's voice sounded weaker by the day, and he was finding breathing difficult unless he lay in a certain position.

I frowned. 'He isn't answering my calls.'

'It's been two days already.'

'Obviously, *something's* upset him,' I said. 'But I'll try again tonight, in case he's just been busy.'

Mark closed his eyes wearily for a second. 'Tell him to get over here quickly, eh?'

I looked at him in alarm. 'Are you feeling that bad?'

'Swallow's been a bit worse the last couple of days.'

'And you're only telling me now?' I said, fear gripping me.

'You had enough on your plate with your mum giving you a hard time.'

I sighed. 'At least she's out of my hair now, for a couple of weeks.' Once she'd realized I was okay and determined to do my own thing despite her objections, she and Ron had set off on a tour of the country.

'I like her, though,' Mark said. 'I wonder if Jenny was anything like her.'

'I don't think so,' I said. 'Jenny was more of an arty, hippy type. What do the doctors say about your swallow?'

'Same as always: won't commit themselves. Good job I've got that advance directive drawn up now. They know what I want when the worst happens.'

I put my hand over his motionless one. I hated to think about that day coming, but Mark seemed to have accepted it.

'But it'd be great to see Alan's photos of Jenny and Paul *before I croak*,' he added in a mock-mournful tone.

'It'd be hard to see them after,' I answered. Gallows humour had become our way of coping. 'Enough of the broad hints; one way or another, I'll get something sorted out tonight.'

Chapter Nineteen

'The cellphone you have called is switched off. Please try later,' the female voice intoned for the twelfth time. I'd been ringing Ewan every fifteen minutes for three hours. After the first eight times, I'd phoned Alan and told him about Mark's deterioration. I slipped in what I hoped was a casual enquiry about Ewan, just in case anything was wrong.

'He's fine,' Alan said. 'The exterior of the lodge is almost finished.'

'Has he said anything about me since I was there?'

'Not really. He… uh… what *did* you do to upset him this time, Ollie? He acts oddly every time I mention your name.'

Great. Clearly Ewan didn't intend to talk to me.

My phone rang just as I cut off after my thirteenth attempt.

'Olivia, your phone's a touch busy tonight,' Pastor's voice breezed down the line. 'How are things going with Mark?'

I tried not to let my disappointment show and filled him in on the momentous events of the past few days.

'Incredible,' he said finally. 'I guess it explains a lot. So now you have to tell Ewan and Alan?'

'Yes, except that Ewan won't answer my calls. I'm thinking I'll have to go over to Hokitika and… well… confront him.'

'That sounds a bit intimidating. You want some company?'

'Thing is, I'm going to have to get over there tomorrow, somehow.'

'No problem. I'm in Picton. Just dropped off Steve and Emily at the ferry this evening.'

'Oh,' I said, feeling guilty. I'd been so caught up in all my own problems, I'd forgotten all about that. 'How did it go? Did you manage to convince them you're happy here?'

'I tried, but they didn't believe me. They're sure I'd be happier around family.'

'And you're certain you wouldn't?'

He was silent for a moment. 'I'm not certain of anything much, right now. It's been good to see them. I need to do a bit of thinking.' Before I was able to respond, he added briskly, 'So what time do you want me to come and pick you up? Early, I guess.'

We arranged for him to collect me at six in the morning. It was a relief to know I wouldn't have to go on my own.

Pastor's old car rumbled down Ewan's drive at just gone eleven. The Toyota and the pick-up were parked beside the cabin, but there was no sign of any workers. As we got out of the car, Ewan appeared from inside the lodge. He started in obvious surprise at the sight of us and then just stood waiting, with a forbidding expression, as we approached.

'What can I do for you?' he asked in a cold, hard voice, looking from me to Pastor.

'I've been trying to ring you,' I said.

'I've been busy. Still am.' He was clearly determined to make this as difficult as possible.

'There's something important I need to talk to you about. This is David… Pastor. I mentioned him to you before. He gave me a lift over.'

'You came all the way over from Blenheim just to talk to me? I find that hard to believe.'

'Believe it, mate,' another voice butted in suddenly.

Both Ewan and I turned sharply. 'Mark!' I exclaimed.

Pastor just looked from one to the other of us in complete bemusement.

'This is Mark?' Ewan asked, looking him up and down. 'He hardly looks like he's dying of anything.'

'For God's sake, get that poker out of your backside,' Mark said impatiently. 'I can't believe any brother of mine could be such a miserable bugger.'

'*Brother*? What the hell are you talking about?'

'Mark is your half-brother,' I said. 'Jenny had a baby with my dad.'

'Even if that were true,' Ewan said after a moment's stunned silence. 'I don't quite get how *this* is Mark. You told me he was completely disabled and on a ventilator half the time, but here he is looking like some sort of Greek god, glowing with health.'

'Thanks for the compliment, bro, but I'm not really here. I just came across to make sure you didn't give Ollie a hard time. She needs your help with Alan. Don't let her down – and don't let me down either. I don't have long.'

He faded out, and Ewan stared at the space where he'd been with an expression of horror on his face, which was far pastier than it had been a few moments earlier.

'What the hell?' he whispered, almost to himself. Then, louder, 'Did he just *disappear?*'

'Yep,' I said. 'Like he said, he was never actually here.'

'Why don't we all sit down and maybe have a cool drink?' Pastor suggested, looking towards the cabin.

Ewan, still looking bewildered, shrugged and led the way over.

'What did he mean, *came across?*' He asked as he opened his fridge.

'It's something he's been able to do since he was a child, he says. Out of body. You and I are the only people who've ever been able to see him.'

He took out some cans of drink absently, staring at me. He turned to Pastor. 'So you couldn't see him just now?'

Pastor shook his head. 'It was a real peculiar experience watching you two talk to the empty air, I can tell you.'

'So the other day – that was him I saw with you?'

I nodded. 'He turned up unexpectedly.'

'You were hugging him though. I mean, a *ghost*?'

'He feels real to me. Probably would to you, too. I thought he was real when I first knew him, until Pastor told me there was no one there.'

Ewan passed us each a can and sat down as though his legs wouldn't hold him up any longer.

'So he didn't tell you about the MND?'

I shook my head. 'I didn't know about it until I went to Blenheim.'

'Or about my mum?'

'I only just found out about that. I put two and two together from things your dad said and because you could see Mark, and then Lisa confirmed them.'

'Lisa! She knew?'

I nodded. 'Thing is, your dad knows Jenny was pregnant by my dad, but she told him it was a stillbirth. He has no idea the baby survived. What's more, he didn't want you to know anything about it, and now I've broken his confidence for Mark's sake.'

He took a gulp from his can. 'He thought I'd be bothered about that?'

'He didn't want to spoil your memory of your mum. But now… Mark doesn't have long, and your dad's the best person to talk to him about Jenny. I wanted to tell you first because of what you said about his depression. I'm afraid telling him she abandoned Mark as a baby and lied about it might… well… send him back down. I don't want to do that to him.'

He sipped his drink thoughtfully. 'Would it, though?' he said, mostly to himself. 'He's so much better now, and what's more, he'd be doing Mark a big favour. In a way, maybe it'll make up for his guilt about your dad.'

'That's true,' I agreed, nodding. 'I think Alan might have known my dad better than any of us, even my mum. He's the only one who can really give Mark what he wants, which is all the gen on both his parents.'

Ewan looked at me properly then, making eye contact. 'I'm sorry. I mean about misjudging you again. Like I already told you, I'm a bit prickly when it comes to that sort of thing.'

'Only a bit?' I said with a smile.

'Okay, more than a bit. So it's bad with Mark then, from what he said?'

I nodded. 'He says his swallow is worsening, and he's struggling to breathe unless he lies in bed in a certain position. He doesn't want to go on if he loses the ability to eat or speak, but… I don't like the way his breathing is going, anyway.'

Ewan eyed me with concern. 'This must be really hard for you.' He got up briskly, perhaps realizing that I didn't want to answer. 'Well, if we're going to make a deputation to my dad today, we'll have to get a spurt on.'

He turned to Pastor, who said quickly, 'Don't worry about me. I just wanted to help Olivia get over here, but now I know she's in good hands, I'll head on back home to Manapouri.'

I walked with Pastor to his car while Ewan phoned his dad, although I wasn't sure what reason he planned to give for our unexpected visit.

'I have to say that all this has given me a lot of food for thought,' Pastor said as he started his engine.

'Religious food?' I asked, a little cheekily.

'Well, kinda. It's all very… intriguing, I have to say.'

'Thanks for all your help today, and I'll look you up again next time I'm in Manapouri,' I said, realizing I'd finally forgiven him for Haast.

'You know you have friends there, if you need somewhere to go after…' he trailed off.

I nodded silently and watched him drive away, wondering how soon I was going to need those friends again.

***

Ewan and I were silent for the first few miles to Westport. Neither of us seemed to know what to say to each other. Eventually he sighed and glanced across at me. 'I really am sorry. I feel a total fool now, but I couldn't have known Mark was… a ghost, or whatever.'

I smiled. 'I'll give you that. I wanted to tell you before, but after what happened when Pastor saw me talking to thin air, it didn't seem like a good idea.'

He nodded slowly, and then frowned. 'Despite what I said earlier, I'm a bit worried about how Dad's going to take all of this.'

'Why did you say we were coming?'

'Just something important. To be honest, I copped out of mentioning that you were with me.'

'Ah. That's going to look good then, us turning up together out of the blue,' I said, raising my eyebrows.

'I don't think he'll mind that; he's forever singing your praises.'

'Your mum… the reason she never told him. Will he be able to understand that?'

He sighed. 'I'm not sure I understand it, really. Why did she give Mark up for adoption in the first place?'

I explained as we wound our way to Westport.

'So how come he kept her name, if he was adopted?' he asked.

'His parents felt it was all he had of his real mum. They didn't want to take that away from him as well.'

'They must have been pretty cool parents. Horrible luck to lose them as well.'

'Yeah, I don't think he ever really got over it.'

We pulled into the drive of the house to find Alan cleaning his car. He started visibly when he saw me and stood watching us with a dripping sponge in his hand.

'Something I should know about?' he asked, looking from me to Ewan and back again.

'Nothing like that,' Ewan said, before I had to.

'It's good to see you again,' I said, and gave him a hug.

'So, to what do I owe this visit?' he asked as we followed him into the house.

Ewan looked at me with an enquiring quirk of an eyebrow. 'I've got quite a long story to tell you,' I replied, 'And I'm not really sure where to start.'

'You already know this story?' Alan asked Ewan, who shrugged apologetically.

'Come on then, Ollie, don't keep me in suspense.'

I sat down on the sofa. 'It's about Jenny – and Mark.'

'How'd you mean? I don't get the connection,' Alan said, sitting down beside me. Ewan perched himself on the edge of one of the armchairs and folded his arms.

I swallowed. 'Jenny didn't lose the baby. She… um… she left him in the hospital in Blenheim. Lisa… well, Lisa knew all about it.'

Alan stared at me in horror. '*Left him*? She wouldn't do that… couldn't, surely.' He paused, clearly trying to take it in. 'Are you saying Mark is… Jenny's child?'

I nodded silently.

'But *why* did she leave him? Did Lisa say why?'

'She was scared and confused, and her parents had been pressuring her to have him adopted. There was all the shame as well, times being what they were.'

Alan washed his face in his hands. He looked like he was struggling not to cry, and I gave Ewan a furtive, worried look.

'Mark's keen to see you,' Ewan said to his dad. 'He wants you to tell him all about Mum, and about Paul. He doesn't have long… that's why Ollie had to break your confidence and tell me about Mum.'

'The MND,' Alan said in a whisper. 'But…'

'Mark's surname is Juniper,' I said gently. 'He spent all these years searching for his parents, especially his mum, under that name. It was just a hunch at first, but when you mentioned the song, I started to wonder.'

'Jennifer Juniper,' Alan murmured. 'It all starts to make such horrible sense. Why she used to get so upset; why she'd never talk about that year; why she never wanted to go back to Marlborough; why she drifted away from Lisa.'

'Are you okay, Dad?' Ewan asked in the kindest tone I'd heard from him yet.

'I don't know – don't know what to think. She lied to me through thirty-three years of marriage. That's a lot to take in.'

Ewan and I exchanged worried glances as Alan stared at the floor, head in his hands, looking lost and defeated, but before either of us had a chance to say anything else, he lifted his head decisively. 'Well, I can't do anything about all that right now, but I *can* talk to Mark, so we'd better get going then, eh? You wouldn't have come here like this if it wasn't urgent, and I'll have plenty of time to think it all over later.'

I was relieved, but it was clear that Alan was making a big effort to contain his feelings. I wanted to give him a hug, but my intuition told me it was the wrong time. Any overt display of affection might set him off, and there was no way he'd want to cry in front of Ewan and me.

Chapter Twenty

My sister Olivia Kimpton. Has a kind of ring to it, I think. Not so sure about *my brother Ewan Jensen*, but maybe he has some redeeming characteristics I don't know about yet. I wonder if I'll ever get to meet my other two sisters.

Here's the funny thing: when I was growing up I used to pretend I had a brother and sister. I guess I was a pretty lonely kid. Out there by the Wairau, it was just my mum and dad and me. Not that I didn't have friends, but they all lived in town. I'm not sure if it started because of that, or because I hated to be confined.

I was about six, and in trouble again. I'd built myself a makeshift raft and I was going to sail it down the Wairau – I might have mentioned my adventurous streak? I'd pushed it out and jumped on, and the current began to pull me downstream. I was so excited – I couldn't wait to get out to sea. Then suddenly there was a shout and a splash from the shore and my dad was swimming towards me as fast as I'd ever seen him swim. I thought it was funny when he grabbed the edge of the raft and dragged it back to the riverbank. I stopped laughing when we got there. He was wet through and gasping and choking, trying to get his breath. When he'd stopped coughing, he loomed over me looking the way he often did back then: worried, cross, exasperated, and bewildered.

'What did you think was going to happen when you reached the sea?' he asked. He was controlling his voice, keeping it quiet; I knew he really wanted to shout.

'I wanted to sail out and see the ships,' I answered.

'*Mark*. It's a little raft made of bits of driftwood. It would have broken up before you even got to the sea.'

'I can swim,' I said proudly. 'I'm the best swimmer in my class.'

Dad ran a shaking hand over his forehead. 'But you're only a little boy, and there's a strong current. You'd drown.' He crouched down to look me right in the eye. 'There are some things you can't do; things that are dangerous. Do you understand?'

I didn't really understand, but I nodded slowly and promised never to do it again.

Dad sighed. 'All right, come on, into the house and straight up to your room. I don't want to hear a sound out of you for the rest of the day. You've got to learn.'

He knew how much I hated being indoors; that's why it was always such a handy punishment. My mum and dad never had to hit me or threaten no dinner. All they had to do was confine me to my room. Not that it wasn't a nice room. It was even quite a big room, full of toys. Mum and Dad weren't rich, but they'd inherited the house from my nan and granddad, and my dad had a good job as a manager at the Lake Grassmere saltworks. My mum was a housewife, but she'd been a teacher before they'd adopted me.

I lay down on my bed and sulked. I didn't want to play with any of my toys, not even my action man. The sun was still shining outside, and it was unfair that I was stuck indoors just because I had wanted to have an adventure. Mum and Dad didn't get it; they were boring: always wanting to be quiet, reading or watching telly. With my eyes tightly closed, I went over the fun I could have been having, how the water felt as it splashed in my face; how the raft rocked in the current; how the sun glinted off the rippling waves of the river. Then, without any warning, I was there, *in the water* up to my waist. My raft lay on the beach a few feet away. I walked towards it with no sense of the water around me. I just seemed to drift to the beach, somehow.

I held out my arms and looked at them – the scratches that I'd got earlier when I was finishing the raft were still livid on my left arm. I was wearing the same T-shirt. My skinny brown legs were bare, and I had sandals on my feet. I took a few more steps towards the raft. It felt like walking, but somehow it wasn't. I tried to touch the wood, but my hands just went through it. Now I was getting scared, but it was a kind of excited scared. I went back to the water and walked right into the middle of the river. It swirled over my head, a bit murky. The sun shone through; a few fish swam by. I lifted up my arms and jumped. My head popped out of the water just in time to see my dad heading down to the beach.

I ignored the river and ran across to him as he stood looking down at my raft. He didn't even look up. 'Hey, Dad!' I called out. He took no notice, just sighed deeply and started to chop up the raft with an axe. 'Dad! Don't, please,' I begged him.

Chop, chop, chop.

'Dad! It took me ages to make.'

Dad sighed again and threw the pieces into a sack. I stopped trying to talk to him and just watched, fascinated. Once he'd filled the sack he put it over his shoulder and headed back to the house. I followed him. My mum was in the kitchen cooking our tea.

'Better burn this lot,' Dad said, dumping the sack near the wood stove.

Mum looked at it and shook her head. 'I don't know what gets into him. He could've been killed.'

'That's what I told him, but I'm not sure it got through.'

'I'm here, Mum, can't you see me?' I said, dancing around in front of her.

'Where does he get it from? That's what I wonder,' my dad said as he sat down at the kitchen table.

'Who knows what those parents of his were like. What kind of mother abandons her baby in hospital anyway? Mrs Juniper, indeed – vanishing like that.'

I stopped dancing around. What was she talking about?

'Like they told us, she must have been very troubled.'

'I often think his dad must have been some sort of explorer or adventurer, the way he acts.'

Dad laughed in a sort of hollow way. 'Bit of a contrast to me, then.'

'Aw, don't put yourself down, Ben. He loves you, even if you'd rather plant a tree than go sailing down the Wairau with him.'

'I hope so, but he gave me one hell of a shock today, love.' Dad ran a hand over his forehead again.

Mum looked up at the ceiling. 'Must have tired himself out – not heard a peep out of him.'

I waved my arms about, dancing between them. 'I'm here, Mum!' I shouted. 'Dad, I'm here!'

She turned her back to me and went back to the cooker. Dad opened the paper. They really couldn't see me. I ran upstairs – at least it felt like I was running upstairs. My bedroom door was shut, but my experience with the water made me bold. First I tried an arm, and there was no feeling at all again. I guess you've seen the film *Ghost*? When he goes through a solid object it looks like he can feel something. I can't. I walked through the door as though it wasn't there.

I was still lying on the bed with my eyes tightly shut. I went right up to myself and stared. I poked a finger at my arm, but as with everything else it went right through. Scared, I watched my body breathe and wondered what was happening. Was I stuck like this forever? I don't know how long I stood there watching myself, but my mum's voice suddenly shouted up the stairs, 'Tea's ready!' and there was a sort of whoosh, and I could feel the bed underneath me again.

I opened my eyes and sat up. Everything looked and felt normal, even down to my mum shouting, 'Mark! Get down here or your tea's going to get cold.' What had happened? Had it been a dream?

I ran downstairs, and this time I felt the jolt of each step, and heard the sound of my sandals as they slapped against the wood. When I got into the kitchen there was the sack full of my raft sitting in the corner.

'Mum,' I said, as she put my plate in front of me. 'Who was Mrs Juniper?'

She nearly dropped a plate in her surprise, but my dad lowered his paper and gave me a stern look. 'Were you listening at doors? It's back to your room after tea for you.'

So that's how I found out I was adopted, and when I found out that whatever room I was shut into, I could always get out.

***

They were great though, my mum and dad, even if they didn't understand me. After that, my childhood got a touch more exciting as I learned how to get *out* at will. I could go anywhere I'd already been, just as long as I got the visualisation right. Otherwise I'd end up back at home. The story of all the things I got up to when I was *out* could fill a whole book. I'm sure you can imagine the sort of fun an invisible kid could get up to, when walls and doors are no obstacle. My childhood was all the richer, but I found out some things a bit early, like what mums and dads get up to in the bedroom at night.

When I was twelve I decided I wanted to be a ranger. It happened when Mum and Dad took me on a camping holiday on Stewart Island. It's nearly all a national park, and it was a paradise to me at that age. I loved camping, although my parents didn't, and we spent the two weeks tramping all over the island. We stayed at DOC campgrounds, and whenever we encountered any rangers, I'd run up to them and start pestering them with questions about what they did. It didn't take me long to realize there was no job I'd like more than one that kept me outside and in the bush, so by the time we headed home to Blenheim I knew that was what I wanted to do. It's another thing you and I have in common; I know you'd love it too.

After I went to Uni and got my own motorbike and could go wherever I wanted, I lost interest in being Mr Invisible for a while. Being able to get *out* was great, but I couldn't smell or touch or talk to anyone. Real life was suddenly a lot more interesting. I had too many girlfriends to count, loved my job with the DOC, and spent all my spare time either out tramping, on my motorbike, or messing about in boats.

I guess I was a bit economical with the truth when you asked me about girlfriends – special girlfriends. There *was* one.

Sam had invited me to a party at his house. You've met Sam – he was the guy you talked to at the Fox Glacier DOC office. We were great friends back then and had some fun times when we were out in the back country. Anyway, he'd invited all the rangers and their partners, and I went with Leona. We'd been seeing each other on and off for a couple of months, but we were already getting bored with each other.

The party was for two new rangers, and when Sam introduced me to Francesca Collins, all I saw was this short, mousy girl with incredibly big, scared-looking eyes. At first sight you couldn't imagine less likely ranger material, and I didn't really take much notice of her. Instead, I was preoccupied with the way Leona was flirting with every man there but me. By the time the party was over, so were we. Weirdly, though, later that night when I lay awake in bed, wondering how come the very idea of a 'steady relationship' seemed to be impossible for me, it was Fran's luminous eyes that kept coming into my mind.

I went into a post-Leona phase of wanting nothing to do with women, although you can guess those never lasted very long, but for some reason I kept noticing Fran. She wasn't my usual kind of girlfriend, so I guess you're going to think I was only interested in the good-looking ones. Well, maybe I was, but Fran was attractive, just not in the typical sort of way.

You'd think I'd have been looking for a permanent relationship, wanting to have a family of my own to replace what I'd lost, or make up for what I never had, but the thought of settling down, moving into a suburban house and having kids always scared the pants off me. Whenever I imagined being married or a dad, I'd feel like I was choking. It seems like I was born with this fear of being trapped, and I've often wondered if that's why I have my gift.

There are some very naughty things that the invisible man can get up to, and, I admit, has got up to in the past. Once I was past my teens, being able to watch people in their bedrooms or bathrooms or picking their noses or scratching themselves when they thought they were alone started to sicken me. I guess I developed a bit of a conscience about it – or I just grew up. Still, there were times when I'd get *out* and go to check up on a girlfriend; that she was really doing what she'd said she was doing. Once or twice I'd caught them out, too.

I have to admit that with Fran being so shy, I was interested in what she got up to when she was off work. I wanted to know all I could about her. So just once, I went round to her flat as Mr Invisible. I felt the guiltiest I've ever felt, spying on her while she watched TV, read a book, made herself a salad, drank herb tea. She didn't do anything dramatic or even really interesting but I kind of enjoyed just being around her. She might be shy and a bit timid, but she was, for me anyway, a calming kind of person. She seemed really at ease with herself, and I was curious about how she got to be like that. I wondered what her childhood was like. In other words, I spent a lot of time wondering about Fran, but she was still quite elusive.

A few days later we were working on some fencing together and I asked her where she was from.

'Picton,' she answered.

'Really? I'm from Blenheim,' I said.

So we got talking about Marlborough, and how it had changed since all the vineyards had sprouted up everywhere, and we laughed when we discovered that neither of us even liked wine. That seemed to have broken the ice, so I suggested a trip to the cinema in Hokitika later in the week. It might seem like a long way to go just to see a movie, but you get used to that sort of thing on the West Coast.

We'd really hit it off, so a couple of months later, we went to Alexandra together. We rode the rail trail, cycled twenty kilometres every day and slept under the stars at night. After that, it seemed natural to rent a flat together. I started to think that maybe this was it; I'd found someone I could really stick with at last. Somehow Fran never made me feel suffocated like the others.

It wasn't until we'd been together for two years that several things went wrong at once.

I came out of the shower one night, flexing my arms and rolling my shoulders. Fran was lying in bed, reading.

'What's wrong?' she asked. 'Your arms stiff again?'

'They just feel a bit heavy and tired.'

'Maybe it's old age creeping up on you,' she said with a small laugh. She put her book down and looked at me seriously as I joined her in bed. 'Speaking of old age,' she began, then hesitated, took a deep breath and went on slowly, 'now that I'm thirty-two and we've been together so long, I was wondering how you feel about… well… about our having a baby together.'

It was like getting hit with a sledgehammer. 'A baby?' I said stupidly.

'Yeah, you know, they're those little squalling things that grow up to be people.'

I turned to stare at her. 'You want to start a family?'

She nodded, and then leaned over to kiss me. 'Don't you? You never talk about it.'

'Well, I… guess it wasn't top of my list.'

I realized I'd said the wrong thing as soon as it was out.

'*Top of your list?* Mark, we're talking about something most people want to do: something normal and natural. I know when we met you said you'd never been much of a one for commitments, but I thought you'd changed by now. We're settled, aren't we?'

I nodded slowly. 'Yeah. Of course we are.'

'You don't want to break up?'

'Of course not. But having a baby – it's a big responsibility. It's…'

'A commitment too far?'

I sighed. 'Can I just think about it for a bit?'

She looked disappointed but just nodded. 'Sure. You go ahead and think about it.'

Only I didn't really get much chance to think about it, because when I went to the doctor about the weakness in my arms, he referred me to hospital for tests.

'What's it likely to be?' I asked, imagining something fairly trivial and easily fixed.

'Hard to say at this stage, but your arms are certainly weaker than one would expect.'

I didn't tell Fran about the hospital appointment. I thought there was no point in worrying her with it, because she always had been a bit of a worrier.

When the tests were done and I was told I had to see a specialist, I started to worry myself, but stupidly I still kept it from Fran.

All I can remember about that doctor's office is the pale blue walls. I never have been able to stand that shade of blue since.

The doctor shuffled papers on his desk, cleared his throat, gave me a sincere look and said, 'I'm sorry, but we've had to conclude that you have motor neurone disease. It's unusual to develop it at such a young age, but there are a few cases a year in this country.'

I'd hardly heard of motor neurone disease; I had no idea what it meant. I sat there, aged thirty-one, and listened while the doctor pronounced my death sentence in a calm and impartial voice.

'You'll gradually lose the use of your arms and your legs. The disease rarely affects sight, hearing or intellect, although some people do report heightened emotions. Eventually, speech, swallowing and breathing are affected.'

'How long? How long have I got?' I managed to rasp out, while the world seemed to pulse around me in a sort of crimson haze of rage and despair.

'It's impossible to tell. The usual expectation is no more than four years, but it could be anything from one year to six. The progression is different for everyone.'

'How did I get it? *Why* have I got it?'

The doctor leaned forward and his expression softened. 'Usually there's no known cause. You've reported that you don't know anything about your birth parents, so we can't rule out a genetic element, but that's actually quite rare, in any case.' He lifted his hands in a gesture that was almost an apology. 'The real answer is that we don't know.'

I walked out of there almost unable to breathe. I was barely aware of what I was doing. *Four years*. Four years in which I'd slowly shrink away to a helpless husk. All my fears about being trapped were going to come true in a big way.

I walked for hours, trying to control the panic, fear and anger. I didn't phone Fran; I couldn't have trusted myself to speak without breaking down, and how could I tell her anyway? She wanted to have babies with me, and I was going to be dead before any kid would even get to know me. No, I couldn't stay with Fran, not with all this to deal with. I'd have to make a clean break and pretend it was because I didn't want to be a dad. She was going to hate me, but it was the best thing. I couldn't see any alternative.

I don't think I need to describe the scenes that went on between Fran and me over the next couple of days. I must have played my part really well. I was so numb, I guess I came over as cold as ice. At first she couldn't believe it, then she got angry, and finally she got hurt as hell. I moved out of our flat, but we still had to work together, and that was hard. I watched from the frozen, detached place I'd been living in since the diagnosis as she gave in her notice, packed up and went to live with her parents back in Marlborough.

I tried to carry on working as though nothing had happened, but I'd changed from cheery, happy Mark to bitter, silent Mark. Sam kept asking what was wrong, but I stayed in that dark place for weeks. Not only that, but my arms were getting weaker and it wasn't as if I were in a job where it didn't matter. I didn't want to tell anyone; I knew how they'd react. They knew me as this tall, muscular, fit and healthy guy. They'd be shocked as hell, and then all over me with pity. I was going to have to leave, and soon. Eventually I told Sam, but I made him swear to keep it to himself. Of course, he was horrified. We'd been best friends for years by then. If anyone knew all about me, it was Sam. He'd been really pissed off with me about Fran, but when I told him about the MND, he understood. He didn't approve, but he did understand.

The DOC found me a desk job in Greymouth, and I left Fox Glacier and the job I loved just six months after the diagnosis. I was going to be closer to hospitals and health care, but forced to be indoors an unbearable amount of the time. I still looked the same, but I felt like a shadow of the Mark Juniper that Fran had known. I'd always been happy-go-lucky, not a worrier or a depressive. I felt like I was walking through clouds of lead every day, and not just because my legs were also getting weaker.

I guess I became a bit of a reclusive so-and-so for a while. While my legs still worked, I got out into the back country as often as I could, but I avoided getting too close to anyone. It only dawned on me slowly that self-pity wasn't doing me any good, that it kind of fed on itself and made things worse, and besides, I still had my gift; I could still get *out.* The real me began to creep back, and the heavy grey fog lifted, even though my body was getting steadily weaker. I was going to use my gift like I never had before.

I did the job in Greymouth for eighteen months, but it got to the point when I couldn't even do that any more. That's when I decided to go home, back to the old house in Blenheim.

After that, with carers coming in a few times a day and both my arms and legs too weak for me to do anything on my own, I spent as much time as possible *out* and revived my obsession with my real parents. Things got quite exciting because, as they say, necessity is the mother of invention. All those years I'd been getting *out,* I'd never really experimented with what I could do. From that first day with the raft, I'd assumed I couldn't touch or move anything, but once I was stuck in the house and *out* became more real than in, I wanted to do more. For one thing, how was I going to check through all those records if I couldn't lift a book or turn pages or operate a computer? It was so frustrating to see the electoral rolls lying there but to be unable to access them.

It took a lot of trial and error, but I did eventually learn how to influence objects. It was a case of realizing I didn't really have arms and legs, that I was just a blob of energy, and all I had was thought. My thoughts had to become my muscles. It used up a lot of my physical reserves, but it meant I could carry out my search no matter how many documents I needed to comb through. Even phones and computers became accessible, but phones really whacked me out, so I didn't use those too often. Not to mention that I had to do any real research in the hours when libraries and archives were closed, to avoid scaring the pants off the staff.

***

Remember that day we met? I couldn't get rid of the horrible idea that maybe I'd made you up. Then I thought, if I'd made you up, wouldn't we have made mad, passionate love or something? You're a beautiful woman, but you were giving out enough 'keep off' vibes for even me to notice. Every time I got *out* after that, I was drawn to you. Three times I was tugged off-target, and every time you were there.

I found out how I looked to you that second meeting on the rail trail when you told me you thought I was twenty-five. I hadn't consciously imagined myself any particular age, but when you said that, I realized that one of my best times ever had been when I was twenty-seven, so I told you I was that age, and you accepted it. Remember handing me your phone number on a piece of paper? Our fingers touched and you didn't even blink. You felt real to me and I to you. I held on to the slip of paper for long enough to memorise the number.

I liked you from the start. You're my kind of girl: active, outdoorsy, independent, and gutsy. If it hadn't been for those 'keep off' signs and my being a bit limited as a blob of ectoplasm, I'd definitely have been up for it, but it wasn't your physical charms that drew me as much as the sense that we were comfortable with each other as people. You were fun to be around, even if sex were out of the question. Good job it was, as it turns out.

I'm not sure if you picked up on the similarities in our backgrounds. Both only children, both suffered tragedy at a fairly young age, both looking for something. I guessed you wouldn't admit that you were a seeker, too, but I could sense it. Why else hang around in New Zealand with nowhere to go? You might not have known what you were looking for, but it was driving you, all the same.

I could tell your dad's death was still bothering you by the way you said *motor neurone disease* like it was a poison you wanted to spit out. It was the same way with my search. Knowing you were unwanted when you were just a helpless baby gets to you, even when you fight it and tell yourself, like I've always done, that I had a great upbringing and that my parents loved me. It's just the fact that once, someone thought you were so much dross, and that person is the only living relative you know about.

I bet you can guess now how I found you that job in Manapouri? I was in Invercargill for a look at the electoral roll, but I thought I'd check around, see if I could pick something up for you. I went around the shops and cafés and anywhere else I could think of. I was a bit worn out by the time I got to the last restaurant and bar. I sat down at one of the tables to give myself the illusion of resting, and noticed a man's voice carrying from a couple of tables away.

'Yeah, she's got pretty sick in the past week. I don't know how we're going to manage. I'm going to try Tim, but I'm not sure how he's fixed.'

'Tim doesn't know much about office work,' another male voice said.

'No, but he's family. He'd do it for nothing. The business is just about ticking over, but there's no cash to spare to pay wages.'

I went over to the table. A couple of middle-aged men were enjoying a drink together, one of them nursing his beer a little mournfully.

'Besides, he knows a hell of a lot about boats,' the mournful man continued.

'Yeah, but not much else,' the other man added with a laugh.

Mournful man chuckled in agreement and drained his glass, and they both got up to leave. I followed them. The lengths I go to for you. It wasn't until I'd endured the whole journey to Manapouri in the first man's car, and then listened in on his conversation with his sick wife about what he'd been up to in Invercargill that I had all the information I needed, including the phone number. After all that, I was relieved to get back home; I really needed a rest.

So that's the kind of thing the invisible man can get up to. Handy to have around, eh? When I was looking through those records for you in Wellington, it never occurred to me that I was going to end up finding my own family.

I don't like to worry you too much, but breathing is getting much harder. That's why I'm recording all this while I still have the breath to talk. We both know what's going to happen when it gets past this point. Speaking of which, I had my will drawn up while you were off chasing Ewan down. I've left everything to you. It's not much, but there's the house at least – you could sell it or something.

Chapter Twenty-One

'So, this Ewan, tell me all about him,' my mum said as she smoothed sun cream over her now tanned legs.

I lay back in the sun lounger and squinted up at the deep blue sky. 'What sort of thing do you want to know?'

'Don't be silly, Ollie, you know perfectly well,' she replied, just as Ron made a big splash off the diving board at the other end of the pool.

'You know as much as I do,' I lied.

'You really are so exasperating,' she said. 'I have it on good authority that there's something going on between the two of you. Why don't you just admit it and be done with it?'

'Something going on?' I turned to her and widened my eyes innocently. 'Ewan's gone back to Hokitika – he's hard at work on the lodge. I don't expect any thoughts about me even cross his mind.'

'Hmph. I hope you don't think I'm that much of a fool, my girl.'

'I'm not even sure he likes me very much. He has *issues* with women.'

'What sort of issues?'

'Being dumped sort of issues. His first wife was unfaithful, several times.'

'I see. Well you're hardly that sort, are you?'

'No, but he doesn't see it that way. He thinks all women are like that.'

'So all you have to do is prove to him that they're not.'

'What makes you think I want to prove anything to him?'

She gave me a considering look. 'Mark told me you and Ewan seemed pretty close that day you brought Alan over.'

'Mum, we're just friends, if that. You shouldn't take so much notice of what Mark says.'

It was quite frustrating that Mark seemed to have taken such a liking to my mum, and vice versa, so much so that since she and Ron had returned to Blenheim for their last couple of weeks in the country, she'd been visiting him on her own. Ostensibly she was meant to be telling him all she could about my dad, but clearly their conversation was straying too often into rather different territory.

I was trying to avoid responding to her hints because while Ewan and I were back on friendly terms, there was still a sense of awkwardness between us, and I couldn't see it shifting in a hurry. Besides, although everyone else seemed keen to pair us up, I wasn't sure what my feelings towards him really were.

'I hope those girls get here in time. It would be such a shame if he never got to meet them,' Mum said, changing the subject abruptly. Ewan's sisters were due to arrive at the end of the week.

I sighed. 'I hope so too.'

Alan had stayed for two days and shown Mark as many photos and told him as many tales as he could manage, but then he'd had to return to work. Since then, Mark's breathing had deteriorated a little more, but he was refusing to use the NIV any longer. 'I just don't get on with it,' he insisted, and the doctors and nurses didn't try to persuade him otherwise. He was having difficulty swallowing even the pureed food the hospice provided, but in any case his appetite was very poor. He could still talk, albeit quietly, but he was sleeping half the day. There was a weight in my chest now that wouldn't go away, and a sense of gloom hung over the bright, sunny February days.

I left my mum sunning herself beside the pool and cycled into town. As she pointed out ad nauseam, I didn't have to cycle to the hospice any more, but I always got a bit restless if I didn't take some sort of exercise, and my antipathy towards cars hadn't altered, so to her suppressed irritation I continued to do so most days.

I always had mixed feelings as I approached the hospice. I looked forward to seeing Mark, but I dreaded finding signs of further deterioration, or worse.

He was in his bed, as he always was now, but he was as irrepressibly cheery as ever.

'So, how's your mum today?' he asked.

'She's happy enough – sunbathing by the pool. What about you?'

'No change.'

'Well just make sure you don't croak before this weekend. The least you can do is stick around for the mother of all family gatherings,' I said, using the irreverent banter that we'd slipped into in order to disguise our real feelings.

'Wouldn't miss it,' he said, but his face was pale beneath the grin.

'Have you been *out* lately?'

'Nope. Not enough energy left over.'

I gazed out of his window at the sunny grounds, but there was no way he was up to getting into a wheelchair now. I turned back and noticed that he'd followed my gaze. 'It's hard, eh?' I said.

'Yeah, but I guess I can't complain – I've had my gift all along, which is more than anyone else in my position does.'

I nodded silently and sat down on the chair beside the bed.

'I've made a recording for you – a sort of last words,' he said with a lift of his eyebrows.

'Oh yeah? Any hideous secrets?'

He grinned lopsidedly. 'You'll have to wait to find out.'

'Speaking of secrets,' I said, 'I'd appreciate it if you didn't keep filling my mum's head with talk of Ewan.'

'It's not exactly a *secret* that you two have got the hots for each other,' he said.

'The point is you're giving her ideas,' I said, realizing too late that I hadn't denied his claim. 'Plus, all I've had from Ewan in the past four days is a couple of texts asking how you are.'

'Disappointed?' he asked, leering at me.

'Certainly not. I hardly know him,' I said primly.

'It's called self-delusion,' Mark pointed out. 'Or denial.'

'Will you just stop it. I'll be too embarrassed to look him in the eye this weekend, with you lot making broad hints all over the place.'

'Hmmm. Well, maybe someone needs to push you two in the right direction.'

'Don't you dare.'

He gave me an innocent, wide-eyed look.

'Got any new questions for me?' I asked quickly, in case he planned to pursue the Ewan issue indefinitely.

We were trying to make the most of our time together, combing our way through my family history, analysing everything I could remember. I knew how important it was to him so I'd taken to making notes every time a new memory cropped up. It was hard at times because the memories weren't always good ones. Nevertheless, Mark wanted to know everything about my dad's MND years, for obvious reasons. I often came away drained from these sessions, and oddly, despite having Mark and even my mum and stepdad around, they left me feeling lonely – or at least alone. I suppose what I was missing was a person to talk to about all this, to share having to go through another MND death, another family loss. My mum ought to have been that person, but although we were getting on better these days, there was still a gulf between us as wide as the Cook Strait between the North and South Islands.

Alan was slowly coming to terms with his own side of the story, but as for Ewan… well, he seemed to have gone back into his shell and the safe solitude of the lodge. They were all due at the hospice at the weekend for the party. The staff were helping us with the preparations to make it a special time for Mark.

Saturday dawned with rain, and lots of it. I sipped a cup of coffee as I peered out of the window of the cottage at the Wither Hills, still brown through the grey haze. At least the parched Marlborough earth might finally green up again, but it was a shame that after weeks of baking sunshine the weather chose *this* day to change.

I narrowed my eyes as I spotted movement at the edge of Lisa's grounds, close to one of the vineyards. Surely that was Alan… and Lisa! They were sharing a large umbrella and appeared to be engaged in a very deep discussion.

Alan had arrived last night and was staying in the main house as usual. There had been quite a crowd of us at the table, with Ewan's sisters having arrived in the afternoon and my mum and stepdad still staying in the larger cottage. Only Ewan hadn't been present; he was due at any moment, having decided to drive over in the early morning yet again. I eyed the distant figures speculatively. Could it be that they had gone out for a walk in the rain simply to be alone? *Very interesting.*

I was still watching them surreptitiously when Ewan's Toyota pulled up outside my cottage ten minutes later. He jumped out and then hesitated beside his car as he spotted the two figures still pacing in the grounds. I opened the front door of the cottage, wondering why he hadn't just gone straight to the main house. 'Is that my dad?' he asked, staring in their direction through the rain.

'Uh-huh. They've been out there for a while. You'd better come in. We don't want them to think we're spying on them.'

'So what do you think that's all about?' he asked, as I made him a coffee. 'Did something happen last night?'

I shook my head. 'Not that I know of. It was a good night – everyone seemed to enjoy Lisa's meal, and there was a lot of chatter and banter with your dad and your sisters. I don't know what happened *after that* of course, but not much I should think, with your sisters staying in the house.'

'Hmmm. I stopped off here first just to check how Mark's getting on. Your texts sounded a bit worrying.'

I handed him the cup and sat down on the sofa, biting my lip. 'I don't think…' I swallowed. 'I don't think it's going to be long. This disease is so unpredictable. I mean, sometimes things go very quickly, and sometimes they take months, but his breathing's deteriorated so much since I first got here that it's frightening.'

He sighed. 'I was afraid of that. Have my sisters only just got here in time, do you think?'

I nodded silently. 'Probably. But at least they *are* here.' I deliberately made eye contact with him. 'What about you? How do you feel?'

He shrugged. 'Still a bit shell-shocked, to be honest.'

'Like your dad,' I said, tipping my head to indicate the window.

'Yeah. He's a bit better now, but it's been hard for him to come to terms with everything.'

'Maybe Lisa's helping him with that,' I said. I wasn't about to disclose Lisa's confidence about her youthful interest in his dad.

He frowned, staring into his cup.

'Something else wrong?'

He looked up at me. 'I'm not really looking forward to this, to be honest. Big gatherings are not my favourite thing.'

Wow. Ewan was actually confiding in me. This was a surprise.

'Not even with your own family?'

He looked uncomfortable and then shook his head. 'Never have liked them.' He drank the dregs of his coffee and then got up briskly. Obviously the confidences were over as soon as they'd begun. 'You coming over to the house? I'd better go and see my sisters; it's been a while.'

I nodded, and once he'd unearthed an umbrella from the back of his car we headed companionably together towards the main house, dodging puddles and trying to keep dry under the continuing downpour. We arrived at the front door at the same moment as Alan and Lisa. Ewan greeted his dad in the usual jocular way, but my gaze was drawn to Lisa. I couldn't help noticing that she looked bright-eyed and a little flushed.

By the time we set off in a two-car convoy to the hospice, the rain still showed no sign of letting up. Alan was taking his daughters and Lisa – he'd been keen for her to come, and everyone agreed that it was probably a good idea, since she'd been the only person who'd known about Mark's existence and might have things to tell him – and my mum had somehow inveigled Ewan into her car. I sat in the back next to him, all too aware of his proximity, while my mum, sitting in the front passenger seat as Ron drove, made a point of commenting on my 'stubbornness' in cycling everywhere, even back at home in England.

'She'd get home soaked to the skin so often I was amazed she never came down with anything,' she said, turning to look at Ewan as though expecting him to concur with her that I was a fool and a Luddite. 'And now, even here, she still insists on cycling everywhere. I don't know what the attraction is. Are you a fitness enthusiast, Ewan?'

I glanced aside at him as he licked his lips a little nervously before answering. 'Well, I think it's good to keep fit. I like a good tramp or a swim. I've never been as much of a cyclist, but I can't see anything wrong with it.'

My mum shrugged, looking slightly disappointed. 'Ollie would have us all live without cars, if she could,' she said, and then screwed her head around to look at me. 'But we'd have got pretty wet and cold without them today, wouldn't we?'

I just raised my eyebrows at her, and fortunately Ron turned into the hospice car park before she had the chance to embarrass me with any further tart comments. Ewan looked my way and gave me a brief smile before we piled out of the car into the still-heavy rain and joined Alan and the others to descend on Mark's room.

Mark was lying in his usual position in the bed when we arrived. After the initial introductions, I held back and watched as his two newly-discovered sisters exclaimed over him, and over his marked resemblance to their mother. He grinned with delight as they perched themselves at his side and settled down to tell him anything they thought might interest him about Jenny. Alan joined them while Lisa and my mum busied themselves with the heaps of food they'd brought along for the picnic they'd planned for later. It looked like it would have to be an indoor picnic, whereas they'd originally hoped to spill out onto the small paved area outside Mark's room, but they obviously weren't about to let the rain spoil their efforts. Alan seemed to have relaxed, too, and he laughed as Julia regaled Mark with an anecdote from her childhood.

Somehow I seemed to have gravitated, with Ewan, to the window. It seemed only fair that I remain in the background, but I wished Ewan could feel more at ease with his half-brother. I turned to him as he stared out of the window at the rain. 'Are you okay?'

He nodded and smiled slightly. 'My sisters are keeping Mark well entertained,' he said, with a tilt of his head towards the chattering group around the bed.

I bit my lip. 'I wish… I wish you'd had more of a chance to get to know him. You two do have a few things in common, you know.'

'Maybe,' he said, and then looked at me seriously. 'You say that as though I won't *get* the chance,' he added, very softly to avoid being overheard.

I sighed and looked across at Mark again. He was talking, but I didn't like his pallor or the way he had to gasp for breath after every few words. 'I think you should take whatever chance you have today,' I murmured.

He must have taken my words to heart, because when the rest of us began to dig into the food later, sitting out on the patio, after all – the rain had finally stopped, and the sun had broken through – Ewan went and sat beside Mark. I couldn't help taking furtive looks in their direction and noted that they were having quite an intense conversation.

'Everything all right?' I asked Ewan when he came to get a drink.

He couldn't quite meet my gaze for some reason, and was I imagining a slight flush on his cheeks? 'Fine,' he replied, pouring himself a glass of Lisa's lemonade. 'But I think he's getting tired.'

An hour later, Mark showed serious signs of flagging. 'Hey, I spend half my days asleep now,' he said, forcing a tired grin. 'It's been a long day for me.'

'It's been a good day, though?' I asked him.

'Yeah, Ollie, it's been a great day.'

I put my hand over his. I wanted to say something more – anything, really, to keep him talking and present with me – but there were too many people around, and besides, his eyes were closing with weariness.

We left him to sleep and headed to our respective cars. I felt anxious and uneasy on the journey back to the B&B; I hadn't wanted to leave the hospice at all. There was a nagging fear at the back of my mind that I'd never see Mark again. His voice had been so quiet, his breathing noticeably ragged. I didn't need my intuition to work out that it couldn't be long.

Everyone else was quiet too. Even my mum failed to think up any more examples of my oddities with which to entertain Ewan. 'I think he enjoyed it, don't you?' was all she said to me.

'He loved every minute,' I replied, and Ewan turned to me with a gaze of surprising intensity. What *had* gone on between him and Mark, I wondered.

When we pulled up at the main house, I said I wanted to be alone for a while and headed towards my cottage, but it was still early evening and the sun hadn't yet succumbed to the clouds that were banking on the horizon. I felt too restless and on edge to stay indoors and my usual need to get some exercise, to be out in the open air for a while, surfaced. I grabbed my bike and set off towards the vineyards, but before I'd gone even a kilometre I came across Ewan, who seemed to have had the same idea except on foot.

He actually smiled as I pedalled into view. 'You really *do* love to bike ride, don't you?' he said.

I grinned back and patted the bike seat. 'Best form of transport, as far as I'm concerned.'

He looked up at the sky. 'You going far? Doesn't look like this spell of sunshine will last long.'

I followed his gaze. There were more clouds gathering to the west, and it looked like they were heading our way. 'Probably just a few kilometres,' I said.

'Don't forget there's another big gathering for dinner tonight,' he said, looking as though it was going to be tantamount to torture as far as he was concerned.

I laughed slightly at his obvious discomfiture, and for once he didn't take offence. 'Has your dad given anything away about Lisa?' I asked.

He shook his head. 'But they seem very close.'

I promised I'd return for dinner and headed down the road. This more vulnerable aspect to Ewan was intriguing. I'd already guessed there was a softer person inside, but for some reason he'd decided to let me see it at last.

The sun steamed the rain off the ground, and the air became noticeably humid as I cycled fast down the long, straight roads. I had a strong desire to cycle as far away as possible from what was happening with Mark, but oddly, I found myself cycling *towards* something. The oasis of trees was in front of me before I'd even thought consciously about where I was going.

The house on the Wairau was very quiet, and this time seemed genuinely empty. I wandered from room to room, looking at the pictures of Mark's adoptive family on the walls. As I studied their features, I had a glimpse of how Mark must have felt. He was connected to them yet not connected. It seemed to be human nature to get a kick out of knowing what our blood relatives looked like. That frisson of pleasure we find in wondering what our ancestors did, about their personalities, could never feel quite the same if you were adopted.

Slightly disappointed that there were no hints of any other presence in the house, I checked my watch and decided there was just enough time to take a quick look at the Wairau before I set off back to Lisa's. The usual almost-silence surrounded me as I clambered down the levee and strolled along beside the fast-moving river. There was only the rush of the river gliding between its banks, the calls of water birds and the wind whipping in warm, humid gusts through the nearby trees. The dark clouds that had seemed distant were coming threateningly closer. I ignored them, sat on the bank, slipped off my sandals and dipped my feet into the water.

As I luxuriated in the rush of cold water across my toes, there was a flutter of something yellow just at the edge of my vision; the same sort of glimpse I'd had the last time I'd visited the house. I looked up, startled, as a little girl dressed in palest primrose appeared. She wasn't looking at me; she was laughing to herself as she skipped down the levee. She stopped beside me, gazing at the river and singing breathily to herself. I watched her in complete bemusement, trying to catch the words, until I realized it wasn't a nursery rhyme or a childish song but a familiar pop song from a few years ago.

'I travel alone, and I am free, yeah this is the life, the life for me. There's no one to give me grief and pain, no one to bring me any rain. Yeah, I travel alone and I am free, this is the life, the life for me.'

Without thinking, I joined in the song. 'But there's no one standing by my side, no hand to hold to keep back the tide. So is this the best way for me to be? Is it enough just to be free?'

She stopped at once and stared at me in open-mouthed astonishment.

'Hello,' I said. 'My name's Ollie. What's yours?'

She put a finger in her mouth. She was a pretty child, aged about five, with curly blonde hair framing a serious and solemn face. After a long moment of mutual staring, she said firmly, 'You can't see me.'

I laughed. 'I think I can. Where are you from? Is there anyone with you?'

''Course there's not,' she said with scorn. 'I'm in dreamland – no one can see me in dreamland.'

I became completely still. 'Dreamland, eh? So how do you get to dreamland?'

She gave an exaggerated sigh. 'I close my eyes and think of a nice place, and then I open them, and I'm there.'

Somehow I managed to keep my voice even. 'And is that what happened today?'

She shook her head furiously. '*I* wanted to go on the glacier. In dreamland, I can do whatever I want and I can't hurt myself. The glacier's my favourite place – it's all blue and white and snowy.'

'But today it didn't work out right?'

'No. It was like before when I came to this house and you were here. How can you be in dreamland too? It's *my* dreamland.'

I lifted my feet out of the water. 'What *is* your name?' I tried again, while I slipped on my sandals.

'It's Evie. *Why* are you in my dreamland?' she persisted.

'It's not dreamland, Evie; it's just the world. You're the one who's different. Like in that song you were singing.'

'My mummy sings that all the time. She says it reminds her of my daddy.'

I nodded slowly. 'Where are your mummy and daddy?'

She shrugged, kicking at a stone, which didn't move. 'My mummy's in the garden. I don't know my daddy.'

I had a sudden choking feeling. 'You've never met him?'

She shook her head again, sadly. 'Mummy says I'm just like him, though.'

I tried to take deep breaths. 'Does she? Did he have blond hair?'

Evie nodded vigorously and sat down on the bank beside me. 'He has blond hair and blue eyes, just like me.'

'But your mummy never sees him?'

'No. He went away before I was born.'

'Did she ever tell you his name?'

'Mark. He was called Mark.' She stood up quickly 'I gotta go – Mummy's calling.'

She faded out, just like Mark used to do. *Mark.* I stared at the water swirling between the brown banks until I realized it was pocked with water droplets and I'd better get moving.

I was pedalling furiously through a steady rain when my mobile rang. I got off to answer it, cursing the fact that there was no shelter for miles.

'Is that Olivia?' the familiar voice of one of the hospice nurses asked.

My stomach clenched immediately. 'Yes,' I replied in a voice that was suddenly hoarse.

'I'm afraid Mark's breathing has worsened in the last half an hour. I think it would be best if you got here as soon as possible. He asked for you, and for his brother, Ewan.'

He asked for *Ewan*? At least that meant he could still talk. Hopefully we'd get there in time. 'Okay, we'll be there as soon as we can,' I told the nurse, and I quickly phoned Ewan to tell him.

'I'll come and get you,' Ewan said, wasting no words.

My legs had become inexplicably weak, but I struggled to cycle on until the now-familiar Toyota turned up on the empty vineyard road. I abandoned the bike at the side of the road and Ewan threw me a towel as I jumped into the passenger seat. 'Courtesy of your mum. She said it was "just typical of Ollie to go out cycling in a rainstorm",' he said, giving quite a good impression of my mum's Edinburgh accent.

I smiled in spite of myself. 'You told them?'

He nodded. 'I don't know why Mark asked for me, though. It's not as if I've really had much time to bond with him, not the way my dad and your mum have done.'

I rubbed my hair with the towel. I was shivering, and not just because I was cold and wet. 'Do you think they'd prefer to be there?'

He shook his head. 'I think they'd all rather remember things the way they were this afternoon.' He looked across at me. 'How are you doing?'

'I'm scared… and I'm going to miss him so much.'

He put out his hand and squeezed mine briefly. I started with surprise and then shivered again. I hoped we were going to get there in time.

Ewan pulled up right outside the door of the hospice, and I ran in, my soaking wet clothes flapping awkwardly around me. The same nurse who'd phoned me took me down to Mark's room. 'He's comfortable, but his breathing continues to deteriorate.'

'He can still talk?'

She nodded. 'But only with difficulty. He won't have the NIV, which would obviously prolong his life.' She stopped in the corridor just a short distance from Mark's room. 'To be honest, I think he's *decided* to go now.' She patted me on the arm and left me to enter the room alone.

I took a deep breath and fought back my tears before I pushed open the door. He was lying in just the same position as before but with a bluish tinge to his skin and lips. Even so, he opened weary eyes as I entered.

'You're wet,' he said.

I couldn't help but laugh. 'I just cycled to your house and got caught in the rain,' I said. 'Mark, listen, there's something I need to tell you about that.'

'Not much time,' he mumbled. 'Where's Ewan?'

I didn't have to answer because Ewan entered the door at that moment.

'Glad you could make it, Bro,' Mark said.

Ewan nodded and stood at the bedside with his hands in his pockets, looking ill at ease. He might not have felt he belonged there, but I was secretly glad he was around.

'Listen, Ollie,' Mark said. 'I've had a great day, with all my *family* around me. You did manage to fulfil my dying wish.' He grinned weakly. 'Took a while, but you did it.'

I bit my lip. 'I need to tell you about what happened at the house,' I repeated. 'Mark, did you ever –?' I stopped sharply as a doctor entered and started carrying out checks.

'You're *sure* you don't want assisted breathing?' he asked Mark, frowning down at the various readouts.

'Nah, I'll be right,' Mark replied, so quietly that Ewan and I leaned forward to catch his words.

Once the doctor had gone, Mark fixed us both with a firm gaze. 'Listen up, you two,' he said, taking hard gasps for air between each word. 'These are gonna be my famous last words.' He looked at Ewan and then back at me. 'Like I told Ewan this afternoon, you two should get it together. Seriously.'

Ewan glanced at me with an expression of embarrassment, and I gave a small, awkward laugh. 'Thanks for the advice,' I said as lightly as I could. 'Mark, I really –'

I stopped in alarm as Mark's eyes closed, and his breathing seemed to pause for a moment. His lips were bluer than ever. I grabbed his hand and held it between both of mine. 'Mark?'

His eyes opened again, slowly, wearily, as though it took all his energy. 'Thanks for being my sister,' he gasped out in a near-whisper.

'That's two lots of famous last words,' I said, squeezing his hand tightly. His mouth twitched as he tried to grin. He seemed to be barely breathing at all.

'I need to tell you…' I trailed off again as his eyes dropped shut, and his breathing stopped. 'Mark?' My voice shook, and I clutched his hand tightly, as though by doing so I could keep him with me. There was another breath and another flutter of his eyelids. I had no *time*, damn it. With tears running down my cheeks, I leaned over and whispered into his ear. 'Thank you for being my brother.'

His eyelids fluttered again as though he'd heard me, but his breaths were becoming less and less frequent, and he seemed to be slipping into unconsciousness. I clung on to his hand, crying mutely, and Ewan stood silently at my side until the tiny, shallow breaths finally stopped altogether. 'I think he's gone,' I murmured huskily. A few moments later, the doctor came in and confirmed it.

I wasn't sure what to do. I just sat there, still holding Mark's hand that had been just as inert alive as it was now, dead. I couldn't help recalling the way things were with my dad all those years ago, but above all I was frustrated that I hadn't been able to tell Mark about Evie before he died. That surely would have meant a lot to him, even if he had had no idea.

I felt a hand on my shoulder and turned to look up at Ewan through a blur of tears. His expression was a combination of sadness, confusion and sympathy. 'Maybe I should phone Dad,' he said gently.

I nodded. 'Yeah,' I said, wiping the tears off my cheeks even as they continued to fall. 'Yeah, better tell them.'

He went out of the room to make the call and, finally alone, I leaned my head on the bed and sobbed.

Ewan returned a few minutes later, by which time I was trying hard to compose myself. He regarded me with concern. 'Your mum wanted to know if she should come, but I said no. I hope that was right?'

I nodded. There hadn't been a time since I was a little girl that I'd actually sought comfort from my mum. 'How did your dad take it?'

'He's upset of course, but he's more worried about you.'

I looked up at him. 'I'll be all right. The worst thing is… there was something really important I had to tell him, and I never got the chance.'

'The thing that happened at the house?'

I nodded numbly, not really wanting to explain yet another 'ghostly' presence.

'Maybe we should go, eh?' Ewan said. 'You're pale, and your clothes are still wet.'

The hospice was warm, but I shivered. I'd forgotten all about my wet clothes. 'Yeah, maybe we should go,' I murmured.

I stood up a little shakily, and Ewan put his hand out to me. I took it gratefully and looked back at the still form in the bed.

Goodbye, big brother.

Chapter Twenty-Two

I woke late the next morning with a sense that something important was missing from the world, and then the memory flooded back. I turned over and hugged my pillow. *At least he went the way he chose,* I told myself, as a few more tears crept out under my eyelids.

There was a hesitant knock at the cottage door, and Alan's voice said, 'Ollie? Are you awake?'

I wiped my eyes quickly and pulled on my dressing gown before opening the door. Alan looked me up and down. 'Are you OK? Did you sleep?'

I nodded. 'What about you?'

'Kind of. D'you want a cup of coffee?' He headed over to the kitchen area before I had a chance to answer. 'Your mum's gone to the hospice to pick up Mark's effects. We didn't think you'd want to do it.'

'Oh,' I said, sitting on the edge of the bed. 'I hadn't even thought about that.'

'It's given her something to do,' he said with a small smile. 'I think she feels a bit helpless.'

I couldn't imagine my tower-of-strength mum helpless, but it *was* the second MND death she'd had to see me through, never mind having all her own bad memories revived.

'What about Carol and Julia – and Ewan? Where are they?' I asked.

'They've all gone out for a bit of a tramp around the vineyards. Lisa's catching up on her gardening,' Alan replied as he busied himself making two cups of instant coffee.

'You and Lisa seem to be getting quite close,' I said, deliberately steering the subject away from Mark.

He handed me a cup and sat beside me on the bed. 'Well, maybe. We've been doing a lot of talking this last couple of days.'

'Just talking?' I asked cheekily, raising my eyebrows.

'*Just talking,*' he replied firmly. 'She's told me… well, she's told me how she used to feel about me back then, when we were at Haast. She said she'd already mentioned it to you.'

I nodded slowly, sipping my coffee.

'Anyway, if we're really going to talk about relationships, how about you and Ewan?'

'Me and Ewan?' I said in an innocent tone.

'The pair of you looked pretty close last night.' He stopped suddenly, staring down at his coffee for a second before looking back up at me. 'I'm guessing you don't want to talk about what happened?'

When we'd got back from the hospice, we'd given a brief outline of events, but I was shivering so much that I'd left Ewan to it and headed to the cottage for a hot shower. My mum had come over later to check up on me, but by then I was so weary from crying that I was already dozing off.

'Ewan didn't tell you?' I asked.

'Only the bare minimum. He's been a bit quiet ever since.'

I sighed. 'Well, Mark did have an ulterior motive for getting Ewan to his deathbed, but if I tell you, you mustn't give me away.'

He raised his eyebrows. 'Okay. I think.'

'Mark wanted to tell us both that we should get together.'

He exhaled sharply. 'That must have been a bit awkward.'

I shrugged. 'Ewan didn't seem as bothered as I'd have expected, but apparently Mark had already brought it up in the afternoon.'

'Hmmm. That might explain Ewan's odd mood this morning. Maybe his walk with his sisters will settle him down.'

I put down my empty cup. 'There's something else – something that happened before Mark died,' I said. 'And there are things about Mark you don't know.'

'Go on,' he said encouragingly.

I outlined Mark's gift and how we'd really met. 'So you really are psychic,' he murmured finally. 'Just not quite the way I thought.'

I smiled sadly. 'I don't see dead people. I assume if I could, I'd have seen Mark by now.'

He gave me a keen look. 'There's been nothing at all?'

I shook my head. 'I've been hoping he'll just turn up like he used to, but no, nothing so far.'

I told him what had happened when Pastor took me to the lodge to confront Ewan, and he laughed. 'Good grief! And I knew nothing about any of this – Ewan thinking you were having an affair, indeed. No wonder he got so moody after that couple of days at the lodge.'

I nodded. 'But now there's another complication to the story. It looks like Mark had a child he never knew about.'

He gasped. 'Wouldn't that be a bit like history repeating itself?'

I nodded soberly and outlined my experiences at the house by the Wairau. 'I tried to tell Mark last night. I wanted him to know before he died, but everything happened so fast that I just couldn't, and now…' I'd started to sob without realizing it. 'He'll never know. He had a daughter, and he'll never know.'

Alan put his arms around me and let me cry on his shoulder. Amid all the pain of loss, Evie's story hurt the most. Mark would have wanted to know he'd fathered a child, and maybe he'd have guessed who the mother was. I didn't believe he'd known about it already; there was no way he would have allowed his own child to grow up without knowing her father. I wished so badly that I'd been able to pass on that last message.

When my tears finally eased, I sat back, wiping my eyes. 'Sorry about that,' I said, still sniffing.

'Don't be – I'm glad to help.' Alan suddenly sat straighter and stared at me. 'My God, I've just realized. This Evie, she'd be Jenny's granddaughter.'

I nodded. 'And I've got to find her. Somehow.'

'Do you want me to book your flight for you?' my mum asked.

'No!' I said, more strongly than I'd meant to. 'I'm staying in New Zealand until my six months are up.' That was one thing I'd decided for certain.

'Is that really a good idea? Wouldn't it be better to make a clean break now? You know you can stay with us until you get back on your feet, and you'll have Mark's house to sell, so you might be able to put down a deposit on something of your own back at home.'

I cringed inwardly at the future being mapped out for me. Back to the call centre, back to a small flat, back to boredom. With New Zealand house prices a lot lower than those in the UK, even if I sold the house by the Wairau, I wouldn't have enough to buy a house or flat outright at home, unless it was minuscule. And whatever else my months in New Zealand might have been, they hadn't been boring.

It was the day after the funeral, and my mum was packing; she and Ron were due to fly home late the next day. Alan and Ewan would also be leaving – Ewan was keen to get back to the lodge after a several-day unavoidable hiatus, and Alan was taking his daughters to Christchurch airport and heading back to the West Coast from there. He'd offered to take me with him, saying he'd be happy to have me to stay for as long as I'd like, but I'd decided to stay on in Mark's house while I sorted out my thoughts and feelings – and, yes, my own plans for the future, in which call centres certainly played no part.

Since the night Mark died, Ewan's attitude towards me had been a sort of careful but distant concern. Maybe he regretted revealing his caring side at the hospice, but I couldn't break through such a hefty wall of reserve in my current fragile state. I wondered if Mark's attempt to get us together had actually done us more harm than good. If Ewan was awkward around me, I was also uncomfortable around him.

'Let's leave it for now, eh, Mum?' I said as kindly as I could. 'There's a couple of things I just want to clear up – and I need to decide about the house.'

'You're seriously going to stay there on your own?'

I sighed. 'Just for a few days. I can't impose on Lisa any longer.' I was also hoping that Evie might turn up and I could winkle some information out of her.

'I don't like to think of you alone out there in the wilds,' Mum said, pressing her lips together. She turned and scrutinised me carefully. 'Does this reluctance to leave the country have anything to do with Ewan, by any chance?'

I shook my head vigorously. 'I've told you before, we're just friends. I don't want to leave the country because I love it here. To be completely honest, I really don't want to go back to the UK at all.'

She continued to stare at me, so intently that it seemed she was trying to see inside me, and then she sat down on the bed suddenly, shaking her head.

'By the time he died, your dad was a defeated man,' she said. 'After all this, I have a bit more of an idea why, and maybe I held him back, made things worse.' She lifted her arms in a hopeless gesture and then reached for my hand, pressing it to emphasise her words. 'If staying here is *really* what you want, if it's that important to you, then fight for it, my girl. And if Ewan Jensen is a part of what you want, then fight for him too. Because I think he wants you. And for what it's worth, I think he'd be good for you.'

I watched in stunned silence as she released my hand, got back up and smoothed out a jumper at the top of her suitcase.

'What makes you think he wants me?' I finally managed to utter in a strangled voice.

She shook her head. 'It's right there in front of you, if you'll only look.'

So now my mum was agreeing with Alan and Mark. Why didn't I see it, whatever 'it' was? And quite apart from that, what had come over my mum?

'Have you thought about getting tested for the MND gene?' she asked in a completely different tone as she zipped up her suitcase.

I sank down on to the bed. I'd been avoiding this problem ever since I realized Mark's MND was probably genetic, but there was no escaping the fact that I was now potentially at risk of developing the disease myself. Mark had had a test for the SOD1 genetic mutation once he'd become aware of the family history, but the results weren't in yet. The problem was that whether his result was positive or negative, I might or might not still be carrying a faulty gene. Maybe I wasn't a carrier of the SOD1 mutation, or maybe I carried it but would never develop MND. On the other hand, Mark's test might be negative for SOD1, but all that meant was his genetic mutation was probably on a gene they couldn't test for yet. What was a person supposed to do when presented with that sort of a picture? Doing nothing seemed like a better option than doing something, because whatever the result, there would be nothing I could do about it. There is no preventative treatment for motor neurone disease.

'The doctors are going to let me know when the result of Mark's test come in. I'll make a final decision on what to do after that,' I said firmly.

'It's your call,' Mum said, and I stared back at her, wondering if some sort of alien duplicate had temporary use of her body.

A little later, I was in my cottage getting ready for Lisa's final sumptuous evening meal when there was a tap at the door. I slipped on my sandals quickly before opening it, and to my surprise found Ewan standing there. I stepped back silently to let him in.

'I um, well… I thought I ought to… I won't get the chance after tonight,' he said, perching himself awkwardly on the only chair and looking everywhere in the room except at me.

'You thought you ought to…?' I prompted.

'I want to clear things up between us. Your mum's just been telling me you'll be heading back to the UK as soon as you've sorted things out about the house.'

I folded my arms. 'Has she?'

He nodded. 'She says she and Ron are going to put you up until you find a job, and you're going to buy a flat back in the UK with the proceeds of the Wairau house.'

What *was* she up to?

'She seems to think you can't wait to leave the country now that… well, Mark…'

I sat down on the bed, facing him. 'I… um… I'm sorry about Mark – I mean, what he said. It really wasn't any of my doing,' I said.

'I didn't think it was,' he murmured, looking at the floor.

'Has your dad said anything about him and Lisa?' I asked, trying to ease the tension.

He laughed slightly. 'Not as such, but I think things are reaching a climax there.'

'What, a getting together sort of climax?'

He shrugged. 'I reckon. They seem very close. Of course Dad's going to be cautious, because he's still grieving for Mum, but…' he nodded slowly, 'I think she's right for him.'

'How do your sisters feel?'

'It's harder for them, I guess, because they haven't been here to see how depressed and lonely he was before, but they're coming around to the idea.'

'So what was it you wanted to clear up with me?' I asked, realizing we'd somehow managed to skirt around it.

He finally met my gaze. 'Damn it, Ollie, I don't want you to go!'

I stared at him while my stomach did odd somersaults. 'Well,' I said, my voice a little husky, 'I don't want to leave either.'

He exhaled sharply. 'So your mum…?'

'Is playing games.'

He laughed, and it was a genuine, amused laugh without the restraint I'd come to expect from him. 'I'm sorry about the way I've treated you up to now,' he said. 'It's not easy for me to trust a woman, least of all one who looks the way you do. When we first met, I was sure… well, I was sure you were another Natalie.'

I grinned. 'If you're talking about the actual day we met, you sent me away with a flea in my ear.'

He looked embarrassed. 'I just couldn't get that idea out of my head, and then everything that happened afterwards seemed to confirm it.'

'It would be nice to…' I started to say, and then hesitated.

'Go on.'

'Well, it would be good to get to know the real you,' I said. 'And I'll be staying with your dad for a while, after I've cleared things up here.'

'Dad *knew* that?' he exploded. 'He just sat there nodding while your mum told me you were off home. It's a conspiracy, that's what it is.'

He was actually smiling, and I laughed, and abruptly, without any conscious intention on my part at least, we were standing facing each other. He looked so much more attractive when he wasn't scowling. A lock of dark hair flopped over his forehead, and I had an urge to brush it back upwards, but instead we just stared at one another for a moment, and then my mum's voice called outside.

'Ollie? Aren't you ready? We're all waiting to start dinner. And do you have any idea where Ewan is?'

The moment of almost-intimacy was broken.

'Won't be a minute,' I said, flustered.

'Hurry up then – Lisa's gone to a lot of trouble.'

'Lisa always goes to a lot of trouble,' I murmured as my mum's footsteps crunched away on the gravel path to the main house.

Ewan smiled. 'And we both know who it's really for.'

'What's the betting my mum guessed you were in here anyway,' I said, and I went into the bathroom to splash some cold water onto my flushed cheeks.

'Well, if she did, there's no point in us making an effort to arrive separately.'

'No point at all. We might as well brazen it out.'

All eyes were on us as we walked into Lisa's dining room, but I wasn't ready to give my mum the satisfaction of knowing her strategy had worked, and obviously Ewan had the same idea, as neither he nor I showed any outward sign of a thaw in our relationship over the lengthy and delicious meal. Besides, my attention was on the body language between Alan and Lisa, and by the time I headed back to my cottage a few hours later, I was sure they were close to becoming an item.

CHAPTER TWENTY-THREE

The following morning, as everyone prepared to depart on their various journeys, my mum managed to catch me in my cottage.

'So did you heed my advice?' she asked, giving me an appraising look.

I raised my eyebrows. 'I didn't really need to after you gave Ewan false information about my plans.'

'Someone had to do it,' she said in an unrepentant tone. 'It did the trick, didn't it?'

I laughed. 'Well, we're proper friends now, at least.'

'That's a start, I suppose.' She sounded slightly disappointed. What had she expected? That we'd have a night of passion together?

'I really hate to think of you all alone in that big old house,' she said. '*Are* you going to sell it?'

I bit my lip. 'I don't know yet. I suppose so, but it seems a shame. It's a last link to Mark.' I hadn't admitted it to anyone, but I was still harbouring the idea that if I were going to see Mark again, it would be there. And there was still Evie, although I'd told only Alan about her.

By some devious means, in the round of who was doing what, Ewan was deputed to transport me to the Wairau house, so the two of us, along with Lisa, waited at The Cedars to see everyone else off.

My mum and Ron were the first to leave, my mum still exhorting me to keep my stay at the house as brief as possible, and to consider very seriously what I wanted to do with my life. Once we'd waved them off, Alan gave me a hug and told me he expected me at Westport within a week or so, and to let me know how things went. Ewan and the girls exchanged deliberately noisy goodbyes while Alan hugged Lisa, and then the three of us watched as Alan's car disappeared down the vineyard road.

Lisa sighed. 'It's going to be *very* quiet around here after all this.'

'I'll come over from Mark's house to see you,' I said, and she gave me a grateful smile.

'I've got new guests coming in a couple of days, so I'll be kept busy,' she said briskly, but her gaze was drawn to the distant dot that was Alan's car. She really did have it bad. I hoped Alan knew how badly.

'We'd better get going,' Ewan said, and I thrust my backpack and a couple of bags, the sum of my New Zealand possessions, into the back of his car.

I thanked Lisa for everything she'd done – and I had a lot more to thank her for than I could have realized I would when I arrived – and hopped into the Toyota. For once I wasn't dreading being alone with Ewan.

'I think we were manoeuvred into this, don't you?' he said as he set off through the vineyards. 'I don't know what they all think happened yesterday, but I've been fielding some very intrusive questions.'

I chuckled. 'My mum seemed disappointed that we didn't spend the night together.'

As soon as I'd said it, I wondered if he'd think me too bold, but instead he grinned and raised his eyebrows. 'You only needed to say.'

I blushed and turned to look out of the window at the familiar rows of vines. The grapes were visible now, although still months away from ripening.

'So do you have any ideas on what you're going to do now?' Ewan asked gently after a couple of minutes' silence.

I chewed my lip. 'There is a thought that's been creeping up on me for a while. I've always felt a bit of a second-class citizen because I didn't go to university. It's meant I could only go for certain jobs, and those weren't much to my taste. So I'm wondering if I could study here, maybe at the University of Otago, where Mark went. If I sell the Wairau house, I ought to be able to fund myself. I could go back to the UK and do it, but I'd far rather stay here.'

He nodded slowly. 'What would you study?'

'That's easy: something to do with wildlife.'

He gave a wry laugh, and I turned to look at him in surprised irritation. 'It's okay,' he said quickly. 'I'm not laughing at you, but at myself. I really got you wrong, didn't I? I never would have put you down as an outdoor girl, although the cycling should have given me a clue. I couldn't believe it when you got stuck into the deck at the lodge.'

I grinned. 'I have to admit I enjoyed seeing the look on your face that day. Not to mention the moment when Mark turned up and told you to get the poker out of your backside.'

'Well I'm glad you found my discomfiture so amusing,' he said dryly. 'I don't think I'll ever get over the sight of Mark disappearing right in front of me.'

I sighed, wishing, for once, that I really *could* see dead people.

'Is this a good time to be alone? Why do you really want to stay at the Wairau house?' Ewan asked, obviously guessing the direction of my thoughts.

'I just need time to think a few things through,' I said carefully. After being wary around him for so long, I couldn't just open up and tell him all my thoughts and feelings. I was still unsure of where we really stood. He'd said he didn't want me to leave, which I took to mean he cared about me, but I couldn't be completely relaxed with him – not yet.

'So where do *we* go from here?' he asked as the tarmac turned to gravel track.

'I'll be in Westport in a few days. I assume you're going to visit your dad at some point?' I answered with a flash of humour.

He laughed softly. 'I assume I am.' He raised his eyebrows in a slightly suggestive manner.

Once we arrived at the house, Ewan hesitated by the door. For a change, he didn't seem to be in a hurry to go anywhere.

'So I'll probably see you at the weekend then,' he said.

I nodded. 'Just let me know if you need any help with the lodge.'

'I always need help with the lodge,' he replied with a smile.

I moved closer to him. 'Well in that case, I'll have to see if your dad's free to bring me down.'

He reached out a hand and touched my arm gently. 'I'm out of practice at all this. It's been a long time.'

Tentatively, I put my arms around him. When he didn't protest, I pressed closer and lifted my face to his.

'I'd forgotten what it felt like,' he said softly, and he kissed me gently at first, then groaned as I slipped my arms around his neck and kissed him back with some passion.

When we separated, he gave me a bemused look. 'If only I'd known you felt like this last night,' he said and raised his eyebrows again.

I smiled. 'That would have given my mum far too much satisfaction.'

He smiled back and then pulled me closer again, for another long, slow, kiss that I didn't want to end. Or rather wished would become something more. When we pulled apart, we were both breathing heavily.

'Damn, I have to go,' he said, looking at his watch. 'I have a meeting with some solar panel suppliers this afternoon.'

The errant lock of hair was falling over his forehead again. This time I risked it and put my hand up to smooth it back into place. Ewan dragged himself away with a gusty sigh. 'I'll phone you later, if that's okay,' he said.

I nodded silently and followed him out on to the veranda. He brushed my hand briefly and ran quickly down the steps of the veranda as though if he didn't, he'd never leave. I watched the Toyota nose its way down the drive and then stood motionless on the veranda, feeling more intensely lonely than I had since that evening on the beach in Hokitika.

Back in the house, I distracted myself by pottering about, tidying odd things here and there. Eventually I settled edgily on the sofa and looked through a set of photo albums that showed Mark growing up, becoming a teenager and finally a grinning man in his early twenties. Then the photos suddenly came to an end, the last album only half full. As I closed the book, a couple of loose newspaper cuttings slipped out of the back. I picked them up from the floor and realized they showed the same smiling, happy couple that had graced the family photos. One detailed the car accident that had killed them, and the other was a joint obituary. I sighed sadly as I returned them to the album and put it back in a desk drawer.

My gaze was drawn to a bag lying on the desk. It contained Mark's final effects from the hospice, but although my mum had given it to me a week ago, I still hadn't looked inside. Now I gritted my teeth and opened it. There were toiletries, his wallet, a couple of pairs of jeans and t-shirts, a few documents, and lastly a small, old-fashioned, voice activated cassette recorder. *Of course*, he'd mentioned making a tape for me. He'd even hinted that there was something important on the tape, so I owed it to him to listen, even if it was painful. I picked up the tape recorder, lay down on the sofa, pressed play and listened to him talk to me in the faint voice that had been all he could manage in the final couple of weeks.

When the tape finished I continued to lie there with my eyes closed, just letting what I'd learned sift through my mind. *Fran*. He'd never mentioned her, never given any clue that there had been someone he really cared about in his past. On one of our first meetings, he'd even made a point of saying there was no one special. *And now this*. Would she still be in Picton? If so, maybe I could find her, tell her what had happened, and how he'd really felt about her.

'Why are you in my dreamland *again*?' Evie's voice demanded from close quarters.

I opened my eyes abruptly. She was leaning over me with her hands fisted on her hips, wearing a pink T-shirt and jeans. 'I'm here *again*, and I wanted to be at the lake.'

I sat up. 'Sorry about that, but I didn't make it happen on purpose.'

'Is this your house?' she asked.

'No, it's Mark's house.'

She sucked her finger for a moment and then took it out and stared at me. 'My daddy's name was Mark.'

I nodded. 'I know it was. This was your daddy's house.'

She looked around her with more interest, wide-eyed. 'Did you know my daddy?'

'Yes, I knew him very well.'

'Was he nice? Mummy said he couldn't deal with 'mitments. What's 'mitments?'

I sighed. 'It's commitments. It means he couldn't stick with something, like staying with your mummy, but there was a reason. Yes, he was nice, but he was ill.'

'My mummy's not very well. She gets really tired 'cos she can't sleep.'

I bit my lip. 'Is your mummy's name Fran?'

She nodded vigorously. 'Do you know her, too?'

'Not yet, but I think I'll be coming to visit soon.'

'But you're in dreamland,' Evie said in a confused tone. 'Mummy doesn't come to dreamland.'

I sat up and regarded her seriously. 'Have you ever told your mummy about dreamland?'

'Yes,' she said hesitantly, 'but she doesn't think it's real.'

'Evie, you need to remember that dreamland is the real world, and you're the invisible one. Only people like you and your daddy can do it. It's a special gift.' I hoped fervently that she would never come to need it as Mark had.

'But then why are you in it, and why isn't my daddy here?'

I tried to explain, but I could see she was just becoming more confused. It was a bit too much to expect a five year old to appreciate such complicated concepts.

Evie frowned and sucked her finger again. 'So who was the man?'

'What man?' I asked, staring at her.

'The man who came the day it rained and rained.'

I took a deep breath. 'What did he look like?'

'He was really tall and his hair was blond.'

'Did he have blue eyes?'

She nodded solemnly. 'I'd tried to go to the glacier, but then I was on this beach, and the man was paddling in the water. He said hello to me, so I asked him why he was in my dreamland. He laughed and said he'd been sick and he didn't know. Then he asked me my name and things. When I said my mummy's name was Fran, he looked funny and sad, but then he said to take care of my mummy, and he was glad he'd met me. Then he started to go fuzzy, and he got fuzzier and fuzzier, then, poof, he was gone.'

I put my hands to my mouth as tears ran down my cheeks. Evie stared. 'Why are you sad? Do you know who the man was?'

'Yes, I know who he was,' I croaked, swiping uselessly at the tears. 'That was your daddy.'

***

I phoned Alan as soon as I guessed he'd be home and told him the whole story.

'It was *the* beach,' I said, fighting back more tears. I'd spent so much of the afternoon crying that my eyes were sore. 'The dream beach. I got Evie to describe it, and it couldn't have been anywhere else.'

'So he knew at the end, after all.'

'Yes. It must have been his last burst of energy. His last trip *out.*'

'I guess so. Ollie, are you okay? I don't like to sound like your mum, but you probably shouldn't be alone right now.'

'I'll be all right,' I said, belying that with another sniff. 'I won't be here on my own tomorrow – I'm going to try and find Fran.'

'Are you sure that's a good idea? Will she even want to know?'

'I think she should know the real reason why Mark split up with her. As it is, she's still thinking the worst about him,' I said. 'And wouldn't it be better if Evie knew more about her dad? And on top of that, there's the MND problem.' Evie, like me, was at risk, now that we knew it was probably familial.

'Isn't ignorance bliss? You should know better than anyone.'

I sighed. 'Yeah, I should. It's hard to have that fear at the back of your mind. I never had it before, because we had no clue that it might be genetic. But yeah, it's true, you do start wondering if every little ache or pain or bit of weakness or stiffness means something ominous, and I have had some darker moments since I found out. But which is worse, knowing who your dad was and what happened to him even if it's hard to live with, or not knowing anything about him? There's only one answer Mark would give to that.'

'So how are you going to find her?'

'Evie didn't know the address, so I'll try to find her the same way I found you and Ewan, by searching the electoral register. I'll go to Blenheim library in the morning.'

***

I had thought I might betray my principles and use Mark's car to drive to Picton, but it turned out to have a flat battery after two years of sitting idle, so instead I caught the Tranzcoastal train from Blenheim to Picton.

The train approached Picton through heavy, ominous clouds that only darkened as we pulled into the station. I hurried to find the address I'd obtained in Blenheim library – fortunately for me, Fran's surname had remained the same – but Picton was in the throes of a ferocious gale. The palm trees writhed, dust slammed into my face and anything not tied down was being flung into the air. In the deserted main shopping street, the shops and cafés were almost empty and many had even closed. An advertising board blew over and hit me on the calf, and I screeched in momentary pain and surprise. This was definitely not the best of days to be at large in Picton. I staggered up a hill against the wind and noticed one of the ferries struggling into the harbour far below. I didn't envy anyone taking the return journey.

Fran's house was a small one near the top of the hill. It was fronted by a neat garden, full of bright flowers. Like me, they were being thoroughly battered under the wind's onslaught. I rang the bell, feeling a little apprehensive.

The woman who opened the door looked stressed. Her big grey eyes had smudges beneath them, and her light brown hair was dragged back into a hasty ponytail. She gazed at me blankly.

'Um, hi. Are you Francesca Collins?'

She nodded. 'Can I help you?'

'I'm… um… I have… um…' I gulped. 'I need to talk to you about Mark.'

A look of intense surprise crossed her face. 'Mark? What Mark?' She paused a moment and then added, 'You don't mean Mark *Juniper*?

I nodded silently.

'I haven't seen him in years. Why would you need to talk to me about him?' Her tone was airy, dismissive, but she was giving me a very careful appraisal.

'I'm his sister, Olivia,' I said.

She swallowed convulsively, still staring at me, but then stood back and let me in. She only found her voice once we were in her living room.

'He doesn't have a sister. I mean, he couldn't find any family.'

I nodded. 'It's a long story.'

It was a relief to sit down on the sofa. My legs were slightly wobbly.

'Even if you *are* his sister, I don't see why you've come to find me,' Fran said as she sat uneasily in an armchair. 'We split up five years ago, and I haven't heard from him since. Why would I want to know anything about him?'

'He died two weeks ago,' I said as gently as I could.

She gasped and paled slightly. 'What of? He was only… thirty-six!'

'It was motor neurone disease.' There's no easy way to give that kind of news, and Mark had been right when he said I spat out those three hateful words on one of our first meetings; I'll never be able to say them easily. 'He had it when you split up,' I said into a stunned silence. 'That was why he ended it. He didn't want to tell you. He thought… well… he thought he'd be a burden.'

'*He thought*!' she cried out at last. 'Why couldn't he just *trust?* He was always so damned self-reliant. I suppose it was his upbringing; you know, being adopted, losing his parents, but now… that's five wasted years of our daughter's life.' Her voice was bitter, distraught even.

'I'm sorry. I know he did care for you. I've brought a copy of the tape he left for me, so you can hear what he said – his last words, as he called them. I think it'll help if you listen to it.'

She took the tape from me a little reluctantly. I wondered why she looked so ill and on edge.

'Is Evie okay?' I asked.

She started and stared at me. 'How do you know her name?'

'We've met,' I said, adding quickly, 'Let me tell you how I met Mark and how I found out he was my half-brother, and maybe that will help to explain about Evie.'

I launched into the tale, and Fran's expression changed slowly from suspicion to interest to disbelief to outright amazement.

'Out of body? You're *serious*? You're saying Evie can do it?'

I nodded. 'Instead of going to sleep right away, she goes to what she calls dreamland – only it's not a dream.'

'You're really not kidding, are you?' she said, her voice strained.

'Are you okay?' I asked, noting that her already pale face was now ashen.

'Mark never mentioned anything about this – in all those years together. Why couldn't he have told me? Yet another secret between us.'

'Didn't you have your own secret, though?' I asked as kindly as I could. 'When you asked Mark about having a baby?'

She put her head in her hands with a little sob. My heart went out to her. All I seemed to be doing was adding to her misery, when I'd actually wanted to help.

When she looked up, her eyes were wet with unshed tears. 'If I'd told him…' her voice cracked. 'If I'd told him, then maybe he wouldn't have broken us up. You're right; Evie wasn't an accident. I thought…' she shook her head. 'I was so stupid. I knew how he felt about being tied down; we'd talked about it at the beginning. So I decided to just do it, and then he'd stay with me because he loved me. I wanted a baby so much.'

'You stopped using contraception?'

She nodded, wiping her eyes. 'I came off the pill without telling him. Women do it all the time, right? I didn't like deceiving him, but I was over thirty, and I was worried he'd never come around to it. I tried mentioning it to see how he reacted, but he looked so stunned that I didn't want to bring it up again. Only I was already pregnant by then, I just didn't know it. I was steeling myself to tell him when he got so cold and weird, and then he broke it off like he'd never cared about me at all.'

My own eyes were damp, and I blinked. 'You never stopped loving him, did you?'

'I tried to. I tried to hate him. It just didn't make sense, unless he'd found someone else, and everyone said he hadn't. So *why*? I decided I'd scared him away by wanting a baby. It never crossed my mind he was ill.'

'It wasn't your fault,' I said. I sighed. 'It wasn't his either. For what it's worth, I think he would have stayed if he'd known, so that Evie could have known her father. At least, in the end, he did know about her.'

Fran looked up at me in surprise. 'How did he know?' she asked in a husky whisper.

I told her about Evie's meeting with 'the man' on the beach at Lake Mahinapua. By the time I'd finished, Fran had begun to sob in earnest, and I joined in. We didn't notice the door opening until Evie ran up to her mother and said, 'Why are you crying?'

'It's all right. We're just sad about something,' Fran said, scrubbing at her face with a tissue as she tried to stem her tears. 'I thought you were having a nice sleep?'

'I was, but…' Evie looked at me properly then. '*You* can't be here,' she said in a puzzled tone. 'You're only in dreamland.'

Obviously my explanations hadn't penetrated very successfully.

Fran lifted Evie on her onto her lap. 'Now what's all this about "dreamland"?' She asked sternly.

Evie stared at me with a solemn expression. 'That's Ollie,' she said, pointing. 'I met her in dreamland, so she can't be here as well.'

'How long have you been going to dreamland?' Fran asked her.

'Not very long. I told you about it, but you didn't listen.'

Fran sighed. 'I thought you were just talking about being asleep.'

'No, Mummy, it's dreamland. I can go all sorts of places. It's fun.'

Fran got the whole story out of Evie piece by piece, including the story of meeting Mark, which had us both sniffing again.

When, eventually, Evie trotted into the other room to play with her toys, Fran said, 'Can you do this ghost thing, too? Being Mark's sister?'

I shook my head. 'I could see him when he was *out,* and obviously I can do the same with Evie, but that's all.'

'It could explain a lot about how Evie's been acting lately. I've been worrying about the peculiar things she says. I took her to the doctor's because she's started sleeping so soundly that I can't wake her up. I've even wondered whether she ought to see a child psychologist.'

'Mark said it took him a while to get the hang of "waking up". When he was *out* he was dead to the world, but he learned how to deal with it.'

She scrubbed her face in her hands. 'I'm not at all sure I want my daughter to be roaming around like a ghost due to some weird gift. I just want her to be a normal, happy little kid. I mean, *invisible*? She could go anywhere, see... well, anything.'

I understood her point; it would worry me too. 'It can be hard, having an ability no one else seems to have,' I said, trying to be comforting, 'But there are compensations. It made Mark's life so much easier over those last five years.'

'If I'd known, *I* could have made his life easier, too,' she said, with a touch of bitterness.

I stayed for a while longer and told her about Mark's last few weeks. As we talked, I realized I liked Fran a lot, and we had quite a bit in common. I wondered why she seemed so strained, and wished I hadn't brought even more problems into her life.

‘I’m still worried about this “gift”,’ she said as I was getting ready to leave. ‘Couldn’t Evie get lost in this never-never land? I mean, be unable to get back?’

‘I don’t know for sure, but I don’t think so,’ I replied. ‘Mark seemed to have it under full control.’

‘But you said yourself he was older. I’m really not happy about all this, least of all with everything else that’s going on.’

‘Everything else?’ I prompted gently.

She sighed. ‘I’m sure you don’t want to hear all my troubles.’

‘Well, I’m Evie’s auntie, so sort of family, and I’m listening.’

‘Yes… I suppose that’s true,’ she said with a slight smile, and she sighed again. ‘It’s all a bit of a mess.’

‘What is?’ I asked.

She bit her lip and avoided my gaze. ‘I might lose this house; I’m struggling to keep up the payments. I could just afford it when I took it on, and I thought it was exactly what we needed. But… I’ve had my hours cut in my job, and it’s just been getting more difficult by the month.’

‘You’re not a ranger anymore?’

She shook her head. ‘I had to take what I could get when I came back here; I’ve been working in a care home for the past two years. Actually I love it, but they’ve had a few cutbacks lately, and I’m one of the casualties.’

I gazed at her with sympathy, and then a thought occurred to me. What about the house by the Wairau?

Chapter Twenty-Four

I kept myself busy over the next few days. I contacted the University of Otago about studying there, visited Lisa as well as Mark's neighbours Miriam and Dave, and consulted the solicitor who had drawn up Mark's will to discuss what I could do for Fran and Evie. Finally, I contacted Fran and asked if she'd meet me for lunch in Picton.

I was a little nervous as I waited in a café near the harbour. I amused myself with watching the ferries and wondered suddenly how Pastor was getting on. I'd spoken to him twice since Mark's death, and although he'd been as kind as usual on the phone, I'd caught a hint that there was something wrong, or at least something he was holding back. I decided to ring him once I was back in Westport.

When Fran arrived, she looked just as pale as ever. I felt she needed to be plied with hot tea and fed with hearty soup, but all she chose was a coffee and a small cake.

'Is everything all right?' I asked anxiously. 'How's Evie?'

She smiled. 'Evie's fine. I'm starting to come to terms with her gift, I think. She's keen to tell me all about her adventures in dreamland, and she's also asking a lot of questions about Mark.' She shrugged slightly. 'I suppose that's a good thing, but talking about him so much brings it all back.'

I toyed with my teacup. 'Did you decide what to do about the MND?'

She nodded slowly. 'I talked it through with the doctor, and I've decided it's not worth going through all the worry of testing, even if we find out that Mark's was the SOD1 variant.'

'That's the way I feel. I can't see the point in burdening myself with all that anxiety.' I just wished I hadn't had to burden her with it.

She sipped at her coffee. 'Was that what you wanted to talk to me about?'

'No,' I said slowly. 'It's about Mark's house.'

She frowned. 'His house?'

I leaned across the table. 'He left his house to me, but… well, knowing what I know now, I feel he'd rather you and Evie had it.'

She gasped. 'But… I can't do that! It must be worth thousands.'

I smiled. 'Quite a few, especially given the location, but this isn't about money – it's about what's right. You heard the way Mark talked about you on the tape, and you know how he'd feel about Evie. He'd want to help. If the MND had never happened, things would have been very different, wouldn't they? You might have bought a house together or even moved into the Wairau house. So I'm thinking that by rights it should be yours.'

Fran had flushed as I spoke, and now there were two red spots on her cheeks. 'Ollie, I… you must need the money. How could I take it?'

'I spoke to a solicitor, and she said the house could be put into trust for Evie, if you'd prefer that. I hadn't decided whether to sell it or not anyway – somehow it seemed like the wrong thing to do – and to be honest, giving it to you and Evie seems like the right thing to do.

Fran smiled at last. 'Got it all worked out, eh?' she said. 'Thing is though, I just don't see how I could take it, even in trust for Evie, not when I know you're not that well off yourself.' I started to speak, but she added quickly, 'What if I rented the house from you instead?'

I leaned back in my seat, feeling deflated. 'But if you did that, you'd still be paying out,' I protested.

'Why are you so sure this would be what Mark wanted? You haven't… seen him, have you?'

I shook my head. 'I wish I had. It's just that it *feels* right.'

'If we lived there and paid rent, we'd still be living there, and we'd have a roof over our heads, which is more than we'll have soon, the way things are going.'

I sighed. 'Okay. A *low* rent, then,' I said, realizing she wasn't going to come around to my way of thinking, no matter how much I pressed.

She grinned. 'A *reasonable* rent.'

I lifted my hands in defeat and smiled back wryly. 'If that's the way you want it, looks like that's the way we'll have to do it.'

Two days later I closed up the house and drove across to Westport. Dave had helped me put the car to rights, and I had to admit that, despite my beliefs, it was pleasant to be independent and able to drive myself, especially as Mark's car was only four years old and had barely been driven. I guessed he'd bought it as a replacement for his beloved motorbike once he could ride one no longer.

'…and that's the situation,' I said to Alan and Ewan that evening as we relaxed after another meal made from food supplied out of tins and packets. 'Looks like I'm going to be Fran's landlord.'

'So she's going to sell her own house?' Alan asked.

I nodded. 'It's not going to bring her in a lot of money, but it'll be a big relief to her. I just wish I'd been able to persuade her to do it my way. It seemed like the perfect solution, and I suppose I wanted everything that had gone wrong to somehow be put right – or at least as right as it can be.'

Ewan gave me an intense look. 'And what about you? Any conclusions about what *you're* going to do now?'

'Well, I've contacted the University of Otago, and they say my A-levels should be sufficient to get a place there. I'd have to pay my own fees, of course, and I'd also have to prove to New Zealand Immigration that I could support myself if I wanted a student visa. Maybe Fran's rent will be enough for that.'

Alan leaned towards me, an earnest expression on his face. 'Ollie, if that's really what you want to do, and Fran's rent isn't enough, don't worry about the money for Uni. I can help you out – I'd be more than happy to do that for Paul's daughter.'

I flicked a glance at Ewan, but he looked surprisingly serene. 'Hasn't the lodge taken all your capital, though?' I protested.

'I'll manage it somehow,' Alan said firmly. 'And speaking of changes, I suppose it's time to tell you both about Lisa and me, and what we've discussed.'

'What you've *discussed*?' Ewan repeated.

'The lodge, to be precise.'

Ewan raised his eyebrows. 'What about the lodge?'

Alan sighed. 'How badly do you really want to be a lodge proprietor?'

Ewan leaned back on the sofa and regarded his father warily. 'I'm not sure how to answer that,' he said slowly. 'You're not thinking of giving up on the whole project, after all the work we've both put into it?'

Alan shook his head. 'Nothing like that. I'm thinking that maybe *you* might rather do something else – go back to teaching, for instance.'

'While you do what?'

Alan coughed. 'Lisa and I could take over the lodge.'

Ewan let out a long whistle. 'So you've asked her to marry you?'

Alan grinned. 'Not exactly. I wanted to see what your feelings were first. Let's just say it's been implied. I know you miss teaching, and there's bound to be a few jobs going in… well… the *Dunedin* area, for instance.'

Ewan and I exchanged amused glances.

'So you've got it all worked out, eh, old codger?' Ewan said.

Alan shrugged. 'I know it's still a while before the lodge is finished, but that gives us plenty of time to get it all sorted out, doesn't it?'

There was definitely something wrong with Pastor. I frowned as I cut off my mobile and looked up at the roof of the lodge where Ewan and a couple of men were manoeuvring a solar panel into place.

'What's up?' Alan said suddenly from my side, making me jump. 'Sorry, didn't mean to creep up on you.'

I shook my head. 'I was just thinking I ought to go and visit Pastor. Every time I talk to him, he assures me all's well, but I just know it isn't.'

'Is it *that* sort of knowing?'

'I suppose it is – he's really troubled, and I'm not sure why he's keeping it to himself. Or maybe that's just it. As he sees it, he's there to help others, and he doesn't want to bother me with his own problems.'

'Didn't you say he'd lost his faith?'

I nodded. 'But somehow he still *thinks* like a pastor, or how he believes a pastor should be. I know he let me down at Haast, but he's been a great support since then, and it feels like all I've done is take… from everyone,' I finished, looking meaningfully at him.

Alan patted my arm. 'Ollie, you're being ridiculous. Think how much you've given to me – and to Ewan. But if you really feel you need to visit Pastor, you don't need my blessing. You should take Ewan with you, though. I reckon he could do with a break.'

I regarded Ewan thoughtfully as he supervised the workmen. At least these days, he didn't come across as brusque and cold – which might explain why he was having less difficulty getting workers to help him. I couldn't deny that the prospect of spending a few days on my own with him appealed to me. It would be our first chance to be alone since declaring our mutual interest in each other. If Alan had detected sexual tension several weeks ago, it was far worse now, and neither of us felt we could share a room and a bed at Alan's, no matter how far from being an 'old codger' he actually was.

'Maybe a few days in Manapouri will do us both good,' I murmured.

'Maybe it will,' Alan agreed, raising his eyebrows suggestively.

I wasted no time putting my suggestion to Ewan, and he was surprisingly keen. Or maybe not so surprisingly, given the circumstances. I booked us into a small cabin not too far from the lake, but I didn't ring Pastor to warn him. It seemed best to just pay him a surprise visit.

Manapouri in March was a little chillier than it had been in December; there was a heavy frosting of snow on the distant peaks. We arrived in the early evening, and the white mountaintops were tinted with pink.

Once we'd dumped all our stuff in the cosy cabin and admired its view of the mountains, both Ewan and I regarded the large double bed speculatively, and then looked up to catch one another's gaze. 'Are you thinking what I'm thinking?' Ewan asked.

I plumped myself onto the bed with a bounce. 'I'm ready for my night of passion, Mr Jensen,' I said, lying back with my arms splayed out across the pillows and giving him an exaggerated suggestive look.

He laughed and lay down beside me. 'Well, it's not nighttime yet, but I think that can be arranged,' he said. The new, relaxed Ewan was so much more fun to be around. I'd finally stopped worrying that I'd do or say something wrong.

I turned onto my side and traced a finger along his slightly stubbled cheek and jaw. He smiled and reached to take my hand. 'Ollie, I love you, you know that, don't you?'

I leaned down and kissed him lightly on the lips. 'I love you too,' I murmured. It was the first time I'd admitted that, even to myself.

He took me into his arms. 'So, did you tell your mum we were coming down here?'

I laughed. 'No, why? Do you think I ought to send her a text? "Hi Mum – in Manapouri with Ewan, finally getting down to our night of passion. We thought you'd like to know."'

He grinned, chuckling with amusement, and for the first time I saw a resemblance to Mark. I kissed him again, and he pulled me closer, and before long all thoughts of my mum had vanished. As the sun set in its red-gold splendour, the two of us finally took pleasure in each other.

***

The next morning, I turned into Pastor's drive with a slight sense of apprehension. I wasn't sure how he'd feel about me just turning up, and the fact that he hadn't confided in me on the phone suggested this was something serious. I was feeling content and at peace with the world after the previous night, and I'd left Ewan behind reluctantly, promising to be back as soon as I could.

Pastor opened his door as soon as I pulled up, and he did a double take at the sight of me.

'Olivia! This is a pleasant surprise,' he said as I stepped out of the car. 'I thought you were busy helping out at the lodge. Why didn't you let me know you were coming?'

I grinned a little sheepishly. 'I thought I'd surprise you. I've been a bit worried; you haven't sounded quite yourself in the last few phone calls.'

'Come on in,' he said. 'You're on your own?'

'I'm here with Ewan. We've rented a cabin for a few days,' I answered as I followed him inside.

'So how are things going with you two?'

I smiled. 'Pretty well.'

'Uh huh. Any chance of you getting married?'

I shook my head. 'We've finally reached a good place in our relationship after all the misunderstandings. I haven't even thought about marriage.'

'And how are things going at the lodge?' Pastor asked as he broke out the iced tea, even though the morning was a chilly one.

I sat down at the familiar table. 'The structure is finished now, pretty much. It's just a case of getting all the equipment installed, the power working and so on.'

'And that's all looking good? Will there be enough power generated to avoid having to go on the grid?'

I nodded. 'Both Ewan and Alan have had a few sleepless nights over getting it all to run according to plan, but apparently they've worked out most of the kinks now.'

It was pleasant to gossip with him about all the latest events and plans for my move to Dunedin and the University of Otago, but eventually the conversation wound down, and I took my chance.

'So what's bothering *you*?' I asked. 'I know there's something wrong.'

He sighed. 'Well, I guess I'm having what they call a spiritual crisis,' he said slowly, fiddling with his tea glass.

I raised my eyebrows. 'How come?' I asked as lightly as I could.

'It's been kind of ongoing since everything that happened with Mark. It really got me thinking, made me doubt a lot of things, especially my decision to run away after Rosalie died.' He paused, frowning. 'And now there's family trouble back in the US. My granddaughter Lindy is skipping school, maybe doing drugs, getting herself into who knows what. It's caused so much friction between Emily and Steve that their marriage is on the rocks.'

'I'm really sorry to hear that. You must be fond of Lindy – you said you missed your granddaughters.'

'Yeah. We used to be pretty close. Guess I feel like I've let her and the rest of the family down. And maybe God, too.'

I stared at him. 'So… you've regained your faith?'

He smiled wryly. 'Let's just say I'm praying again. And I'm wondering whether I ought to go home after all. Should I carry on hiding out here when I'm wanted back home?'

'Sounds like you already have your own answer,' I said.

He rested his chin on his hands. 'I guess I do,' he said softly. 'I love it here, but I've been running away for long enough. It's time to face up to things, and my family really needs me now.'

'I'll miss you,' I said.

He reached out and covered my hand with his. 'Same here. It's been a real pleasure knowing you, Olivia.'

Chapter Twenty-Five

I hammered in the last nail and stepped back to view my handiwork with a sigh of satisfaction. The rustic-looking wooden sign I'd carved myself read 'Serenity Bush Lodge'. It had taken quite a while for everyone to agree on a name, but I thought it was just right.

'Looking good,' came a voice from behind me.

I turned to regard the source. 'Thank you, Mr Jensen,' I said with a slight curtsey, and I went to join him in admiring the now completed lodge. The river ran high nearby, wood smoke drifted out of the chimney, and the sun glinted off the solar panels on the roof.

'It looks amazing,' I said. 'And we made it with a week to spare.'

Ewan grinned. 'And at last we get to be our own first guests. I thought those beds were never going to arrive.'

I laughed. 'It certainly will be a relief to finally escape from your old cabin,' I said. 'I've never stayed in a luxury eco lodge before.'

He put his arms around me. 'It's just a shame it won't be truly luxurious, since we still have to do our own cooking and cleaning.'

I leaned into him. 'Never mind – we have it all to ourselves this way.'

'Hmmm... I wonder how we're going to entertain ourselves? Where was that game of Monopoly again?'

I laughed, and we headed arm in arm into the lodge. The scent of the still-fresh timbers permeated the air, reminding me strongly of all those days spent sawing and hammering. 'I still can't believe it's finished,' I said, looking around at the communal area with its nooks and sofas and large dining table at one end.

'It'll be hard to adjust to being a teacher again, that's for sure, after over eighteen months of hard labour,' he said.

'Isn't being a teacher hard labour, too?'

'It is when it's teenagers,' he agreed, 'but I must admit I'm looking forward to it.'

He'd found a job teaching biology at a high school in Dunedin, and we were in the process of renting a house together. I'd already had one semester at university, but I'd come back to Hokitika to help out during the vacation.

I headed into the state-of-the-art kitchen area and started brewing up some coffee while Ewan sat at the table and stretched out his legs. His boots were crusted with earth from the garden. 'I got a lot done this morning,' he said. 'I reckon the lodge will be able to source most of its own fruit and veg by next year.'

His mobile rang, and he took it out of his pocket, raising his eyebrows in surprise. 'It's Dad.'

I smiled to myself as I got out the coffee cups, wondering how Alan could spare the time.

'Uh huh. That's great,' Ewan was saying. 'So you'll be back on Thursday? Yes, it's all done – we've installed the furniture now. Yes, Ollie's fine. Have I what?' He looked across at me with an odd expression on his face as he listened. 'Uh, no, I haven't,' he said in an awkward tone. 'Yep, yep. Okay, we'll see you in five days.'

I gave him a questioning look as he put the phone down. 'So they're all right, then?'

'Having a great time, apparently. They're in Perth now. Honeymoon of a lifetime, he says. Shame he and Mum didn't have much of one.'

'So what was he asking you?'

He looked tense for a moment, and then he suddenly relaxed and smiled. 'If you must know, he was asking me if I'd popped the question.'

'Popped the question! No wonder you looked so embarrassed. Do you want to pop the question?' I asked with a cheeky grin, setting the coffee cups on the table.

He reached across to take my hand. 'Do you want me to pop the question?'

I clasped his hand tightly and leaned over to kiss him on the cheek. 'Ewan Jensen,' I said in a firm tone, 'I don't mind if we're married or not. I'm not going to abandon you. I love you.'

'Well in that case, will you marry me?'

I didn't hesitate. 'Yes, I will.'

He gave a delighted laugh. 'Then that is highly satisfactory, and we must arrange a date forthwith.' He pulled me towards him until our lips almost touched. 'Unless, of course, you want a wedding with all the trimmings, and your mum and Ron over from Scotland, and my sisters over from Oz, and Evie for a bridesmaid, and…'

'Will you let up!' I said, settling on his lap and putting my arms around his neck. 'Let's just sneak into a registry office one day or something,' I murmured, brushing his lips with mine.

'How very unromantic of you,' he said with a smile, and then he gave in and kissed me properly and very satisfactorily.

EPILOGUE

It was mid-November; it would have been Mark's 40th birthday, and the old house by the Wairau resounded with laughter; the rooms were full of people. We'd invited everyone, from my mum and Ron to Mark's half-sisters. Somehow they'd all managed to make it.

Evie was outside, skipping among the trees with Carol's young sons, and I was in the kitchen, trying to help my mum, Fran and Lisa to prepare a buffet meal for fourteen.

'Sit *down,* Ollie,' my mum said in an exasperated tone. 'I've told you we have it all under control. You're getting too big now to be on your feet so much.'

Fran flashed me an amused look across the kitchen but kept quiet.

'I'm only seven months, Mum, and I feel fine.'

'Well, we know better, don't we Fran? Now if you won't sit down, why don't you go and find that husband of yours.'

I sighed and decided to leave them to it. My mum was clearly in her element, but once I reached the veranda, I wasn't so sure about Ewan. He looked a little cornered as he listened to Ron talking about his golf handicap. My mum and Ron had moved on from amateur dramatics to golf, in a big way.

I slipped on to one of the old sofas beside Alan, who grinned and said, 'She seems very happy.' He indicated Evie, now nine years old.

I nodded. 'She was showing me her room earlier – the same one Mark used to have. I'm sure he'd be happy to know they were living in his house; I think I did the right thing.'

'Of course you did,' Alan said.

'Hey, budge up, old codger,' Ewan said, having just made his escape from Ron, who was heading towards the kitchen.

'Interesting conversation?' I asked innocently as he squeezed between us.

'Fascinating. Did you know there's more championship links golf courses in East Lothian than anywhere else in the world?'

I coughed. 'Um… no.'

'And Mary Queen of Scots played at Musselburgh Links?'

'Well, I never,' I said, opening my eyes wide.

'Yes,' he said, nodding earnestly. 'I'm beginning to wonder if I ought to find the nearest golf course here in New Zealand. Get Ron and your mum to introduce me to the game.'

'Ewan Jensen, if you think…' I started to say in mock anger, just as Evie ran across to us, with Carol's youngest son following behind.

'Auntie Ollie,' she said, 'when will your baby boy be born? Jack wants to know.'

I stared at her. 'In about two months, but we don't know it's a boy yet. It could be a girl.' Ewan and I had chosen not to learn the baby's sex when I'd had my scan.

Evie was shaking her head vigorously. 'No, it's a boy.'

Ewan leaned forwards to make eye contact with her. 'What makes you so sure, Evie?'

She regarded the three of us with utter seriousness. 'He's got a boy's – you know – thingy,' she said, and then she dropped the solemnity and giggled slightly with girlish embarrassment.'

Before any of us could respond, one of the other children shouted to her from across the garden, and she and Jack ran off blithely, leaving us staring at each other in bemusement.

'What d'you make of that?' Alan said.

I bit my lip. 'I'm not sure. Unless…'

'…Evie has gifts that go beyond the one we know about,' Ewan finished for me.

'A combination of mine and Mark's,' I said slowly. 'Although I don't recall ever predicting the sex of babies in the womb.'

'D'you think she's right?' Ewan asked.

I placed a hand over my round belly. 'I *know* she's right.'

Mark Alan Jensen was born ten weeks later.

THE END

Acknowledgements

Once again, my very special thanks to Tori Howell for being the first person to read the manuscript, for giving me invaluable feedback and encouragement as well as advice on medical matters. Thanks to my mum and sister for their usual support.

Thanks also to the MND Association for providing me with helpful information and to Sue Cook of Rough and Tumble Bush Lodge in Seddonville, New Zealand for advice related to building a lodge. In addition, I can't miss out the people and the landscape of the South Island of New Zealand in general for inspiring this book.

And of course, many thanks to everyone at Snowbooks for publishing the book!

About the Author

Jill Rowan was born in Hertfordshire but now lives in the Shropshire countryside. She gave up a career in accounts in order to pursue her passion for writing. She is a keen photographer and natural history enthusiast with a special interest in spiders. She also likes to engage in desultory gardening, lazy walks and leisurely cycle rides. She has obtained both a BA and a BSc with the Open University and has studied subjects as diverse as astronomy, creative writing, languages, environmental science and religion. This is her second novel. Her first, The Legacy, was published in 2011, and she is now working on her third.

About motor neurone disease

Motor neurone disease is a rapidly progressive, fatal disease that can affect any adult at any time. The cause of MND is unknown, and there is no cure. The disease leaves people unable to walk, talk or feed themselves, but the intellect and the senses are usually unaffected. It affects approximately one in 15,000, which means there are around 5,000 people living with MND in the UK at any one time. Half will die within 14 months of diagnosis.

If you would like to help people with motor neurone disease, there are associations in both the UK and New Zealand.

The MND Association of the UK co-ordinates support, guidance and advice for people affected by MND, while promoting research into causes, treatments and a cure. They can be found online at www.mndassociation.org and their address is PO Box 246, Northampton, NN1 2PR, England.

The Motor Neurone Disease Association of New Zealand helps to support people with motor neurone disease and their carers. They have fieldworkers around the country who provide information, advocacy and emotional support and help people to have access to the right health services at the right time. They have a website at mnda.org.nz, and their address is PO Box 24-036, Royal Oak, Auckland 1345, New Zealand.